D1020138

Ghost of a Chance

Also by Linda Crawford

Vanishing Acts
Something to Make Us Happy
In a Class by Herself

Ghost of a Chance

Linda Crawford

**ARBOR
HOUSE**
New York

Library of Congress Cataloging in Publication Data

Crawford, Linda.
Ghost of a chance.

I. Title.
PS3553.R286G4   1985   813'.54   85-1321
ISBN 0-87795-677-4 (alk. paper)

The author acknowledges permission to reprint lyrics from
"Do I Love You," by Cole Porter. Copyright © 1939 by Cole Porter.
Copyright renewed, assigned to John F. Wharton, trustee of the Cole
Porter Musical and Literary Property Trust. Chappell & Co., Inc.,
owner of publication and allied rights. International Copyright
secured. ALL RIGHTS RESERVED. Used by permission.

For Ryna

Special thanks to Gloria Safier and Peg Parkinson for their invaluable support.

Chapter One

SHE should have known, Kate thought when she looked back. There were portents she might have discerned in their very first meeting had she been paying attention. Beryl's smile, for example, the way it flashed and died so quickly, always missing her eyes. The first few times it appeared Kate mistook it for a tic and attributed it to the fact that Beryl had recently been locked in a bank with an insane gunman. That could lead to all sorts of abnormal manifestations, Kate imagined. Only when she had seen it several times did Kate realize it was an expression of pleasure. Or the moment near the end of lunch when Beryl's fork snaked across the table to Kate's plate, speared a plump grape that had been part of the garnish, and sped back to Beryl's mouth, depositing the grape within. Beryl seemed utterly unaware of what she had done, but Kate wasn't. Surely she might have read that as a clue. And what about Beryl's suggestion that she use the pen name Kathryn Koob on the book about her ordeal that she and Kate had met to discuss?

1

"It sounds familiar," said Kate.

"Of course," Beryl replied. "She was one of the hostages in Iran."

"Oh, yes." Kate was nonplussed by Beryl's notion of appropriating the woman's name. "But I don't think—"

"A foremost female hostage. It would show my identification with her."

"Yes, I suppose so, but—"

"Besides," said Beryl, "I just think it would look better on a book than Beryl Swarr."

Kate couldn't argue with that, although she wondered if Koob was really that much better than Swarr.

That she was not put off by these signs, nor alerted by them to future danger, indicated just how distracted and desperate she had been, distracted by the upheaval between her and Jason, desperate for work that she would not have to generate herself in her somewhat fragmented state. In fact, far from being a menace, Beryl looked like a miracle. And Kate had actually been touched by her, by her earnestness, by her hideous hat made of imitation leopard skin in aviator cap style, by the streak of butter that glistened on her chin throughout lunch, escaping every swipe of her napkin. When Beryl described how at the darkest moment of her trial she got down on her "hands and knees and prayed to God," Kate was moved, even as she pictured Beryl on all fours. When Beryl admitted that after captivity her regular life seemed rather vapid, that she indeed suffered quite a letdown upon returning to it, Kate was stirred by her candor.

Beryl Swarr had a tale to tell quite by accident, though she quickly began ascribing it to more directive influences, variously and obliquely identified as "something larger than

me," "a force," "some power." She worked as a bank teller
in Harbor View, Michigan, a resort town on Lake Michigan. There were two other tellers at People's Bank & Trust,
one of them Lana Van den Haag ("pronounced *hog*," said
Beryl, making two short, porcine noises, apparently to make
sure Kate grasped it; Kate made a mental note to tell Beryl
she needn't do that), whose cage was next to Beryl's and
whose spurned suitor arrived at the bank one summer afternoon with a shotgun under his arm, his waist girdled with
hand grenades, like ripe fruit heavy on the bough, and a
pack on his back that contained two revolvers, extra ammunition, and more grenades. He said he just wanted to talk,
but Lana, made skittish by the display of armaments, refused, screamed loudly, and ran for the door. The suitor,
Rodney Flint, shot her in the back, gunned down two bank
customers in the ensuing panic and, after clearing out everyone else, took Beryl hostage. She lived in the bank with
Rodney and the three dead bodies for ten days.

At first this situation was attended to primarily by newspapers and television stations in Michigan and by the wire
services. But eventually it became the focus of national interest, thanks not only to its duration but to Beryl herself.
For hers was the voice that spoke out from the armed camp
within the bank, hers the face that appeared several times
daily at the bank door to report Rodney's demands and to
serve as go-between in his negotiations with the police. And
there was unanimous agreement that she acquitted herself
very well indeed.

Newspaper accounts described her performance as
plucky, gallant, poised. Television images spoke for themselves: Beryl, head at an indomitable tilt, feet planted resolutely, standing before the bank speaking through a bullhorn

. . . Beryl, Rodney's arm round her neck, his gun at her temple, gazing clear-eyed toward the crowd . . . Beryl, when it was all over, walking briskly past the ambulance that had been sent for her, giving its hood a sharp, dismissive rap.

Within days of her return to home and family, Beryl received calls from several agents and publishers, urging her to consider doing a book about her experience and offering to furnish her with a writer who would help in the endeavor. One of the agents was Kate's.

Kate had begun her career as a novelist, but quickly realized that she could not live on the meager profits gleaned from fiction and turned to ghost writing to supplement them. The ghost work, for reasons spiritual and psychological, as well as economic, had taken over Kate's writing life and, although she kept intending to return to the world of fiction, she had not yet done so.

Her first ghost job was the autobiography of a Hollywood movie star of the 1940s who, in a drink-and-drug drenched rage had bludgeoned to death her domineering mother, and after serving a prison term for her crime and repairing at its conclusion to a cloistered nunnery where she lived in a state of general abasement, had upon publication of her book felt sufficiently redeemed to relocate to Beverly Hills and begin resuscitating her career.

Kate also ghosted something called *Hum Your Way to Health,* an unpromising project that she leapt at in order to prove to herself that her recent marriage to Jason Wylie would not keep her from pulling her own financial weight, a matter that was extremely important to her, less so to Jason, a successful writer of detective fiction. The writer of record was a therapist who contended that the vibrations set in motion by a daily regimen of humming certain tones and tunes could realign the body's energy patterns in such a way as to ensure emotional well-being.

Her most recent ghosting effort had been *Women and Transplants: A Feminist Perspective,* written for Ulrica Forstman, a doctor who viewed the sharing of organs among women as a metaphor for the sort of interfemale relations that might develop if patriarchal strictures were truly cast aside. And it, surprisingly, managed to find a respectable and quite enthusiastic audience. But it nearly finished Kate.

Ulrica, a Viennese woman of immense bulk and colossal ego, was given to demanding gestures of fealty, such as having Kate call her at the end of the day to read what she had written, or asking that Kate eat the same food as she when they lunched together. Kate indulged her for a time because of Ulrica's elevated reputation, the size of the advance, and because Kate felt she was being tested and that, once she passed the test, Ulrica would desist. But Kate's compliance seemed only to whet further Ulrica's appetite for obedience. When she asked Kate to come to her house and watch her while she did some reference reading ("It will mean something to me. It is not important that you should know what"), and Kate refused, a struggle ensued between them that was truly dreadful.

"What she really wants is my heart," Kate fumed to Jason. "She wants to tear it out of my body and transplant it into hers. No, my heart wouldn't be enough. She wants all of my organs. She wants my soul." But Kate hung on, offering up finally to Ulrica no part of herself but simply a competent and, mercifully, completed manuscript.

And soon after it was delivered Kate vowed never again. Jason backed her up.

"You're miserable when you're doing these things," he

said. "We don't need the money. Why don't you write a novel?"

Kate was, in fact, planning to begin one when the trouble in their marriage surfaced, leaving her in too weakened a condition to reject the Swarr project when her agent suggested it. She said yes because it was, like Mt. Everest, there. It would allow her to say to herself, to Jason, to anyone else she was trying to impress with her solidity, that she had launched a new project. That, in turn, would make her feel more intact than she was. It would allow her to underscore, for her own benefit and Jason's, her financial independence, which now seemed more important than ever. And the work itself would cause her to become engrossed in something other than her own distress. She couldn't possibly write a novel, feeling as she did. She would have only one subject—married man has affair, protests it has nothing to do with love for wife, but wife, nevertheless, is devastated—and it was not one she could approach with any dispassionate distance or writerly control. Besides, hadn't it been done before? Roughly several times a year?

Kate first saw Beryl poised in the doorway of a restaurant in Kate's downtown New York neighborhood. Kate had told her that she was tall, had gray hair, and would be wearing purple, a completely useless description, as it turned out. She was sitting down, so her height was irrevelant. Two days earlier she had decided that her silver gray hair, so stunning when it had arrived in her early twenties, now, as she approached forty, made her look older than she was, so she had returned to the light brown of two decades ago. The lavender and rose sweaters she'd been wearing ever since Jason told her about the affair (she had no idea why she had settled on these but they lifted her spirits slightly and, superstitiously, she stuck with them) looked awful with her new hair, so she had worn a black dress with a high neck that made her feel stark and efficient. While Beryl scanned the restaurant looking for Kate, it gave Kate a few moments to study her.

She was a bit on the round side and the impression her clothes gave of straining against her body, indicated that the gain of several pounds might have been recent. Perhaps eating to assuage residual trauma, Kate thought. When Beryl unhooked the chin strap and peeled off her hat, her fair hair fell into a fringe across her forehead and lank drapes along her cheeks. As she searched for Kate, her blinking blue eyes and darting head motions gave her a feral look that vanished when Kate waved to signal Beryl to her table.

"At the last minute I decided on a disguise," Kate said, as Beryl approached.

"I see," said Beryl, apparently accepting this as plausible, cutting off Kate's inclination to explain.

"What I think I should do," Beryl said, after she had gotten settled, "is to tell you the whole story in my own words."

Did Beryl actually realize that this might be one of the last times she would use her own words to describe what had happened to her? Did she recognize that from now on the words would be Kate's? If so, that made her rather astute. It also made her wholly different from anyone else Kate had written for.

Each one of them had believed that he or she had written the book Kate had been hired to write. The Hollywood star had thanked Kate for "pulling the book out of me," as if it were a full-term fetus that needed only the technicality of delivery in order to spring to life. The humming therapist

7

Linda Crawford

had confided to the book's editor that he had enjoyed the process of writing a book so much that he was thinking of doing another. Ulrica admitted only to having had "a little help with arranging and such, not my strong suit," managing to put Kate's task roughly on a par with sorting mail and making her own absolute inability to impose order on anything, including a sentence, seem a slight eccentricity.

"Why don't you write the book yourself?" Kate asked Beryl when she had finished telling her story.

"Me?" It was obvious this had never even occurred to her. "I have trouble writing a grocery list."

Kate, though she should have known better, was disarmed.

She also asked Beryl why she wanted to do the book, a question she always asked even though she didn't think she had ever received an honest answer.

"I'll be honest, Katherine," said Beryl.

"Kate."

Beryl's smile burst across her face, then vanished. "Other people first suggested this to me. And I wasn't sure it was all that good an idea. It was a pretty exciting story, I guess, but who was I? I mean, what happened to Beryl Swarr in People's Bank & Trust in Harbor View, Michigan, might not be all that interesting to people. But then, the more I thought about it, the more I began to see that maybe if I told my story it might help all those other people who've been hostages."

"Are there a substantial number of them?" Kate asked.

"You'd be amazed."

"I would."

"I did some research and I figured out that a hostage incident occurs in this country once every 106 hours."

8

"I had no idea."

"Now some of those you hear about—the bunch in Iran, me, some others—but plenty of them get no coverage at all. That doesn't mean that those hostages aren't hurt just as bad though. They come out of these incidents with very poor feelings about themselves. They think it was their fault, that they should have done something they didn't, or that they shouldn't have done something they did."

"Also," said Kate, struggling to get back to surer ground, "it's simply a terrific story. It's got everything: conflict, suspense, human interest."

"The more I thought about it," Beryl continued, as though Kate hadn't spoken, "the more I began to think that maybe something greater than me put me in that situation for a reason."

"And the reason is the book?"

"I've begun to think so, Katherine."

"Kate."

"The rictal grin flared and fizzled. "I hope I'll have your help."

Kate, when she was feeling defensive about missing clues in her meeting with Beryl, did note that she had gone virtually sleepless the night before. She and Jason had begun the evening with an attempt to have a cordial and civilized meal together, their first in more than a week. The days following the revelation of his affair were filled with guerrilla warfare: a display of firepower from Kate—sometimes a hit-and-run maneuver, sometimes scorched earth—Jason responding with silence, return shelling, or the occasional search-and-destroy mission when he felt Kate had gone too far.

"It's one thing to have an affair, but it's another to have it

9

with a child typist," Kate said, referring to Tabitha Waxberger, a twenty-six-year-old whom Kate herself had visited
upon their household when she hired her to transcribe some
tapes for *Women and Transplants.*

"Are you trying to tell me that you'd feel differently if she
had been my age and in my professional bracket?" Jason replied.

"Jason," said Kate, hoping to wither him with her voice,
"I am not trying to tell you anything." And she swept out of
the room.

The morning after the revelation Kate stood outside the
closed bathroom door strafing Jason, who shaved within.

"How could you fall for that little snake who wormed her
way in here, so ingratiating, so efficient, so helpful, baking
her awful whole-grain bread while she ripped off a page a
minute in the other room? . . . Oh, God, I was wrong to call
her a typist—she was a typist-baker, the little hyphenate—
and bringing along her special Uruguayan coffee beans that
she decaffeinated by hand, café au lait every morning at ten,
exotic fruits and cookies for that midafternoon slump. . . .
She made herself indispensable, didn't she? And we know
what treats she brought you! Jesus! I can't bear to think
about it. And what about her name, Jason? Tabitha, for
Christ's sake—part of the Kimberly generation. . . . I love
you, Tabitha . . . I love you, Tabbie . . . Bitty . . . Titty, Tits,
Toots . . . oh, the little pet names . . ."

Jason opened the door. There were flecks of shaving
cream in his dark hair, which curled furiously from damp-
ness; his face was nicked and bloody in several places.

"I never told her I loved her," he said, evidently shocked
that Kate would assume this treason of the word along with
his admitted apostasy of the flesh.

"What is that supposed to be, a principle?"

He looked as though Kate had slapped him. "No, it is simply a true statement."

Kate's attempt at an airy laugh came out like a strangled bark. "Forgive me if my regard for your notion of truth is a little low at the moment."

"I can understand that it might be, but—"

"And forgive me if I reject your understanding." She turned and headed down the hall.

"Just one thing," Jason called after her.

Kate stopped but kept her back to him. She didn't really want to see him standing there in his towel, looking winsome and pathetic at once. It had been hard enough to keep from reaching out to touch his shaving wounds.

"The bread was good," said Jason. "You liked it."

"The bread was awful," Kate corrected him. "I said I liked it."

"Why did you lie?"

"How dare *you* ask *me* that?" Kate resumed her progress toward her study, which she entered, slamming the door behind her.

After a few days the hostilities between them subsided into a grim cease-fire, marked mainly by weary silence, broken only occasionally by a brief exchange.

"I deserve everything awful you feel about me," said Jason. "Does it help to know that I'm just as horrified as you are?"

"No, Jason, it doesn't and you're not."

They lived side by side, circling each other with wary politeness. They slept next to each other at night, their bodies stiff and unmoving, taking care not to touch, as if to do so might ignite a blaze that neither was prepared for.

At one point Kate felt she was ready to hear more about Jason's affair and asked him to tell her. She had the sense that if she heard every squalid detail and survived she would be all right. It couldn't be worse than torturing herself with questions.

She learned that Jason and Tabitha first coupled during an evening three months earlier when Kate was unexpectedly summoned by Ulrica, who had become hysterical because Kate had omitted from the latest chapter Ulrica's thesis about transplant metaphors in popular songs.

"Come at once," Ulrica growled over the phone.

"Couldn't we discuss it now," Kate suggested, "or the next time we meet?"

"This is a grave and urgent matter, much too important for the telephone. I sense you are trying to shape the manuscript to your own design."

"I assure you I have no interest in that."

"Come," Ulrica commanded and slammed down the receiver.

"I guess I'd better go to keep her pacified," Kate said to Jason. "I don't want things to blow up this near the end."

"God, Kate, wouldn't it be easier just to write what she tells you? Then you wouldn't have these scenes. It's her book, after all."

"Jason," said Kate, through clenched teeth, "nine times out of ten I *do* write what she tells me. But it's also in my best interest to make it seem that this book is the product of a balanced mind. And I think a section on the transplant imagery in "My Heart Belongs to Daddy" undercuts that impression, don't you?"

"Isn't Tabitha staying for dinner?"

Kate had taken to feeding the young woman on those evenings when she worked until close to dinnertime.

"Everything's ready," she said. "There's lasagna in the oven, salad, bread."

"I'm not worried about dinner," said Jason, who cooked as often and as well as Kate. "But I don't want to spend the evening with her."

"Tell her you have work to do. Ask her to leave when dinner's over."

He didn't do that, Jason later told Kate, because he was angry, angry at the general air of distraction that had enveloped Kate ever since her association with Ulrica began, angry that Kate had thrown temptation directly into his path, for Jason had not missed Tabitha's decidedly flirtatious emanations even though Kate, in her heedless state, had. When he added an excessive amount of wine to his anger and sense of neglect, Tabitha began to look less like a ravening waif and more like a realistic option. When she told him how much she liked his latest detective novel, *Theobold and the A Capella Gang*; when she, in fact, told him that it seemed to her more like a "real" book than other mysteries she had read, Jason succumbed.

"I had no idea her critical faculties were so well developed," said Kate. "Move over, Benjamin DeMott."

Jason gazed at her, silent and long-suffering."

"And I had no idea you were so easily seduced. Do you mean that all these years I had only to mention you and the kingdom of literature in the same breath and you would have been mine?"

"I was yours anyway."

The candor and simplicity of his statement brought everything inside Kate—her rage, jealousy, disgust, hurt—to a halt for a moment. She knew what he said was true and that it still applied. She also knew she was not yet ready to accept it.

13

Jason rushed to tell her that the act had taken place in his study, not in their bed, presenting this as though it were a mitigating circumstance and he a true protector of the marital covenant. Kate took little solace in it, however, imagining the wild and acrobatic possibilities each piece of Jason's office furniture might have afforded the impassioned pair. It would have been less inflammatory to picture them in bed. Jason also said he felt perfectly awful when it was over. But not so awful that he did not do it again, perhaps a dozen times over the next two months.

And then one day, he reported, the scales fell from his eyes. He saw that Tabitha was not the luscious goddess of his obsessed fantasies but simply a rather pretty, though pallid, young woman with a nice laugh, thick blond naturally curly hair, remarkable typing speed, and quite resistible charms. It was not a sudden realization of his love for Kate that caused him to perceive Tabitha clearly. He had never lost sight of that.

Kate spent several days absorbing what Jason had told her, producing for each scene he had described a little film that she ran over and over in her mind, some melodramatic, some farcical, some pornographic: Jason leering drunkenly and grotesquely across the dinner table at Tabitha; Jason looking haggard and stern as he tells Tabitha that it's over, he's sorry, that he loves only his wife, who is ten times the woman Tabitha will ever be (Kate felt the scene needed this last to round it out so she added it); Jason's and Tabitha's naked and entwined bodies writhing atop his desk, so anesthetized by lust that they fail to feel the tape dispenser, the stapler, the magnetized paper clip holder biting into their sweating flesh.

It was the pornographic film that Kate played most often,

of course, but gradually, as she screened it time after time, the images began dimming from wear. After nearly a week their power was sufficiently attenuated for her to consider trying to talk to Jason. So she suggested they have dinner together the night before she was to meet Beryl Swarr.

Jason cooked, and he made Kate's favorite things, an obvious but nonetheless affecting gesture. He put the food in serving dishes, which he ordinarily spurned as unnecessary but which Kate favored. He inquired whether or not she would like candlelight: she said no. When they sat down, lit by the gleam from the Tiffany lamp that hung over the table, Kate saw for the first time the toll the last ten days had taken on Jason. The lines on his craggy face had deepened; his eyes looked hollow and haunted. His nervous exhaustion was evident in the tremor of his hands. The dishes he passed to Kate bobbed toward her like flotsam in a choppy sea.

Kate was delighted to find that she was hungry for the first time in days and began eating with zest. Jason pushed the food around his plate while he laboriously worked his jaws over the original mouthful.

"Swallow, Jason," she said finally, alerted by the clicking of his jaw.

He did so, with difficulty. "You're going to leave me, aren't you? I know it. You may as well tell me and get it over with."

Kate laughed. She couldn't help it even though it obviously stung him. "Why would I do that? Because you touched someone else's body?"

"Repeatedly."

"Wouldn't it be ridiculous to give up everything we have because of that?"

"I guess you'll have an affair then, to retaliate . . . and I'd understand, Katie, I really would."

"Don't say that."

"All right, I wouldn't understand."

"I mean Katie."

"I can't call you Katie? You're not going to leave, but you won't let me call you Katie? I think it might be very hard to reestablish things between us if there are a lot of rigid rules."

"I'm sorry you feel that my request that you avoid a certain form of address is the equivalent of 'a lot of rigid rules.' "

"Why are you talking like that?"

"I'll talk however I goddamn well please and you'll call me whatever I goddamn well want to be called. I think I'm entitled to that, don't you?" Kate's voice had risen progressively as she spoke and she now heard her final shouted query echoing in the air.

It had driven Jason to the kitchen and Kate could hear him trying to make purposeful noises as though he had gone there for some culinary reason. Kate, even when angry, rarely raised her voice. Until the last several days, it had happened perhaps half a dozen times in the eight years they had been married.

"Do you think it's likely that you would be tempted to have an affair to even things up?" Jason asked, after he returned to the table.

"Probably not," said Kate. "I hope I'd be mature enough to think it through ahead of time and realize what the consequences might be. Besides, Jason, I don't consider this some sort of game, where we keep score."

"Neither do I. You know that."

"Then why do you keep asking me if I might have an affair? The important thing here is not what I might do in the future but what you did in the past."

"I guess I'm frightened."

"I get the feeling you're less concerned with what I'm feeling than with what you think you might feel if you were in my shoes. Well, let me tell you something. It's pretty awful in my shoes. You really can't imagine how awful. And as much as I've hated you lately I wouldn't wish it even on you. It's the worst thing I've ever felt."

This time Kate ran for the kitchen, astonished to find tears streaming down her face. Crying was also uncharacteristic of her. When Jason appeared in the doorway, she waved her arms savagely, signaling him to go away. When he didn't move, she picked up the large wooden spoon to which a strand of vermicelli still clung and brandished it over her head, causing the pasta to drop onto her hair. When Jason smiled, Kate threw the spoon at him and he withdrew.

A short while later they again resumed their meal, but it wasn't long before another exchange flared into conflagration. And the pattern persisted all evening. Near midnight, when a mutual declaration of love degenerated within moments into name-calling (Kate called Jason a child molester, he called her a WASP), Jason said they needed a cooling-off period, announced that he intended to do his cooling in their house in the country, and left.

"Coward," Kate hollered. "You can't even take your punishment." But her words just bounced back at her from the closed door. And she realized quite quickly that she was relieved. At the moment, Jason stood for pain and betrayal. She was glad to have the reminder out of her sight.

Nevertheless, when she got into bed she missed him

terribly. She moved over to his side; she punched his pillow into a comfortable position beneath her head; she used his slippers to travel back and forth to the bathroom, first for aspirin, then for cold water, then for the heating pad that might relax her back and make her drowsy, a washcloth to dampen and place over her burning eyes, water again, more aspirin after four hours passed. She felt like an experimental rat performing in its assigned track but failing to receive its reward. During the hours that she heaved herself about in bed, she may have entered the sleep state once or twice, but, if so, the periods were exceedingly brief and superficial.

So perhaps it was not surprising that Kate failed to detect Beryl Swarr's true nature during their meeting a few short hours later. And by the next time they met, a month later in Michigan, the deal was made, the die cast.

Chapter Two

FOR two weeks, in Harbor View, Kate immersed herself in the life and times of Beryl Swarr. She recorded Beryl's account of what she referred to as My Incident, apparently to distinguish it from those other incidents that occurred once every 106 hours, a statistic Beryl continued to use but failed to substantiate. She recorded Beryl's chronicle of her life before the Incident, one Beryl summarized as "about the norm, just a regular American life." She discussed with Beryl, and recorded, her sense of the long-range consequences of the hostage experience, embryonic at this point but moving toward formulation. ("My Incident made a profound difference in my life, Katherine. I am just not the same person.")

Kate became acquainted with Beryl's husband and children, her parents, her friends and old schoolmates, and the townspeople who were terribly proud of their most celebrated citizen. She looked at all the videotape shots during the ten-day siege and talked to the Harbor View police, the reporter who had covered the story for the *Harbor Herald*, the officers, other employees and customers who were present at People's Bank & Trust that fateful day. Only Norma Van den Haag, mother of the unfortunate Lana, sounded a dissonant note in a chorus of approbation for Beryl.

"If she hadn't talked that maniac into surrendering," Norma told Kate, "he would've been shot down like a dog, which is what he deserved. And if she hadn't turned the whole thing into a big TV special it would've ended about nine days sooner and I would've got my baby's body back right away instead of having it rot away in there."

When Beryl heard what Norma Van den Haag had said, she allowed that it must be very disturbing to think of a loved one's body going untended.

"Of course, I did what I could for Lana," she added. "I made Rodney put her back in her cage and cover her up, but Norma would have no way of knowing that. She really hasn't been reachable since this whole thing happened."

Beryl had wanted Kate to stay with her, but when Kate demurred, she got her a room at the Wooden Shoe, a motel built in the shape of a Dutch clog. Beryl had quit her job at the bank to devote her full energies to what she had begun, rather alarmingly, to call the Work, and their days quickly settled into a routine.

Kate arrived at the Swarr home about nine o'clock and she and Beryl spent the morning recording. Generally, Beryl asked someone to join them for lunch, "people from my background," she called them. Nearly every one of them professed to have spotted early on Beryl's potential for pluck and to be unsurprised that she had become what her father called "Harbor View's numero uno." Only Beryl's mother, seeming bewildered by all the fuss, failed to weigh in with a tale of her daughter's mettle.

When Beryl introduced "my writer" to her mother (Kate

had considered asking her to drop the possessive pronoun but decided to let it go), Acacia Wease squeezed her eyes into slits of suspicion.

"Do you mean to tell me that just because some wacko nutcase locked Beryl in the bank for ten days you're going to write a book about it?"

"Well, it's Beryl's book really . . . but yes, I guess . . . in a way . . ."

"That's mother for you," said Beryl. "She takes everything with a grain of salt."

Kate wasn't sure that was how she would have described Mrs. Wease's stance, but she was glad to be off the hook.

In the afternoons Kate spent a few hours by herself. At six o'clock she returned to Beryl's for dinner. Afterward, they usually recorded for another hour or two. When Kate told Beryl she needn't feel obligated to feed her every night, Beryl said she felt it was important for Kate to see her in her "family setting."

The family was Beryl's husband, Stanley, and their two children, Melody and Lance, and they lived in a well-tended ranch house in one of Harbor View's newer sections. Stanley, whom Beryl described as being "in cement," was a large, genial man who obviously adored his wife. When she spoke he seemed to absorb her words greedily, as if they fed him in some essential way. When he talked about her his eyes gleamed. Passing by her in a room, his hand invariably reached out, touching her arm, her hair. His homage reminded Kate of Jason's efforts to demonstrate his love when he'd returned from his two weeks in the country. They had been so intemperate and strenuous that Kate finally had begged him not to try to make things up to her. Stanley's devotion, by comparison, seemed utterly effortless, as if he had been worshipping Beryl all his life.

And that, it turned out, was not far from the truth. The Swarrs and the Weases had lived next door to each other and Beryl and Stanley grew up as playmates. Stanley had known from the age of six that his intentions regarding Beryl were far-reaching and when he said so ("Beryl's not my friend, she's my girl friend and I'm going to marry her"), everyone thought it was adorable, including Beryl. When they were teenagers, however, and he continued to insist on his grand design even though Beryl was dating other boys, it became oppressive. But even when Beryl spread her wings and went off to college three states away, and for the next two years of vacation brought home with her a young man she had met there, Stanley didn't lose hope. And when the young man threw her over, and she quit school and came home to Harbor View, Stanley was there and Beryl was grateful to have him. Stanley had never gotten over his good fortune.

It was more difficult to ascertain Beryl's feelings for him. She depended upon his adoration; that was evident. ("Stanley is my biggest fan," she told Kate more than once.) She accepted his displays of affection the way a sovereign accepts tokens of allegiance from a subject, graciously and as her due. But at those somewhat rare times when Stanley's focus was elsewhere, Kate noticed Beryl gazing at him quizzically, as though he were a stranger. She was also sharp with him sometimes. "I have a great deal on my mind, Stanley," she said, increasingly often, and, Kate noticed, rather menacingly.

Melody was thirteen and pugnacious. "I'm Melody Swarr and I look just like my mother," she said, opening the door to Kate on her first visit to the house.

"Yes, I can see that," said Kate.

"People don't always," Melody replied, obviously a

young woman unwilling to leave things to chance. "But our personalities are completely different."

"In what way?" Kate inquired.

"I'm nice and she's not." Melody turned away into the house as her mother loomed behind her.

"Pay no attention," said Beryl. "It's just a stage. And personally I believe it's been brought on by living in the glare of publicity."

Kate had had no idea that the glare had been sufficiently bright to alter a child's personality.

"And that worries me about the book, by the by," Beryl went on. "How will she feel when everybody sees her mother on the 'Today Show,' 'Good Morning, America,' 'Merv Griffin'?"

This was the first direct clue Kate had gotten to Beryl's expectations. Should she tell her it was unlikely that there would be a problem with massive nationwide television exposure? Make a speech about the number of books competing for limited media coverage? Caution her not to get her hopes too high?

"Oh, she'll probably take it in stride," she said.

Lance, who was ten, appeared unaffected by those forces that Beryl claimed had caused his sister's bellicosity. In fact, his mother's experience with an armed killer had, it seemed, given her a new luster in his eyes and he seldom passed up a chance to brag about her exploit.

"You'd think I was a character on one of his favorite TV shows," said Beryl, coloring with pleasure.

Dinner with the Swarrs was an onerous occasion. Beryl, in Kate's honor, had taken great pains to come up with some special dishes and she served each of them with a lengthy explanation of its preparation.

"For this one," she said on the first night of Kate's visit,

Linda Crawford

"you take a can of clams, a can of shrimp, and a can of
crabmeat and you mix that with a package of frozen spinach
that's been chopped, a package of egg noodles that you've
cooked before, some mayonnaise, Worcestershire sauce,
sweet pickle relish, and heavy cream and put it all in a casserole, dot with butter or margarine, sprinkle with grated
cheese, and bake for about forty-five minutes or until done."

"What do you call it, sweetheart?" asked Stanley.

"Seafood Rockefeller," said Beryl. "Serve with a green
salad and warm French bread," she added.

"The salad and bread sound good," said Melody.

"You will eat what you are given, young lady," said Beryl.

"I didn't say I wouldn't. I just said the salad and the
bread sounded good."

"I know very well what you said and what you meant."

"Now she's a mind reader," said Melody disparagingly.

"Mel," said Stanley, a mild warning in his voice.

"You haven't even tasted it," said Lance. "How do you
know you won't like it?"

"Did you hear what's in it?" Melody squealed.

"That's enough," said Beryl, smacking two fingers against
the table edge with surprising ferocity.

The next night they had beef Mexicali. "You fry some
ground chuck and onions, add a package of frozen cooked
corn, a can of kidney beans, chili powder to taste, put in a
casserole with grated Jack cheese, crumble corn chips on
top, and bake for about forty-five minutes or until done.
Serve over minute rice dotted with pimiento pieces. This
goes nicely with a fruit sherbet for dessert."

The third night it was chicken vegetable muffin bake, a
combination of chicken "bitelets," green beans, carrots, cel-
ery, cream of chicken soup, and Bisquick balls.

24

"Maybe it would be easier to eat if you didn't tell us what's in it," Melody said, when her mother finished listing the ingredients.

"We eat our food, Melody," said Beryl. "We don't discuss it."

"*You* discuss it," Melody whined. "You say how you made it and what's in it. That's discussion."

"Button up and eat," Beryl ordered.

"Do you always cook so elaborately?" Kate asked.

"Well, I know you're used to all that New York food," said Beryl, making it sound like an alien cuisine.

Kate, despite the nearly inedible results, was touched by Beryl's efforts on her behalf.

On the fifth night, after the presentation of the flounder surprise, Melody's fury turned on Kate.

"She's doing it for you." She spat out the words, making it clear that she held Kate responsible for the gastronomic torture to which she was being subjected, implying that it was within Kate's power to stop it.

"Melody Swarr, you may leave the table this instant and go to your room." Beryl's mouth was grim, her eyes stony.

"Oh, please don't—" Kate began.

Beryl shifted her gaze to Kate, stopping her cold.

"You mean I don't have to eat?" Melody's face was suffused with hope.

Beryl barely missed a beat sidestepping the trap. "And you may take your surprise with you and return your plate when it is empty."

As Melody slunk away, her mother called after her, "I will hear toilets flushing, I will check all wastebaskets, the ground outside your windows, shoe boxes, sweater bags, mattress holes . . ."

Noting the ease with which the list of hiding places grew, Kate realized Beryl must have ransacked her daughter's room a time or two in the past.

"And remember, fish smells," Beryl wound up.

Kate tried to beg off dinner the following night, but Beryl wouldn't hear of it. Melody must not be allowed to think that she wielded such power; surely Kate could understand that. But she did manage to avoid dinner with the Swarrs twice during the following week by pleading pressures of the Work. And before returning to New York she took Melody out for a large, greasy cheeseburger and a malted milk.

During their work sessions Kate and Beryl went through the Incident time and again, Beryl never flagging in her re-telling, Kate's questions each time opening up new avenues for speculation and embellishment. Kate viewed the video-tapes several times. And by the end of her two-week stay in Harbor View, she felt as though she had been inside Peo-ple's Bank & Trust the day that Rodney Flint, unhinged by rejection, entered and in a few short moments irrevocably changed Beryl Swarr's life, to say nothing of Lana Van den Haag's or, for that matter, Kate Wylie's.

She did not see Rodney immediately, Beryl reported, be-cause she was busy with a customer and he presented him-self at Lana's window. Her first hint of trouble came when she saw Lana moving away from the window, onto the floor of the bank.

"Hey," Beryl remembered calling to her, "you can't just leave your cage like that."

And then she saw Rodney, shotgun trained on Lana, who was making for the door, and she heard a thunderous noise and saw Lana fall. Rodney moved quickly to the door, blocking the only exit, yelling at everyone to come into the middle of the bank where he could see them. They huddled there, Lana's dying form and Rodney's agitated one before them.

"It was touch and go at that moment," said Beryl, "extremely touch and go. He was waving the gun around and yelling. We were staring death in the face, no question about it. Mr. Dana, the president, started praying and that made Rodney even crazier. 'Not a sound,' he screamed. 'Not one sound from any of you.' And there wasn't, believe me. We weren't even breathing. And then this noise came from Lana, like a gurgle and a sigh at the same time. And that really got to Rodney. He just sort of collapsed by her body and called to her and said he didn't mean to hurt her and he was sorry. I guess Bill Fosheim thought that was the time to make a move because he just lunged out of the group and threw himself toward Rodney, trying to reach one of the guns, but he wasn't fast enough. Rodney shot him right in the face. And Mrs. Mallory, another customer, couldn't take it and she started to scream and run for the door, and he shot her too."

Rodney, apparently calmed by the carnage, herded his captives away from the bodies and asked them to form a straight line. When they had, he began to dismiss them one by one until only Beryl was left.

"I knew before he said a word that I would be staying," she told Kate, unable to conceal entirely her pride at the dubious honor of being chosen. "I saw it in his eyes."

"Why do you think he picked you?" Kate asked.

Beryl considered carefully. "I believe he must have known that I would be the best spokesperson. I don't know if he ever saw any of the shows I did with the Harbor View Players—I had parts in *A Thousand Clowns* and *Redhead* and a few other things—but I believe he just felt that I had a gift for communication. And also, you must remember, something larger was at work at that moment. Rodney wasn't the only one doing the choosing."

Rodney, with or without help, wasted no time establishing Beryl as his go-between with the forces outside the bank. One hour after he had gunned down his erstwhile girl friend, Beryl stood in the doorway of People's Bank & Trust facing Harbor View's entire police force, television cameras from nearby Muskegon, and a large crowd of horrified and fascinated citizens. Rodney's shotgun, pointed at her head, was visible in the murky space behind her.

Beryl's eyes flicked rapidly from side to side. She tugged repeatedly at her clothing. ("I never was comfortable in that skirt and wouldn't you just know I'd have worn it that day.") Her mouth worked frantically, as though she were taking a running start toward speech. But only when a policeman started toward her along the front wall of the bank did she find her voice.

"No!" Her piercing shriek pinned him in place. "Go back," she pleaded. He retreated at once.

Then, glancing down at a piece of paper in her hand, Beryl began to speak.

"Mr. Flint has asked me to tell you that this bank is now an armed fortress and I am his prisoner." Her voice caught as she described her own status, but she composed herself, hauled downward sharply on her skirt, and continued, gaining in steadiness and volume as she went along. "I will die if there is any attempt to rescue me or capture him. He says that he has nothing to lose by killing again. However, if everyone does what he says he has promised not to harm me. He will have more to say later on."

As Beryl scuttled back into the bank, a voice in the distance wailed her name and Stanley could be seen arriving at the edge of the crowd. But it was too late for him even to glimpse her.

The first night was the worst, Beryl said. She and Rodney were "on very different wavelengths" and Beryl was distressed by what she called the "inhumane conditions" of her captivity, meaning the bodies lying about on the bank floor, the lack of food, and the fact that Rodney tied her up when he wanted to sleep. Her appearance the following morning made it evident that she was somewhat worse for wear. Her hair was matted against her head, her face, devoid of makeup, looked pale and indistinct, her clothes, dampened by the already soaring temperature, flattened against her body in patches.

"Mr. Flint has asked me to tell you," she began, but before she could complete Rodney's directive, two policemen surged toward her from the right and attempted to surround her, scoop her up and sweep her off to the left. Rodney's bullet caught one in the back of the head and he fell immediately; he winged the other in the shoulder, which spun him away from Beryl. She crawled back into the bank on her belly.

"That was the turning point for me," she told Kate. "I got down on my hands and knees and asked what I should do and the message came back loud and clear: God helps those who help themselves. There wasn't going to be any rescue. I was on my own. I realized Rodney probably didn't want to kill me because he could've right then and there but he didn't, and I decided I wasn't going to give him any reason to. I also realized that I'd better take charge of certain things because he wasn't too tightly wrapped and he just wasn't going to think of them."

Beryl told Rodney he had to clean up the mess, that she

29

would not allow herself to be physically restrained (he had her word that she would not try to escape), and that she planned to order breakfast, and he had better do the same because low blood sugar wouldn't help anything. Rodney, perhaps to give a sign of cooperation to match Beryl's swift return to the bank after the abortive rescue effort, perhaps simply unable to resist her purposefulness, agreed on all counts.

When she emerged from the bank soon afterward, the police shouted their support through bullhorns. ("Try to remain calm, Mrs. Swarr. We have everything under control.") Stanley called out his encouragement. ("Hang on, sweetheart, we'll get you out of there.") And the crowd sent a sympathetic murmur rolling toward her. Beryl held up her hand for silence.

"We'd like some food in here," she said crisply. "Bacon, eggs over easy, and home fries for Mr. Flint, and some O.J. and two Egg McMuffins for me, four coffees, two black, two with cream and sugar." Order given, she disappeared into the bank. And so began what Norma Van den Haag bitterly called "The Beryl Swarr Show."

Beryl appeared several times a day with communiqués from Rodney and herself. His generally involved strategic concerns: everyone must stay at least one hundred yards away from the bank; the crowd must be dispersed at night so as not to interfere with his sleep; the authorities should arrange his safe passage out of the country. Hers focused primarily on housekeeping matters: she asked for the cot she kept in her attic, along with the new yellow flowered sheets she had bought the week before on sale; she regularly requested changes of clothing. ("Stanley, bring down that pretty pink shift with the spaghetti straps and my white patent leather sandals.")

Kate began to understand that it was during Beryl's incarceration, not its aftermath, that her weight gain had occurred. She ordered her meals with meticulous attention to detail, emphasis on volume, and great relish. ("I'd like a bucket of extra crispy chicken from the Little Red Hen, all white meat, and that doesn't mean wings, some potato salad from the deli, an order of those delicious fried mushrooms from Walt and Vivian's, and a chocolate marshmallow almond sundae with chocolate, coffee, and fudge-ripple ice cream from Sweettooth.")

"Boy, Beryl's really packin' it in, isn't she?" someone in the crowd remarked after hearing one of her orders broadcast through the bullhorn.

He was quickly hushed by the other onlookers.

"Why shouldn't she?" one asked.

"What else's she got to do?" said another.

When Kate asked Beryl if she thought the stress had made her overeat, Beryl looked at her blankly for a few beats, then seemed to catch on.

"Oh, that's the camera," she said. "It puts on at least ten pounds."

The crowd was now confined behind police barricades in the park that lay directly across the street from People's Bank & Trust. The police and the television cameras were stationed just in front of the barricades, although Beryl had gotten Rodney to agree to let the cameras come in somewhat closer when she was making a statement. Often when she came out of the bank and picked up her bullhorn, reporters shouted questions at her. The first day or so these flustered her, but soon she was handling them like a pro.

"Mrs. Swarr, are you angry that the police have been unable to secure your release?"

"I recognize that their hands are tied," said Beryl, her

amplified voice floating out over the town. "We had a stalemate from the very beginning and you saw what happened
when a rescue attempt was made. But I'm working on things
from the inside and I hope to have something to report on
that soon."

"How would you describe Flint's state of mind at this
point?"

"Mr. Flint is stable and calm, sleeping well, doing little
things around the bank that I need help with. He's being
very cooperative."

"What's the hardest part of all this for you, Mrs. Swarr?"

"Being away from my home and family."

"How much more can you take? How long do you think
you can hang on?"

"As long as necessary."

As the days went by, crowd participation took on the air
of a political rally, with Beryl as the favored candidate.
When she appeared signs popped up all over the park:
WE'RE WITH YOU 100 PERCENT. HARBOR VIEW SALUTES
SWARR. BERYL'S OUR GAL. YOU HAVE OUR PRAYERS. And
lest she feel insufficiently supported by these messages, or be
unable to see them all, the citizens in the park also chanted
a message of solidarity whenever she appeared: "Here's the
word from Harbor View/Beryl, Beryl, we're with you."
Beryl, responding in kind, flashed the crowd a victory sign.

During an impromptu press conference early one evening, Beryl entertained a question about Rodney's treatment of her.

"Other than laying down the basic guidelines that I'd be
killed if I tried to escape, Mr. Flint has never threatened
me in any way. In all our dealings he has been polite, courteous . . ."

The rest of Beryl's words were obscured by a horrendous

noise. The cameras swiveled quickly in its direction and showed Norma Van den Haag stretched over a crowd barrier, hands pummeling two policemen who had apparently attempted to halt her forward rush, face contorted by the howls issuing from her mouth.

"Shut up! Shut up!" she cried. "Somebody shut her mouth, make her stop . . . shut up . . . shut up."

The police attempted to haul Norma away. People in the crowd rushed to vilify her.

"She's crazy. Get her out of here."

"Shut *her* up."

Beryl called for restraint. "It's all right, everybody. Just stay calm. Norma, can you hear me?"

The only reply was the sound of Norma's ongoing scuffle with the police and her now wordless keening that vibrated in the heavy dusk.

"Norma, listen to me. Lana did not suffer. She died instantly."

A mournful and monumental moan rose up and pushed against Beryl's words.

"She felt no pain," Beryl continued, "none at all. And that's certainly something to be grateful for . . . a real blessing."

"Mother of God," Norma cried, "please . . . shut up."

"Get her outta here," called Beryl's partisans. "Take her away."

"Please, people," said Beryl. "She's had a terrible shock. She doesn't know what she's saying."

Norma's shouted denials gradually receded as she was carried away.

Beryl struck many different emotional notes during her appearances. She was at times somber ("Enough blood has been shed in this tragic incident and I intend to see that no

more is spilled"), playful ("Well, at least the bank has air
conditioning so maybe it's not such a bad place to be in this
heat"), reassuring ("There is absolutely no cause for alarm
or concern about my state of mind. It is A-OK"), impatient
("I will not answer any further questions about a rescue attempt. It is simply not an option"), inspirational ("I do feel
certain that if God hadn't wanted me to be in this situation
he wouldn't have made me a teller"). She was never dis-
pirited or morose.

The day the children came was, many felt, her finest
hour. Rodney had decreed that none of Beryl's family be allowed any contact with her. She had explained that that
would be cruel and unusual punishment for Stanley ("He'd
go crazy if he had to stay away. You know how it is to feel
that way about somebody") and also unnecessary ("You'll
hear everything we say to each other. There's no way we
could conspire against you"). Despite misgivings, Rodney
relented in Stanley's case and allowed him to stand in the
crowd and exchange a few words with his wife during her
appearances.

But there came a time, as the days passed, when Beryl
wished to see her children also and asked Rodney if she
might. He decided to permit them to come but told Beryl
where they must stand, how long she could talk to them,
what she should say. ("Nothing soppy, just get a look at
them and tell them you're fine and that's it.")

Beryl was waiting outside when Melody and Lance were
delivered to a spot just in front of the crowd barrier. They
stood, squinting at their mother through the bright afternoon sunlight, uncertain how to behave. Beryl was uncharacteristically quiet, gazing back at them. Lance broke
the spell.

"How're you doin', Ma?" he called to her, raising his hand in a small salute.

"Just fine, dear," her voice boomed back at him. "How about you?"

"Don't worry about me," he said.

"How are you, Melody?"

Melody, in obvious torment, grunted something unintelligible.

"Speak up, honey," Beryl prompted through the horn.

"I'm fine," Melody screamed.

"Time's up," Rodney hollered.

"I want you children to cooperate with your father and do whatever he says, all right? Remember, I'm just fine and I love you."

Beryl leaned down, put the bullhorn on the pavement, and turned to head back inside. But just as she reached the doorway, she whirled around and ran toward Melody and Lance, arms outstretched. A cry from inside the bank stopped her about halfway across the street.

"I got a grenade here," Rodney screamed. "And I'm takin' out the pin and if you don't walk back this way I'm gonna let it fly and it'll hit you and your kids and lots of other—"

Beryl, facing the bank, hands on hips, shouted him down. "Just hold on there, Rodney. Just simmer down. I probably shouldn't have moved so fast. But it wasn't a trick, it was just an impulse. I just wanted to give my kids a hug. I'm sure you can understand that. Now I want you to put that pin back in that grenade, set it down, and just relax. I'm coming right back inside, but first I'm going to walk over to my kids for just a minute."

The silence, from the bank, from the crowd, was absolute

35

as Beryl approached her children and crushed them to her. Lance wrapped his arms around his mother's waist, Melody kept hers at her sides. Beryl bent her head to theirs. Soon she straightened up, wrenched herself away, and strode back toward the bank, the flapping of her sandals on the pavement the only sound. As she reached the doorway, the crowd broke into applause. Beryl paused for a split second as the noise reached her, then, without turning, raised a hand in acknowledgment before vanishing from sight.

It appeared the police had already conceded that their best, perhaps only, chance lay in letting Beryl manage Rodney. But if there were any remaining doubts about the wisdom of such a course, this incident erased them. As police chief Garrett McGee said to reporters, "Mrs. Swarr seems to be able to handle this fella and we believe she's the one who can bring this thing to a peaceful conclusion."

"Should that be the responsibility of the hostage?" he was asked. "Isn't that the job of the police?"

McGee just grinned and said, "We're counting on Mrs. Swarr."

Beryl had determined quite early in her ordeal that Rodney's surrender was the only sensible outcome, the only one guaranteed to keep them both alive. And she was interested in Rodney's safety as well as her own. She had, she told Kate, become rather fond of him.

"Oh, I could see he had problems," she said. "One of them that made my job tough was a trust problem he had with women because of the way Lana had treated him. I knew he was disturbed, all right, but he also had other qualities. He could be very, very sweet."

Beryl attempted during the first few days to overcome Rodney's trust problem by following his commands to the letter, demonstrating her reliability at every turn. When she felt that he had begun to have a little faith in her, she broached the idea of surrender. Rodney went into a paranoid rage that lasted the better part of two days. He cursed and reviled Beryl, held loaded guns to her head, lashed her to the cot at night and took away her snack privileges. ("He said I couldn't eat between meals and he watched me like a hawk to make sure I didn't.")

"Of course, I didn't let on to the outside about any of this and I think that impressed him and he eventually calmed down and we got talking again."

Beryl told him it was unlikely that he would ever get out of the country. Even with her for cover, a sharpshooter could easily pick him off the minute they walked out of the bank. Escape wouldn't necessarily solve his problems either, she pointed out. He would be hunted for the rest of his life, as surely as if he were a Nazi in South America. Surrender, on the other hand, might work in his favor in any legal proceedings. At the very least it would probably keep him alive. Rodney was not convinced, but neither did he punish Beryl this time. She knew then, she said, that if she were patient and persistent, she would triumph. She was both, and finally the break came.

At noontime on the tenth day of the siege Beryl, well-coiffed, carefully made up, and wearing a fresh seersucker suit, emerged from the bank and picked up the bullhorn.

"I'm very pleased to be able to make the following announcement: I will be bringing Mr. Flint out of the bank shortly. He will be holding a revolver to my head. Do not be alarmed by this. It is simply a precaution he feels he must take. A police car should be parked in front of the bank with Chief McGee and another officer inside. Mr. Flint and I will proceed to the car and there I will place him in the chief's custody. All other police officers and members of the audience must stay behind the barricades. Your cooperation is of the utmost importance. Thank you."

Minutes later, when the official blue and gold car was in place, the scene unfolded just as Beryl had outlined. She and Rodney stepped into the midday haze. He clutched the protective shield of Beryl's body to him by an arm encircling her throat. The shiny black barrel of a gun bit into her temple, one blond tendril wrapped round it as if to hold it in place. Together they shuffled forward, Beryl's unblinking eyes straight ahead, Rodney's feverish ones darting about in search of danger. They reached the car without incident and the chief took Rodney's gun away from him and guided him into the car, which drove off. For just a moment, Beryl stood alone. The crowd seemed to hold its collective breath. Now that it was over would Beryl founder, become hysterical, fall apart? The answer came as her arms flew above her head, fingers of each hand separating to form a V.

Soon only these waggling symbols were visible as Stanley, the press, ambulance attendants, and police surged forward. Then even her hands disappeared. At the center of the crush Beryl answered reporters' questions. Yes, she felt relief that it was over. No, she never lost faith. The support of the crowd and "something bigger than all of us put together" had sustained her. She was not bitter that the police had been unable to free her. She felt only sympathy and compassion for the entire Van den Haag family and it was well known that the loss of a loved one could, in some instances, cause derangement. She looked forward to sleeping in her own bed, taking a shower, eating some of her own home cooking, and returning to "normal life."

Once the press was satisfied ("Thanks a lot, Mrs. Swarr." "Anytime, happy to do it"), Beryl rejected offers of an ambulance or a police escort and, with Stanley's arm around her shoulder, made her way across the street. Her progress through the crowd in the park was halting as everyone, it seemed, wanted to touch her, congratulate her, give her a message. And it was delirious. The crowd cheered, waved signs and banners, chanted Beryl's name, and sang "God Bless America" and Harbor View High School's fight song.

Nor did the adulation stop here. In the days that followed Beryl was feted by the Rotary; the League of Christian Women; the Harbor View police, who made her an honorary member of the force; MAFIA (the Michigan Association of Financial Institutions of America), which, in a burst of high good humor, made her "honorary godfather"; the Girl Scouts, and a group of neighbors ("We're just proud to be on the same block with you"). Restaurants in town, grateful for the invaluable publicity they had received when Beryl ordered in their food, offered her free meals. Letters poured in from all over the country. A parade in which Beryl rode atop a float constructed to resemble People's Bank & Trust climaxed Beryl Swarr Day, a panegyrical orgy that lasted from dawn to dark.

All this, of course, delayed Beryl's return to normal life, and when it did finally come she found that it was neither as satisfying as she had remembered, nor as comforting as she had anticipated. She told Kate she found herself feeling restless and perturbed. And after a few weeks of this disquiet, she got in touch with Kate's agent.

"I knew there was something important that I was supposed to be doing," she said. "I just felt I had something to say."

39

"Did you know what that was ... specifically?" Kate asked.

"Well," Beryl replied, "I suppose that's really up to you in a way. You're the writer."

Flying back to New York, back to beginning to write, back to continuing to inch her way toward Jason, Kate, looking over her notes, came upon a list of titles that had emerged from a postdinner session one evening at the Swarrs'. Curiously, Stanley's choices—*The Siege at People's Bank & Trust, Ten Days in a Bank*—tended to emphasize the setting of Beryl's ordeal rather than her part in it, revealing perhaps that he still found it almost unbearable to think of his wife in such straits.

"Oh, Stanley, those'll just end it up on the shelf with all the money books," Beryl said, demonstrating that she was already beginning to grasp some elementary marketing concepts.

Lance favored such straightforward titles as *The Hostage of Harbor View* and *The Beryl Swarr Story*. Melody basically refused to participate although she stayed in the room glowering at them and making noises of disgust whenever a suggestion was made. At one point, having apparently reached the limit of her endurance, she rose and began to shuffle out of the room, muttering as she went, "Why don't you just call it *The Little Piggy and How She Grew*"?

"What's that, Mel?" her father asked.

"Never mind," said Beryl, hands unconsciously moving to smooth out the fabric that pulled across her stomach. "Just let her go."

Beryl's own choices veered from the rather melodramatic—*Hostage to Fate, No Man Is My Jailer, Date with Destiny*—to the intensely practical—*How to Survive as a*

Hostage: A Commonsense Guide to Being Held Prisoner.
Kate told her that, despite the once-every-106-hours statistic, this last would limit their audience severely. Beryl also
suggested *The Lady and the Gunman* ("That would be
great for the movie," she said, once again demonstrating the
scope of her expectations) and *A Teller in History* ("It's sort
of a steal from Lee Harvey Oswald's mother, but I think it
gives a good perspective").

Kate could not, at this point, say she hadn't been warned.
Certainly she was no longer in the dark about Beryl's sense
of calling, nor about the vacuity of her mission, nor about
her addiction to the limelight. But all that really had nothing to do with her, Kate told herself, closing her notebook,
settling her head back against the seat, feeling the sedative
hum of the airplane's engines. Beryl's inflated notions aside,
there was a good story here, and there was a contract for a
decent sum of money. Kate would simply write the book
and be done with it. After all, to be responsible for Beryl
Swarr's book was not to be responsible for Beryl Swarr. Was
it?

Chapter Three

KATE suspected that she had been drawn to writing in the first place by her need for the illusion, however temporary, that she was in control of something. Quite early in her childhood she began composing tidy and harmonious stories about imagined people that served to balance the rather disorderly unfolding of her own life.

In her stories families were large, parents rigidly dependable, schedules regular. Meals were eaten on time, promises kept, cupboards, drawers, and shelves, all of them clearly designated, prominently featured. (" 'Please bring Mother the green thread from the sewing drawer, dear,' Mrs. Wetmore said to her daughter Patricia." " 'Hang it up in the coat closet,' Jake's mother told him." " 'You will find the knife in the silverware drawer where we always keep it,' Betty reminded her sister Honey Bee.") This undue emphasis on organizational principles and routine did not make for very dramatic reading, but Kate found her tales soothing, an antidote to the reality created by the vagarious natures of her parents.

Kate's father, Lucius Cadwalader, eldest son of a wealthy old Philadelphia family, had seized his inheritance at the earliest possible moment and used it to propel himself away from his family and its world. His father had pulled strings to keep Lucius out of combat during the war. When it was over, Lucius headed directly for devastated Europe to see what he had missed. From there he traveled to Russia, back to the states through Alaska and Canada, down the west coast into Mexico and Central America, then back again to the United States via the Gulf, and across Texas, Louisiana, and Mississippi. There, in a small town on the Alabama border, he fell in love and briefly came to rest.

His repose lasted long enough for him to court and marry Carabel Langford, daughter of the hotelkeeper, but soon after that was accomplished, he was on the move again, ostensibly taking his bride north to meet his family. Carabel, whose childhood had been somewhat precarious in terms of finances and family connections, was greatly excited by this prospect. When they got as far as Maryland, however, near Frederick, to be exact, Lucius was arrested by the area's rich Civil War history and by increasingly sharp recollections of his family's members.

They were Carabel's opposite—she was gentle and lush, they were unyielding and austere—and he feared exposing her to them, as though they might somehow poison her reserves of warmth and softness on which he'd come so quickly to depend. So they stopped short of Philadelphia—a disappointment to Carabel, the first of many—and settled in the Maryland countryside in a large antebellum brick-and-wood house surrounded by a great green sea of endlessly stretching fields. Kate was born there a year later.

During her childhood, Lucius's inheritance dwindled, Carabel's hopes of being clasped to the Cadwalader family bosom receded, and both of them found ways to retreat from the pain these circumstances caused them. Lucius spent long hours in the barn, inventing contrivances of dubious value; Carabel read a great deal. The idea that Lucius might work to ease their economic difficulties apparently never occurred to either one of them. In fact, they made none of the common concessions to a fall in fortunes: the housekeeper stayed, they dressed exceedingly well, Lucius maintained a wine cellar of some distinction. They did cut back on their food budget (he espoused the virtues of organ meats and began to grow a variety of vegetables), the house and its furnishings became somewhat dingy with wear, and occasionally Lucius sold off a small piece of his original acreage. Despite the strains between them, they remained, for the most part, tender with each other, avoiding overt discord except when the subject of his family arose. Still, signs of conflict did exist.

Lucius loved food cooked with garlic; Carabel developed an allergy to it so severe that if a clove were opened in her presence she suffered a horrendous gastric disturbance that lasted for days. He enjoyed putting "his girls," as he called his wife and daughter, in the car and driving over to Baltimore to see an Orioles baseball game; she became unable to travel any farther than the library in Frederick, where she picked up at least a dozen books a week.

Lucius frequently cloistered himself in the large front parlor of the house, playing a recording of the Verdi Requiem, conducting it vehemently with his beautiful ivory baton, emerging at the end of a session, drenched and drained. When she heard the Dies Irae thunder through the house, Kate liked to sneak out onto the front porch and peer in through the gauzy curtains at his sinuous silhouette. "Your daddy just loves all that death stuff," her mother, who was often reading in a hammock on the porch, would say mildly. "I'll never know why."

Carabel, for her part, hung in the living room two large samplers from the mid-nineteenth century that told heart-breaking stories of grief and loss. One listed the brief lives—two days, sixteen days, four weeks—of three children, the dates of their arrivals in, and departures from, this life stitched onto the cloth by their mother, one Mary Derby-shire. The other memorialized a young husband "struck down by God" only one week after his wedding, his new wife's sorrow embroidered on a pale ground in somber threads. ("Morbid things," Lucius would say whenever he noticed the samplers. "Don't know why your mother wants them around.") One had to wonder, as Kate did, if these needlework messages in any way reflected Carabel's ideas of motherhood and marriage. She also wondered if her mother had declined to have more children because she hadn't deemed her first experience worth repeating.

Kate, in her early childhood, viewed both her parents as enchanted creatures. Lucius took her along when he visited Civil War battle sites, describing to her in detail the clash of opposing armies and the resulting bloodshed and desolation. Antietam was Kate's favorite and she never tired of her father's ardent account of what had happened there. Long before she really understood what death was, Kate found the idea of so much of it, in such a short time, compelling. He also taught her everything he knew about baseball, another of his passions. By the time she was ten or eleven, Kate knew the statistics on all "the Birds," as Lucius called the Orioles, and held her own easily with him in discussions of the strategic fine points of the game. She could also throw a good fast ball and, with the wind behind her, swat the ball in the air all the way over the cornfield and into the beans.

Carabel, whose concerns were more interior, read to Kate from whatever novel happened to be in her hands: Pearl Buck or Jane Austen, Louis Bromfield or Henry James. Her tastes were omnivorous, her appetite for fiction was voracious, frequently carrying her through two or three books a day. This made Kate's acquaintance with any one book necessarily brief and fragmentary. She might hear a snatch of, say, *The Idiot* in the morning, but by the time she arrived home from school in the middle of the afternoon Dostoevsky could be finished and Carabel deep into *Bleak House, The Caine Mutiny,* or *Alice Adams.* But Kate didn't mind being robbed of resolutions and continuity. And more than the sound of any particular author, it was her mother's voice she remembered, washing over her, holding Kate against her with a web of words.

As Kate grew older, however, the discord between her parents infringed more and more on her notions of each of them. She could not help but feel her father's sense of failure, visible in his increasingly neglected appearance and in what Kate perceived as a doleful downward pull at the corners of his eyes. Nor could she ignore the air of hopelessness that hung about her mother like a cloud of scent. When Terlitha, the housekeeper, was found dead in her bed one morning, and Lucius propped up her body in the front seat of the car and drove her to the next county, where her long-estranged brother lived and where death duties and burial costs were lower, saying she had expired during the ride, Kate could see her mother's humiliation.

One day Carabel took Kate and left Lucius a note saying she was leaving for Philadelphia, there to bring her existence and that of her daughter to the attention of his family in hopes of securing some financial relief. Although she turned back just outside of Frederick (trying to push beyond her self-imposed travel limit left her weak and shaking), Lucius found the note and Kate sensed the shame and rage it had produced in him.

By the time Kate left home to go to college, she had resolved to establish her financial independence as swiftly as possible and never again to relinquish it, to forego having children, and to avoid marriage. She was adamant about these intentions, tenacious in their pursuit, and successful in their execution until she met Jason Wylie when she was almost thirty years old. And because he so heartily approved of her first two resolutions, Kate found it hard to resist him when he challenged the third.

They met at a party given for the publication of a book of a mutual friend. Kate had just published her first novel, Jason his sixth. Within half an hour of their meeting, Jason knew he wanted to marry Kate, even though he had already tried marriage once and failed at it. He managed to keep his desire to himself for a few more hours, however, not apprising Kate of it until he took her home later that night. She was sorry, she said, but she wasn't going to marry anyone. Nor was she going to surrender her independent financial status. Nor have children.

He was absolutely in favor of financial independence, Jason asserted. Being sole breadwinner during his first marriage had done nothing for his ego or his notion of his own

47

masculinity. In fact, he said, he'd found it rather a strain. He had worked for a newspaper during the day, written his novels at night, and regularly begged Natasha, his wife, to consider gainful employment. An emigrée from the Soviet Union, she pleaded language difficulties, even though she had been in the United States for nearly fifteen years and spoke, to Jason's ear, adequate, though heavily accented, English. Whenever they had a discussion about work, however, Natasha's speech shattered and broke into a series of halting, nearly unintelligible phrases. As for children, Jason said, he had two and considered that enough. Would she please think about marrying him?

During their courtship, which lasted nearly a year, they covered this ground, and other disputed territory, over and over again. Why had he married such a dependent woman? Kate asked. He'd been attracted not by her dependency but by her exotic foreignness. Why was she afraid to make commitments? Jason inquired. She wasn't afraid; she was simply prudent. Wouldn't he backslide on the financial and progenitive issues once she was in his clutches? Was she going to hold herself separate and apart all her life just because her parents' marriage had been odd and strained? Back and forth they went, their attachment to each other deepening as they argued.

Jason asked Kate to meet his mother. She agreed.

"She'll like you, but she'll be suspicious," he told Kate.

"Because I'm not Jewish?" she asked.

"Because you're a writer. She thinks there's a tiny little Philip Roth hidden inside each of us, longing to get out and expose our families to shame and ridicule. It doesn't matter that I've written six books that are distinctly not autobiographical. She still doesn't trust me. Every time I start a new book, she says, 'I hope this will be another nice story.' That's her way of saying it better not be about her, or my father, whom I don't even remember, or Uncle Morris or Aunt Adele or any of the rest of them."

Rose Wylie questioned Kate closely about her work. Did she go in for "drawing things from life"? Rose wondered. Or was she able to employ her "creative powers"?

Kate said she hoped her first novel had been imaginative.

"I was always under the impression," Rose said, "that a novel was a novel because the things in it were made up. But that's not the case today. Am I right or am I wrong?"

Before Kate could answer she went on. "You don't look like the sort who'd have to stoop to feeding off other people just to make a splash for yourself."

"I certainly hope not—"

"But looks don't mean much today," Rose said. "People have gotten pretty good at pretending to be one thing when they're really another. Am I right or am I wrong?"

"Well, I think I'm—"

"I've never seen much point in that," Rose cut in. "Sooner or later the real thing shows through. Why postpone it? Right from the beginning you may as well let people know where you stand. Am I right or am I wrong?"

"Right," said Kate.

"It was a great success," said Jason, as they left Rose's apartment.

"It was? How could you tell?"

"As we were leaving, she whispered to me 'much better than the Communist.' And she liked Natasha. At least she wasn't a writer."

Jason met Lucius and Carabel when Kate took him down to Maryland for a late spring weekend. She had not been eager to make the trip, but Jason had. The few times in her life that Kate had exposed her parents to friends of hers had been excruciating.

She had, from an early age, suspected that certain aspects of her parents were anomalous. Viewed through the eyes of her eighth-grade friend Alice Louise Archibald, for instance, they were undeniably so. Lucius's and Carabel's eccentricities glared at Kate in a harsh new light. She was sure that Alice Louise's mother did not bring a book to the dinner table with her, nor talk about the characters therein as though she'd seen them at the market that afternoon. She was sure that Alice Louise's mother, not her father, went to the market. And did Mr. Archibald make contraptions for measuring portions of food, or shelling pistachio nuts, or hemming skirts automatically? Kate doubted it. The very things that made her parents so magical to her seemed, through outside eyes, grotesque. Kate hated herself for this response, but she also hated her parents for their part in producing it.

"You have to understand that they're not just regular people," Kate said to Jason as they approached the Cadwalader house.

"You mean like my mother?" he asked, silencing her.

Kate had already fallen in love with Jason. She knew that, even as she continued to dispute its implications. She had fallen in love with his face, its dark handsomeness offset by a slight crook in his nose from a childhood break, with his enthusiasm for whatever lay in front of him, with his fascination with the dark side of human nature, and with his air of solidity and his comfort with absolutes, both things notably absent from her past.

During the weekend in Maryland, she fell in love with the

easy way he entered that past. Jason's presence enhanced Kate's parents, rather than diminished them. Seemingly without effort, he appreciated those things that set them apart. Kate knew, before the weekend ended, that the fight was over.

"You win," she told him, as they drove back to New York.

"Thank God," he replied.

Kate had never regretted her decision. Not even when Jason, as she had feared, began attempting to undermine her financial independence by urging her to say no to ghostwriting the story of the first teenage correspondent on a network news program, and offering to support her during the writing of a novel.

"For God's sake, Katie," he said, "it's only temporary. And it's for your sake. I just want you to be happy."

"Do you know the atrocities that have been committed in the name of rationales like that? I knew this would happen eventually."

"Yeah. I've just been biding my time, waiting to subvert you."

"I'm sure that's not your motive. It just feels that way."

"Look, if you want—"

"Don't say 'look.' I hate it."

"If you want to write anchor boy's autobiography for a miserable twelve-thousand-buck advance just so that you can cling to the idea of economic autonomy, be my guest. At least it should be short."

"He's not an anchor."

"Well, surely he will be after the book comes out."

"I'm not doing it. It's repellent."

"Ah, sweet reason restored."

51

"This doesn't mean I won't do another ghost project sometime."

"Of course not, unless you find you like being kept."

(Kate, as it happened, did begin a novel, but soon abandoned it in favor of the humming book, which was, she explained to Jason, repellent in a different and more manageable way.)

Nor did Kate regret marrying Jason when he had the affair with Tabitha Waxberger. She certainly wished he hadn't, but her energies, quite quickly, went toward attempting to restore their union rather than deploring its existence.

So, unfortunately, did Tabitha's. Unable to accept Jason's rejection of her as final, she dogged him, in the streets, via the U.S. mails, by telephone. The various voices she adopted on the phone were ill-disguised and Kate took to saying "he's not here, Tabbie" to virtually any unrecognizable party, generally causing a hang-up. This only backfired once, when Rose called and Kate mistook her for Tabitha doing a Rose imitation.

"Who's Tabbie?" Rose asked.

"Oh, it's not important," said Kate, nonplussed.

"Was she that girl who cooked for you?"

"She wasn't a cook."

"She made me kasha muffins. I remember it very well."

"Yes, she did bake things."

"She gave me her recipe for soybean nut loaf. Very nice."

"I hired her to transcribe tapes, not cook."

"And now she's working for Jason? What does he need transcribed? I don't see why he needs to do research if he's making up stories from his imagination."

"No, she's not working for either one of us."

"But she's calling . . . for Jason."

"Well, I thought she was, but it was you."

"I'm surprised we sound so much alike."

"My mistake."

"You know what I think? I think she's probably after Jason with no good in mind and she calls and bothers him and bothers you and you're too polite to tell her to take a powder. Am I right or am I wrong?"

"Wrong." It was the first time Kate had answered Rose's perpetual question in the negative and it stopped her in her tracks.

Recognizing finally that she was not making any headway with Jason, Tabitha turned to Kate, asking if she might come to see her. Kate, pitying the straitened creature, and hoping she might somehow bring the whole lurid episode to a close, agreed.

She opened the door to someone she barely recognized. Unrequited love had ravaged Tabitha. Her hair had lost its spring and shine and shrouded her face in dingy hanks. Her skin, never highly hued, was now devoid of any color whatsoever. Her lithe, young body seemed to have caved in on itself and she stood with shoulders sagging, abdomen sunken. Kate could not help herself: she reached out, took the young woman's hand, and drew her inside.

"Have you been eating, Tabbie? You don't look well," Kate said.

"Can't," Tabbie managed to croak before making her way to the kitchen, where she unloaded from her backpack a batch of still-warm buckwheat brioches and a thermos of Tanzanian coffee.

"You didn't have to bring anything," Kate protested.

Tabitha shrugged and moved automatically to the cup-

Linda Crawford

boards to take out plates and cups, to the refrigerator to remove butter, jam, and milk.

"Sit down," Kate chided her. "Save your strength."

Tabitha subsided into a chair and looked up at Kate with haunted eyes.

"We had something so beautiful," she said, tears streaming down her chalky face. "You'd never understand."

Kate, her pity quickly displaced by the recollection that this forlorn and desolate soul had possessed and ravaged Jason on the desk in his study, felt like taking a brioche and stuffing it into Tabitha's mouth, which was slowly widening to make way for a horrendous wail. Instead, she tore the roll open, slapped some butter and jam inside and shoved it across the table.

"Eat," she ordered.

"Let him go," Tabitha whispered. "Release him. I know he wants his freedom, but he's very obligated to you."

"As I am to him."

"And you want a relationship that's based on that?" Her upper lip twisted into a tremulous sneer.

"Yes, I do. Based on that and other things."

"What other things?" Tabitha bawled.

The sound so unnerved Kate that she pulled the brioche back across the table and took a large bite of it herself. "You wouldn't understand," she said finally.

"Release him," Tabitha cried. "Let him go."

"Tabbie," Kate said softly, "Jason and I don't want to be released from each other. You'll have to find a way to recognize that."

"I can't," she shrieked. "I can't, I can't."

Kate tore off another mouthful of brioche and chewed it while she watched Tabitha scream. Eventually, the young

54

woman fell silent, and soon thereafter she went, leaving behind the brioches and making Kate promise not to give any to Jason. Within a few days she resumed calling, using her own voice, and asking for Kate.

"I just wanted to let you know that I'm feeling better," she said. "I think I'm starting to let go a little."

"Good . . . I'm glad to hear it."

"Things are definitely on the upswing."

"Great."

"I ate a complete meal yesterday, slept four straight hours."

"Tabbie, you don't have to tell me—"

"That's the most I've eaten or slept in weeks."

"Terrific. Listen—"

"I'll keep you posted." And she hung up.

Kate didn't have the heart to do the same to her when the calls continued.

She did not even regret marrying Jason when those things that had drawn her to him in the first place—the fact that he was decidedly not a dreamer, his sometimes literal nature—became irritants. That, she supposed, was an irony integral to the married state. It might provoke her, but it never caused remorse.

But when Jason broached the possibility of presenting Kate with a child, a full-blown adolescent son, she questioned the wisdom of having chosen him as a mate.

The child was Igor, oldest of Jason's children with Natasha and now, in his fifteenth year, well beyond his mother's disciplinary capacity. Kate had first known Igor as a sweet, rather shy seven-year-old. He and his sister, Ludmilla, had spent time with Jason and her over the years until Natasha moved to California, at which point, according to Natasha,

55

Igor began immediately to run amok. Now Natasha, who had always been loath to let Igor out of her sight, was begging to have him taken off her hands.

"My God, Jason," said Kate, "I never even wanted one of my own, but to take on somebody else's—"

"Mine, Kate. You don't have to make him sound quite so anonymous."

"Well, yours, yes . . . but barely. He's really Natasha's child. And to take on somebody else's child when the damage is done and I'm not even the one who inflicted it . . . I'm not sure I'm up to that."

"You underestimate yourself. You'd be great."

"Don't bother with the flattery."

"But you've been wonderful with the kids when they've visited."

"I'm not good with teenagers. They make my throat constrict. Couldn't we take Ludmilla instead?"

"She's not the problem, Kate. Igor is."

"He doesn't even like me."

"He doesn't like anyone."

"I don't think I want to live with someone who doesn't like me. Besides, we're just getting over the Waxberger thing. I don't think we need to put another strain on ourselves."

"That seems to me like a pretty selfish point of view."

"Right. And one of the reasons I didn't want children was so that I would be able to have such a point of view. It never seemed to bother you before."

"There are certain responsibilities that go with being a parent."

"I never noticed those bothering you before either."

"Don't get nasty."

"It's just an observation."

"I know I haven't been an especially conscientious father, but now I have a chance to rectify that."

"Couldn't we wait until I finish *Captive Courageous?*"

"He's in trouble *now*. I want to help him now. Just sleep on it, Katie. We can talk again in the morning."

At six A.M. Kate was awakened by a ringing phone and picked it up to hear a series of guttural noises that sounded like large dogs tearing at one another. Assuming it was Tabitha in the throes of a relapse, she muttered, "sleeping, Tabbie," and was about to replace the receiver when an unmistakably Slavic note stopped her.

"Kaaa-taa-ree-na." The voice spun out an elongated filament of sound.

"Natasha? Isn't it the middle of the night out there?"

"What difference? For me, it is always darkness."

"Oh, things can't be that bad."

"My rope is gone, Kaataareenaa."

"Your rope?"

"The boy needs the hand of his father. Without it, he is destroyed . . . I am destroyed . . . little Luddy is destroyed. If Jason will not help—"

"Of course he'll help," Kate said, suddenly filled with guilt. "Of course he will." She felt Jason's body curl around hers. "We'll call you later to make arrangements."

She hung up the phone and lay very still, feeling his warmth surround her.

"Thank you, Katie," he said against the back of her neck.

His gratitude overwhelmed her, dissolving a restraint that had existed ever since the affair, and Kate abandoned herself to him completely. It was the kind of lovemaking, she thought afterward, that should lead to the conception of a child.

But when Igor arrived, just one week later, he looked like

anything but a blessed event. Kate sent Jason alone to the airport to meet him because she thought they should spend some time together without her. But when they arrived at the apartment it was evident that relations between them had already begun to deteriorate.

Igor shambled in, his head thrust forward at a truculent angle, his eyes ranging warily over his new surroundings. After submitting reluctantly to Kate's tentative embrace, he stripped off his leather jacket to reveal a T-shirt that bore the legend DON'T MESS WITH ME on both back and front. When Kate showed him to his room, he elected to stay in it.

"What did you say to him?" she asked Jason, whose facial nerve was twitching visibly beneath the skin of his cheek.

"I didn't *say* anything to him," he said defensively. "I just let him know that we have certain ways of doing things around here and that he would have to accommodate himself to our way of life, not the the other way around."

"Maybe it wasn't the best thing to lay down a lot of rigid rules on his first night."

"I did not lay down any rigid rules, Kate. You know, for a child hater you're very quick to take his side."

"I'm not even going to dignify that with a response."

"Look—"

"Don't say look."

"He needs limits. He needs discipline. He's here because his mother can't supply those and I can. Tonight I started supplying them. That's all."

"He also needs love," said Kate.

"Of course he does," Jason said. "I already told him I loved him—twice."

The lines were quickly drawn. Jason was eager to give Igor what he called a "framework" of clear goals and expectations. Igor, instinctively, was determined to resist his father's suggestions. Kate hovered uneasily between the two of them, urging Jason not to be too harsh, trying to converse naturally with Igor despite the glottal barrier that dropped into place whenever she encountered him. She knew she was trying too hard—to like Igor, to make him like her, to regulate Jason. She knew she should just let go, allow things to take their own course, simply be herself, whatever that might be. But she could not.

Her only peaceful moments came when she was working, shut away in her study spinning out the saga of Harbor View's numero uno. It was relaxing to write of Rodney Flint's insanity, Stanley Swarr's tortured nightmares, Norma Van den Haag's despair, Beryl's fortitude. But Kate's own reality waited outside this sanctuary and eventually, at some point each day, she had to come out.

She and Jason tried not to carp at each other in front of Igor but, away from him, they had frequent arguments, which he must sometimes have overheard. ("You know nothing about raising children, Kate. How could you? You weren't *raised*. You just evolved and the two people you lived with watched . . . sort of. What did they ever teach you? What Oriole pitcher finished the most games in 1961? The number of Union dead at Gettysburg?" "You're desperate to show how involved you are, Jason, because you're compensating for years of neglect. It's guilt that's driving you, not love." "Taking responsibility sometimes means taking a hard stand, Kate. That's part of being a grown-up." "It may also, Jason, depending on who's doing it, be part of being a sanctimonious S.O.B.")

One night after an especially nasty and clamorous argument Kate went into Igor's room. He lay on his bed reading, a nest of clothes propping up his head, his pillow tossed in a corner of the room next to several stacks of books, some empty yogurt cartons, and a tangle of sneakers and jeans.

"I'm sure you heard us." Kate forced her voice through the narrowing laryngeal passage, causing it to emerge in a high, manic-sounding burst.

"Don't worry about it," said Igor, keeping his eyes on his book.

"You're not responsible, you know."

He gave a sardonic snort that caused the pages of his book to riffle. "How many times did you two fight about me before I was living here?"

Kate was about to protest that they weren't really fighting about him, but she realized it wouldn't wash. She was used to seeing Igor upright, guard in place, poised for attack. Lying on the bed, he looked smart and sad and strangely fragile.

"I shouldn't have come here," he said.

"Of course you should have," squeaked Kate. "We're just all of us going through a period of adjustment."

"I told my mother it wouldn't work out," he continued.

"Of course it will," she countered firmly, feeling for the first time that she might really want it to. "But we all have to be patient with each other. Aside from my parents, I've never lived with anyone but Jason, and I suspect I'm probably not very good at it."

"You're doing all right," said Igor.

Kate was flooded with a warm sense of pleasure, as though he had handed her a lovely and unexpected gift.

"I'm the problem," he said. "I just don't get along with people."

"Sometimes I've had ideas about myself that weren't

true, but I've carried them around for years anyway," she said.

"I'm okay if I just stick with myself, but when I get involved with other people, forget it. I'm a troublemaker. That's why I got sent here and that's why you'll ship me back when you can't stand it anymore."

"That's not true," said Kate, stunned by Igor's bleak view of his prospects. "We'll work things out. I'm committed to that and so is your father. You and I have done okay for the last ten minutes, haven't we?"

"Ten minutes!" He laughed scornfully and turned his body away from her, toward the light, and stared down at his book again.

"It's a start," said Kate. "We've gotta start somewhere."

Resisting her impulse to approach him, to reach out and touch the shoulder blade that poked up sharply beneath his T-shirt reading GIMME A BREAK, Kate turned to go. Igor's voice stopped her as she reached the door.

"Do you really know who finished the most games in '61?" he asked.

"Hoyt Wilhelm," she said quickly, then opened the door and closed it behind her.

Chapter Four

BERYL'S communications to Kate, during the months she was writing *C.C.*, as Beryl called it, were incessant. Every few days a letter or phone call relayed her observations and reflections. Some of these bore very specifically upon the Work; others had a decidedly personal cast, charting Beryl's psychic fluctuations and indicating a deep immersion in self-help literature, as well as an eye on her own future place in same.

She wrote:

> *Growthful journey exciting, though painful. No pain, no gain. But energy positive, ready for what's ahead. Great release in focus on Work.*
> > *Freely yours,*
> > *Beryl*

> *Recognizing need to prioritize as time approaches to step onto larger stage. Inner self-nurturance foremost.*

Know that for sure. Support zones helpful, of course,
but ripening comes from inside out.
                                    Yours in freedom,
                                    Beryl

Just below the sign-off of each letter, Beryl drew the symbol of a broken shackle.

Kate wondered about Beryl's curious reluctance to employ personal pronouns (was it an identity problem that her rapid development had failed to address?), her choppy style (it was as though her evolution had left her breathless), some of her phraseology. She suspected that "inner self-nurturance" probably meant Beryl was doing pretty much whatever she pleased, and Stanley and the children go hang. She did ask about "support zones," but when Beryl said that meant friends, Kate decided not to inquire further. Beryl's parlance had nothing to do with her, she told herself. She was responsible only for the woman who would appear in the book.

Beryl, of course, was also filled with ideas for *C.C.* and she disgorged these to Kate regularly as well: she knew *C.C.* was "factual" (her term for nonfiction), but was there any need to spell out in detail the food she had ordered while imprisoned in the bank? She'd remembered that as Lana left her post and Beryl chided her for doing so, Lana had called out, "Shut your mouth, Beryl," and perhaps that *should* be included. (Kate had the sense that Beryl subconsciously saw Lana's brutal demise, in part at least, as punishment for her cutting remark.) She was thinking of using her maiden name, Wease, on the book in order "to protect Stanley and the children." Did Kate think it had as much "punch" to it as Swarr? (Kate replied that she thought it was a toss-up, punchwise.)

Whenever a hostage incident occurred, anywhere in the world, Kate could count on hearing from Beryl. The day the siege began at the Libyan embassy in London, Kate received a message on her answering machine saying, "Keep an eye on developments in London, Katherine. A hostage angle could develop there." When that failed to occur, Kate sensed that Beryl was somehow disappointed. She sent Kate a large packet of clippings on the gunman who killed three and took a man hostage in the Quebec legislature. She peppered Kate with notices from obscure papers about what she called "spurned suitor incidents," events for which she had a soft spot, as her own experience had had its genesis in such rejection. When seventy-three hostages were taken by rebels committing a supermarket robbery in El Salvador, Beryl picked up the phone.

"Are you following the Salvador story?" she asked Kate, who had made the mistake of answering rather than letting the machine take a message.

"How can I avoid it?" Kate replied. "It's on the front page nearly every day."

"No, no," said Beryl impatiently, "I don't mean the fighting and the Communists and all that. I mean the people in the market."

"The market?"

"Seventy-three shoppers being held, Katherine. This is a big one. Could make Iran look like kid stuff."

"I'll watch for it in the paper," Kate said wearily.

At first when she began receiving these reports, Kate had tried reminding Beryl that they were just telling one woman's story, not conducting a study of the hostage phenomenon. However, Beryl's need to see herself in a global context (she called other hostages "my brothers and sisters") continued unabated, the bulletins and clippings kept coming, and Kate eventually stopped protesting and simply ignored them.

She worked along steadily, making her main character less frenzied and bombastic, more modest and appealing, than Beryl herself was proving to be. And progress was rapid, as she spent long hours locked away in her study in an effort to finish the book as soon as possible, and to avoid the tensions of the household.

Jason, too, was involved in a new book, *Theobold and the Dim Sum Murder Case*, but making an effort to get on with Igor despite their shaky start. He took him along to Chinatown while he wandered about soaking up color for his novel. He even took him out of school to go to Wednesday matinees of Broadway plays. He bought tickets whenever the Rangers were in town.

Igor, who did not like Chinese food, the theater, or hockey, tried to conceal his lack of interest in these activities, but inevitably, at some point in every outing, it surfaced. Jason, unable to accept how different from him his son was, fell to lecturing him on the value of whatever they were doing. At the end of nearly every one of their excursions they arrived home in strained silence.

"Why don't you do something he likes?" Kate asked after one of these unsuccessful ventures.

"Like lie in bed and read?" said Jason.

"There must be something else."

"Believe me, I've asked, but all I get is 'whatever you want, Dad,' which is useless because he hates everything I like."

"I'm sure that's not true, Jason," Kate said. Then she reconsidered: "Or if it is, I'm sure it's not personal."

"Perhaps if you stopped hiding out in your study, *you* might be able to discover what it is he enjoys doing."

"I'm not hiding out," Kate protested. "I'm working."

But she recognized the truth in Jason's comment and vowed to herself to try harder with Igor. Despite their one rather friendly exchange that afternoon in Igor's room, Kate and he had quickly fallen back into a mood of mutual unease. Their suspicions prevented anything spontaneous from occurring between them and they treated each other gingerly, with excessive politeness and marked restraint.

Sometimes Kate glimpsed something in Igor—the way he tilted his head when he looked at Jason, as if he were trying very hard to listen to sounds beneath the surface; his vigorous humming of the Russian national anthem when he was in the bathroom and thought he couldn't be overheard; the careful way he folded the napkins in a triangular shape when he set the table—that stirred her and made her want to reach out and touch him, but she stifled the impulse, fearing her own inexperience with children and the possibility of Igor's rebuff. She sometimes caught Igor looking at her intently, remembered his grin when she'd told him Hoyt Wilhelm finished the most games in 1961, and understood that Igor might have similar feelings about her that he needed to curb for his own reasons. But when the breakthrough between them came, it happened in a most unexpected way.

Kate arrived home late one afternoon after running errands to be met at the elevator by a wild-eyed Igor, who grabbed her arm and pulled her close to him.

"There's a woman inside who says she wants to surprise you," he whispered desperately. "She's been here about an hour."

Kate stripped off her coat and hung it on one of the pegs

set into the wall in the entryway. As she did so she noticed an extraordinary garment, a voluminous, quilted, screaming red coat, taking up several of the pegs, and wondered who would wear such a thing. Walking into the living room area, she found her answer.

"Beryl!"

"I wanted to surprise you." She was wedged into the corner of the large oyster-colored sectional sofa, a rust pillow tucked beneath each arm, looking very pleased with herself.

"You have," said Kate.

She felt she ought to shake Beryl's hand, kiss her cheek, but she didn't really want to, and as Beryl made no move toward such a greeting, Kate simply lowered herself onto the sofa, looking at Beryl expectantly.

Something was different about her. Was it the makeup, rather more extensive than any Kate had seen her wear in the past? Her clothes perhaps, obviously new but managing nonetheless to look vaguely secondhand? Her hair? Yes, it was the hair, permed into a cap of tight little curls that seemed to sit atop her head, rather than emerge from it.

"Iggie took very good care of me while we were waiting," Beryl said, assaying a wink that looked like a sign of perturbation rather than playfulness.

"It's Igor actually—"

"He and I got to know each other quite well."

Igor was standing behind Kate, but she could feel him rolling his eyes upward in his characteristic gesture of disgust.

"I had no idea your husband had been married before," said Beryl.

"No. Why would you?" Kate replied.

"Nor that he was of the Jewish faith."

"No, I don't suppose that would have come up either."

What was Beryl doing here in Kate's house, pumping her stepson about things that were none of her business?"

"When did you arrive?" she asked.

"Just a few hours ago, and I came directly here. I needed to touch base."

The idea that Beryl considered Kate, or her home, a base of any sort was alarming. "Well"—Kate said.

Beryl flipped the pillows out from beneath her arms and leaned forward urgently—"I think I'm going to love the Apple."

Igor had moved into a chair beside Kate and she had to take care not to look at him for fear of cringing or laughing or rolling her own eyes. In just moments, he had become, unquestionably, the ally and Beryl the disruptive, disconcerting presence.

"You've been here before and enjoyed it," said Kate.

"But not to *live*. I already feel different, knowing it's my city."

"You're moving here?"

Beryl's head canted to the side (for a moment Kate expected to see her hair slide off onto the sofa); a coy smile pulled up the corners of her mouth. "Aren't you almost finished with *C.C.?*"

"Yes, as a matter of fact, but that has nothing—"

Beryl interrupted her, oozing, "And isn't this where it will be published?"

"Of course, but you don't have to actually *be* here, to *live* here. . . . I've told you there's a long period when nothing happens. I turn in the book and silence descends for months. The silence may continue even when the book's published. Most books get very little attention, you know, and sink into—"

68

Beryl cut in again. "That's enough of that negative energy."

"Beryl, I'm just being realistic."

"I know you're trying to protect me against disappointment, and I appreciate that." She patted the sofa next to her as though it were Kate's hand. "But I'm not going to be disappointed. C.C. has a great future in store. I just know it. And I'm going to be right in the thick of things to make sure it gets the attention it deserves."

Kate decided she had warned Beryl for the last time. From now on she could guide herself through publishing's treacherous waters. And if she got dashed on the reef . . .

"It will be a big change for Stanley and the children," Kate remarked.

"Oh, they'll get along just fine. Melody's a lot better at doing things around the house than she pretends to be."

"They're not with you?"

Beryl tossed her head backward, causing Kate to worry again about the beanie of hair, and gave a noise imitating mirth. "Can you imagine Stanley here? And it's certainly no place to raise children."

She gave Igor a quick, uncomfortable glance, and then flapped a hand in his direction as though erasing her comment.

"You've left them?" said Kate.

"I've just decided to take some space, Katherine, and focus on my primary relationship—mine with myself."

"How is that different from leaving?" Igor asked. Kate could barely resist leaning over to pat him on the back.

"These things are hard for young people to understand, Iggie," Beryl said.

"It's Igor," said Kate. Why did Beryl insist on calling Igor by a nickname and absolutely refuse to use Kate's?

"Try me," said Igor.

"I'd love to find a place like this," said Beryl, ignoring him and looking around the spacious and elegant loft.

"You wouldn't need this amount of room, would you?"

"Oh, I'll be doing my share of parenting when the children come for vacations. And perhaps when they're here Iggie will show them around the city."

"Probably not, if you keep calling him that," said Kate.

Beryl blinked rapidly, but then sailed on. "Friends are so important in a strange place, I think."

Kate knew what was coming and felt her shoulders stiffen. A sharp pain shot up her neck, traveled across the top of her head, and lodged in her right temple.

"I hoped to spend my first night here with friends," Beryl said pointedly.

How could Kate refuse? Beryl had fed her almost nightly for two weeks. On the other hand, Jason would despise Beryl. She couldn't just spring her on him. The shock would be awful, the evening unbearable.

"Do you remember that my class is coming here tonight to see that tape on Africa?" Igor said belligerently, vigorously defending against the prospect of another broken promise. "You said they could and you said you'd feed them."

Kate had never heard Igor mention his class. And as far as she knew he hadn't a friend within three thousand miles.

"Is that tonight?" she asked.

"Damn right it's tonight," he snarled at her.

"Then of course we'll do it," she said soothingly. Casting a helpless glance Beryl's way, she asked, "Will you take a rain check?"

"Good quick thinking," Kate said to Igor when Beryl had gone. "Thanks."

"What a turkey." His eyes orbited their sockets.

"Sorry you got stuck with her."

"No problem," he said. "But what a humungus turkey."

Kate and Igor never mentioned the new rapport that sprang between them as a result of facing Beryl together. But Kate no longer experienced a strangling sensation when she talked to him, and Igor regularly made references to the encounter.

Beryl collected on her rain check three days later, arriving in her enormous red coat, which looked as though the hanger had been left in it. When Beryl stepped away, leaving it in Kate's hands, Kate realized the coat could stand up perfectly well by itself, but the cats, thinking it a new and exotic household tree, would doubtless try to scale it and scratch it ragged.

"Nice coat." Kate hung it up, unable to stop herself from uttering the lie because something about the coat's hideousness, Beryl's choice of it, her ridiculous appearance in it, touched Kate. Beryl had had this effect on her from the beginning, and it was unnerving.

"Brand new," said Beryl. "I went shopping in Grand Rapids just before I left and there was a sale and—"

"I want you to meet Jason," Kate said. "Come in."

It wasn't true, of course. The last thing in the world Kate wanted was for Beryl and Jason to meet. But it was bound to happen sometime and Kate had prepared the ground as thoroughly as she could.

"This will only happen once, I promise you," she'd assured Jason. "It's an obligation I have to repay, but once it's over, that's it. You won't like her, but I hope you'll be nice to her. She's annoying but harmless, and just try to remember that anybody can put up with anything for a few hours."

"Of course I'll be nice to her," said Jason.

71

And he was, though it could not have been easy. Beryl focused a great deal of attention on him, taking pains to mention those few Harbor View citizens "of the Jewish faith," noting what fine folks they were, what solid relations she'd enjoyed with them. When she learned that he cooked, she subjected him to a detailed accounting of a dinner party she had given just before coming to New York. (Was it a farewell dinner? Kate wondered. Did it include the husband and children she was about to leave?) All the way through her description of apple-celery kabobs, fish cobbler, and banana grape mold, Jason never once recoiled; he even managed to look interested. When Beryl urged him to tell her the plot of one of his novels, he obliged.

Kate herself did not do nearly as well. It was evident early on that the cats made Beryl skittish. Yet when the large calico, who liked to creep up behind people and chew on their hair, practiced this perversion on Beryl, Kate did not call her off. When Beryl brought up *Captive Courageous*, her favorite topic, Kate changed the subject as quickly as possible. She served Beryl a slightly smaller piece of dessert than everyone else. This woman, whose horrible coat moved Kate in some inexpressible way, also made her feel pitiless. She knew Beryl would never notice any of her small cruelties and that somehow made it all the worse.

"This one's really a beaut, Katie," said Jason, as he, Kate, and Igor cleaned up afterward, as easy and relaxed with each other as they had been since Igor's arrival. ("Nothing like a common enemy to bring people together," Jason remarked later.)

"Oh, she's not so bad," said Kate, feeling guilty for the slights, recognized or not, that she had inflicted on Beryl.

"Yes, she is," said Igor.

"An area of agreement," said Jason, tossing his arm across his son's shoulders and giving a squeeze.

"Yes, she is," said Kate.

"She makes me think fondly of Ulrica Forstman," said Jason.

"How quickly you forget," Kate replied. "Forstman was a viper, a lunatic. Beryl's just absurd."

"And noxious, I suspect."

"Oh, God, Theobold on the case, sniffing out evil. Look, the bad news is that I have to deal with Beryl a little bit longer. The good news is that you don't."

"You're not going to let her get involved in your life, are you?" Jason asked.

"Of course not," said Kate. "Don't be ridiculous."

But in making this quick dismissal, Kate failed to take account of either Beryl's rapaciousness or her tenacity. She tried very hard to keep Beryl at arm's length, but Beryl succeeded repeatedly in bending Kate's arm backward and closing in.

Beryl's first concern was finding a place to live and during the search she called Kate several times a day to check on the caliber of neighborhoods, prices, details of rental contracts. She settled finally on a vastly overpriced and unnecessarily large three-bedroom apartment in the east eighties.

"Isn't that a little steep?" Kate asked, when Beryl told her what she would be paying. And more than a little grand? she added to herself.

"I'll need a place where I can work, as well as entertain," Beryl answered.

"And parent, when the kids are here," said Kate.

"That's right. It's a space for a multidimensional life."

"I guess I hadn't looked at it quite like that. But it's still a lot of money."

"It may seem like that now, but it won't be as soon as C.C. starts to sell."

Kate, maintaining her vow of silence, said nothing to squelch Beryl's expectations. Nor did she ask exactly what work Beryl would be doing in her new place, nor whom she would be entertaining. She visited the apartment a few weeks after Beryl had moved in in order to bring her the completed manuscript of *Captive Courageous*, and to drink the glass of champagne with which Beryl insisted they celebrate her new home and her new book.

She met Kate at the door, flushed with pride, wearing something akin to a piano cover that indicated she might have gained more weight in the time since they'd seen each other. The apartment was furnished with a curious mix of pieces, some of them massive and somber, others so flimsy they looked as though they would topple at a touch. In the living room, for example, sat an enormous low mahogany oval, in its center a black cast-iron cavity easily three feet in diameter. Kate presumed this was a coffee table even though it more closely resembled an elaborately mounted barbecue pit. Behind it was a rattan sofa standing on legs that could have belonged to a foal, so uncertain did they look. In the master bedroom, a heavy maple bureau stood cheek by jowl with a set of wispy, free-standing filigreed shelves. Tiny glass-topped pedestal tables were set down next to giant overstuffed armchairs. It was hard to believe that all the furniture in the apartment had been chosen by the same person, and Kate wondered if it reflected conflicting aspects of Beryl herself: the stout and the slight, the forceful and the frail.

Beryl read the manuscript that night and called Kate the following morning.

"I just love her," she said, speaking of herself as she appeared in the book. "She's so strong and courageous, but at the same time so appealing. I really admire the way she handled herself."

Did Beryl's retreat into the third person indicate an unexpected modesty or a dangerous psychic split? Kate decided she didn't really care. She was simply relieved that her work with Beryl was at an end, and that she could now gracefully withdraw.

Beryl, however, having established her base of operations, went into training for her new role as a published author. And she kept Kate posted every step of the way. Each time that Kate was fed up, about to turn her away, something happened that revealed the little teller lurking inside the persona Beryl was creating, and Kate was lost, submersed in feelings of responsibility and obligation.

With an eye on the promotional tour that she was anticipating, Beryl first addressed the question of her girth, which had become considerable.

"I wanted to let you know, Katherine, that I'm going to start doing some very serious body work," she said one afternoon on the phone.

"Please don't feel you have to tell me what you're doing all the time," said Kate.

"Oh, I don't," said Beryl, "but I know you're interested and I'm happy to clue you in."

"Beryl, we had one sort of relationship while we were working on the book together, but that's behind us now."

"I certainly hope you don't think I'm the type that would

75

just cast you aside because I'd gotten what I wanted from you." There was a touch of acerbity in Beryl's voice.

"No, but circumstances change, people change—"

"That's just not my idea of friendship."

The word made Kate's blood run cold, and she fell silent.

"Anyway," Beryl went on, "I've joined a club where I can work out and run and swim and use the machines. And I'm also practicing food sensitivity."

"Oh?"

"It's important for me to be conscious of what I put in my body," said Beryl, "what foods have value for me, what foods don't, what portions are helpful, what aren't."

"Is this anything like a diet?" Kate asked.

"That's such a destructive notion, Katherine. It has such self-hating connotations: 'reducing,' 'losing.' I feel very diminished when I conceptualize it that way. I mean, just think of the word itself: *di*-et. Die. Die! Do you hear it?"

Kate could hardly not as Beryl's voice had risen to a shrill pitch. "What is the point of food sensitivity? To lose— sorry, to take off weight? Do you use the word *weight*?"

"You see!" Beryl pounced on Kate's penultimate question and ignored the last. "Negative connotations again. You're talking about subtraction, Katherine."

"And what are you talking about?"

"My sense," said Beryl, "is that I want to change my body configuration. Food sensitivity is one of the tools I'm using to help me achieve that goal."

Kate decided not to pursue the subject further. However, when she saw Beryl some four weeks later (unable to cut her loose entirely, Kate tried to limit their contact primarily to phone conversations, but every so often she was coerced into a face-to-face meeting; short of telling Beryl that she never wanted to lay eyes on her again, there seemed no way to avoid it), it was evident that food sensitivity had proven a great success. Beryl was at least twenty-five pounds lighter and gave no sign of having reached a plateau. "One twenty-four and counting," was how she put it to Kate, with one of her large, unwieldy winks.

Kate wondered why it was acceptable now to bandy about figures and indicate future diminution, and guessed it was probably because the figures were considerably lower than they had been several weeks ago.

Along with Beryl's new body configuration had come a change in wardrobe and hairstyle. She was wearing a flax-colored linen outfit that consisted of an oversized, billowing jacket, with a metal collar and heavy hardware fastenings, and wide-legged pants cropped just below the knee. On her feet she wore little mesh boots that rose an inch or so above the ankle and resembled nothing so much as tiny basketball nets. Giant black stone circles were affixed to her ears. Both wrists were weighted with highly polished black stone bracelets.

Her hair had, apparently, been straightened and now stood straight up from her head in streaked stalks. Wisps had been left to curl around her ears and down the back of her neck, like threads from an unraveling hem. The color, apart from the streaks, had been darkened, and produced in Kate a determination to let her own silver gray hair grow back in.

Beryl's top front teeth, which Kate recalled as rather crooked, were now completely straight. There hadn't been time for orthodonture and Kate didn't even want to contemplate the other possibility. (Even Beryl wouldn't have done *that*, would she? Kate couldn't bring herself to ask.)

With the exception of the teeth, Beryl had chronicled these changes for Kate over the telephone ad nauseam, but there was no way she could have been prepared for the spectacle Beryl presented. During the first half hour of their lunch Kate kept her eyes averted slightly, fearful of flinching if she took in Beryl head on.

Where had Beryl gotten the money to finance her transformation? For as horrid as the clothes and hairstyle were (and, for that matter, the furniture in her apartment), Kate knew they were not cheap. Was Stanley bankrolling his wife's metamorphosis? Was there really that much money in cement? Kate wondered if she secretly envied Beryl for being able to take money from a man even though she no longer lived with him. At least Beryl didn't have to write other people's books in order to convince herself that she was an upstanding, solvent adult. She hadn't even had to write her own.

Beryl had indicated that she wanted to talk to Kate about something far too important to discuss on the phone. Kate waited expectantly through the first half of the meal for Beryl to broach the topic, but Beryl, as she ate her lettuce, tomato, cucumber, sprout salad, spritzed with lemon, prattled on about the number of pounds she was "pressing" at the club, discussions she'd had with the publicity people at Waverly Press, publisher of *Captive Courageous* (Beryl had refused to accept the idea that there was a period during the publication of a book when nothing happened, and had made herself a regular visitor at Waverly's offices), and the state of negotiations with several agents she was interviewing (she was looking for someone who would be "nurturant" and also only take seven and a half percent).

Beryl had insisted they meet at a place called Grains 'N

Greens ("it's best for my food sensitivity"), and Kate hated it. It reminded her of Tabitha Waxberger, whose calls had dropped off lately only to have the slack taken up by Beryl's, and Kate's mandible was clicking from eating her way through a melange of raw vegetables. (Zucchini and broccoli were one thing, but eggplant and potato quite another.) It was the restaurant's boast that none of its food was cooked. Kate wondered what that portended for the grains, but her jaws were throbbing too much for her to frame the question.

Finally, over barlaccino for Kate ("We slowly brown our own pearl barley, stone-grind the rich roasted kernels to a fine consistency, prepare a flavorsome brew with sparkling spring water, mix with steamed soy milk, and *voild!* Barlaccino"), and hot water and lemon for Beryl, the Subject was raised.

"It's romantic," Beryl blurted.

Kate had one mad moment of panic that Beryl was describing their meeting. But she was quickly disabused of the thought as Beryl hurtled on.

"He's my dance instructor and a wonderful man aside from that, an Indian Indian, but he's been in this country for a while and he's well connected here, has some very nice friends, very continental and sophisticated and from all walks of life. I want to give a little dinner party to introduce him to some of my friends and I'd like you and Jason to come."

"I had no idea you were studying dance," said Kate, beginning at the top, saving the worst till last.

"I just started last week, but I feel I've known Ram— R-A-M but it rhymes with bomb—for years."

"The romance is rather sudden then."

"It just happened, Katherine. It was just one of those things, as the song says."

Kate prayed Beryl wouldn't hum a few bars, but she did, complete with swaying shoulders and snapping fingers.

"What kind of dance does he teach?" Kate asked, when Beryl quieted down.

"It's a mixture: Hindu, Sikh, Parsee."

"I thought those were religions."

"Well, I suppose the dancing reflects other things," said Beryl, apparently unconcerned that Ram may have been imprecise with her. "The thing I like about it is that it's not terribly strenuous. After all the heavy work I do at the club I need something to mellow me out, as Ram says."

"That old Indian expression."

"Oh, he's completely Americanized. He came here years ago when his family was killed in an uprising. An American couple found him wandering on the road outside his village, the only survivor of an incredible massacre. They brought him to the United States and he lived with them in California until he came to New York ten years ago."

"That's quite a story."

"Exactly what I said when I first heard it. I told him he should do a book."

"Well, I don't know if—"

"I also told him I knew somebody who could write it." Again, the wink.

"Oh, I don't think I'd be—"

"And he said the most wonderful thing. He said, 'I would rather dance than write.' "

"That's certainly something in his favor. How did you find him?"

"He had an ad posted on the board at the club and it just caught my eye. For some time I've felt the need to get in touch with a quieter part of me, what Ram calls *jiva*, the inmost heart."

"And the dancing helps you to do that?" Kate could not entirely conceal her skepticism and Beryl, uncharacteristically, noticed.

"It's not jitterbugging, you know," she said tartly. "It's just movement, based on the principles of organic kinesis." She threw her hand in the air, signaling the waiter that she wanted another cup of hot water and lemon, dismissing Kate's line of questioning.

Kate backed off. "You've met his friends?" she asked.

"He's talked about them so much I feel I've known them for years."

"And you want him to meet yours." Kate knew very well that Beryl did not have a wide acquaintance in the city. Aside from the publicity people at Waverly Press, the only other people Kate could recall her mentioning were her doorman and a woman at the club whom Beryl felt leered at her when they were showering.

Beryl's smile flashed on pointedly, remained rather longer than usual, then died.

"Who will be at the party?" Kate asked, knowing the answer before she heard it.

"You and Jason. I don't want to overwhelm him with a lot of people all at once."

"No," Kate agreed, "that wouldn't make sense."

How could she say no? If she did, there would be no party. Anyway, Kate thought, she'd like to scrutinize Ram, who sounded improbable, to say the least. On the other hand, how would she get Jason to go along? He was already

81

intolerant of her involvement with the woman he'd taken to calling the Swarr.

"We'll look forward to it," Kate said, shriveling internally when she saw the pleasure her lie produced.

"Wonderful. Next Friday at seven-thirty." Beryl dropped her voice and leaned across the table toward Kate. "I think you'll see immediately, Katherine, why he makes me feel validated as a woman."

Kate wasn't sure she knew what that meant, but in order to deflect any further unsavory confidences from Beryl, she actually ordered another barlaccino and chattered about its uniqueness and flavor until she was certain the matter of validation had receded from Beryl's mind. The rest of lunch passed without incident.

Coming home, Kate considered her approach to Jason. There was no way to make an evening with Beryl sound palatable. She had better just ask him, head on, no embroidery, no cajoling. He would do it for her if she explained why she couldn't say no. Why couldn't she? she wondered.

On the other hand, Jason had recently seemed resentful that Kate was getting on with Igor so well, while he and his son continued to clash. (Just two nights ago Kate had taken Igor to a Mets game at Shea Stadium while Jason stayed home sulking.) He might be feeling punitive, without even knowing it, and seek revenge by refusing to go to Beryl's. Perhaps Kate should shame him, raise the specter of Tabitha, remind him of the debt he had accrued through that tawdry little incident. Surely one wretched evening with Beryl was small price to pay for a two-month affair. Of course, Jason had already spent one wretched evening with her. He could argue that his debt was paid. If all else failed, Kate supposed she could use the enticement each of them always used as a last resort: it would be good material.

When she arrived home Jason was in his study. Kate flung open the door and planted herself in the doorway.

"I need a favor from you," she said combatively.

"How could I refuse when you ask so sweetly?" said Jason, peering at her over the top of his new half-glasses.

"Then it's yes?" said Kate. "No matter what?"

"Give me a clue."

The words jammed in her throat.

"Just one," Jason prompted.

Kate couldn't bear to say it.

"Could we have sex on your desk," she blurted, "the way you and Tabitha did?"

"We never did that." Jason sounded genuinely shocked.

"You mean you've been saving the desk for me?" Kate batted her lashes at him.

"Is that what you pictured, the two of us on top of my desk, for God's sake?"

"Or was it in the chair?" Kate's eyes swung to the soft caramel-colored leather chair in the far corner of the room.

"C'mon, Katie."

"Up against the bookcases?"

Jason pulled off his glasses and set them on the desk.

"Under the parson's table?" Kate moved toward it and slapped her hand down on one of the diagrams covering its surface. (Jason made detailed schemata for every aspect of his Theobold books.)

He rose and came out from behind his desk. "You're getting warm," he said.

"Yes."

"On the floor," he said, taking hold of Kate and pulling her down with him onto the red, blue, and gold Persian rug.

83

They made love there, on the desk, in the chair, against the bookcases, and ended up on the floor again.

"That was really the favor, sex on the desk?" Jason asked.

"No." Kate ran her fingertips over Jason's face, thinking how she never tired of it, in fact loved it more each year.

"The sex was just to soften me up?"

"No, it just came over me. I was seized by lust. Actually, I've had it in mind for quite a while."

"Lust?"

"Sex on the desk. I couldn't bear to think she'd done anything with you that I hadn't."

"Oh, God." Jason squirmed in recollection. "It seems impossible. I can't believe it happened."

Kate supposed that while he was roasting in the fires of regret it was as good a time as any to raise the matter of dinner with Beryl. "Jason, about that favor."

"It's the Swarr, isn't it?"

"How did you know?"

"Something happens to your voice when you mention her."

"I didn't mention her. I was just thinking of mentioning her."

"Let me guess. You want her to move in with us. You want the three of us to plan a vacation together. You want me to accompany her on her promotional tour."

"I want you to go to her house for dinner."

"Oh, Kate," Jason howled, "you said *never again*. You promised."

"I know I did, but she has an Indian boyfriend and she wants him to meet her friends and she doesn't have any so she asked us. I couldn't say no."

"Why can't you get rid of the beast? What's the hold she has on you?"

"There's no *hold,* Jason. I feel responsible because I wrote her goddamn book, and now she thinks she's going to become a star and probably save some souls along the way. And really all she is is a pathetic little sponge who lived with a killer for ten days and who's conned herself into believing that that gave her the answer to life."

"But you're not responsible for her conning herself," he said.

"Face it, Jason. If you give someone a book with her name on it she's bound to think she has something to say."

"You didn't give her a book, Katie."

"No, I just wrote it, that's all."

"And if you hadn't, someone else would have."

"Oh, God, where are your absolutes when I really need them?"

"Katie, the most important thing here, which you're missing entirely, is that the Swarr is about as pathetic as a shark circling a bloody stump."

"And I'm the stump? Nice image, Jason. Thanks a lot."

"No, darling, of course you're not the stump. But she's definitely the shark. Mark my words."

"How about it?" Kate asked. "Will you go?"

"Did you say there was an Indian boyfriend?"

"He makes her feel 'validated as a woman.' "

"Really? What does that mean?"

"I didn't want to ask. He's also teaching her Hindu, Sikh, and Parsee dancing."

"Any chance we might get to see some of that?"

"You'll go?"

"Katie, you know I've never been able to resist the old Sikh two-step."

Chapter Five

THE day before Beryl's dinner party, Jason and Igor had a ferocious row that ended with Igor storming out of the house. Jason had seen his son coming out of a movie during school hours. Confronted later, Igor lied about where he'd been that afternoon and all the other afternoons when, as Jason determined by a phone call, he'd also been missing from classes. Trapped in the lie, Igor squirmed, saying that school was pointless, the teachers incompetent, the subjects irrelevant. Jason raised the specter of the future and inquired of Igor what possibilities it might hold for him if he failed to complete the tenth grade. Igor said Jason was a fossil. Jason said Igor was an escape artist, just like his mother. At least she had the capacity for understanding, said Igor. To a fault, Jason replied: fifteen years of "understanding" had made Igor who he was today, someone with no sense of responsibility to himself or others, no ability to set goals or to discipline himself to achieve them, and possessed of a system of behavior based solely on the principle of self-indulgence. Far better all that, said Igor, than to be like Jason—rigid, narrow-minded, insistent that everything be done his way. A parent is supposed to set standards, Jason pointed out. If that was true, Igor asked, why had Jason neglected the task for so many years?

The evening before Beryl's party, Kate found Igor in his room in an advanced state of drunkenness. She heard a thumping noise and looked in to find him ricocheting off the walls like a ball in a squash court. Jason, fortunately, had retired to his study to read about tong wars for his Theobold book and he did not hear the pounding.

As Igor flew by her, Kate reached out and caught hold of his shirt, arresting his motion. Then she steered him toward the bed. He collapsed onto it, his head coming to rest on the heap of clothes that served as his pillow. Kate, spotting his real pillow beneath a pile of debris in the corner, got up to retrieve it, but Igor stopped her with a shout.

"Doan wan it." He waved his arms wildly to emphasize his point.

Kate hesitated, then tugged the pillow free and marched it over to the bed.

"No," he said, "al-lur-shick."

"You're allergic? To the pillow?"

Igor's head bobbled in a loose-necked nod.

Kate felt overcome by sadness. Had Igor been afraid, unable, unwilling to tell them even that, that he was allergic to his pillow? And what about her? Had she been so anxious not to intrude on him, so fearful of dealing with him, that she'd rationalized that sleeping with a misshapen pile of clothes beneath his head was a teenage tribal custom? The pile now seemed to her a symbol of the awful things that could happen to people when they didn't talk to each other.

Igor, words heavily slurred, body twisting with drunken exaggeration, pleaded with Kate not to tell his father that he'd gotten drunk. Jason already believed he was no good; this would clinch it for all time. Jason already hated him; this would set the seal on his hatred.

Jason did not hate Igor, Kate protested vehemently; he loved him. He loved him very much, and wanted him to do well, and wanted the two of them to be able to understand and enjoy each other. Igor vowed he would try harder, do better. Kate didn't promise not to tell Jason; nor did she say she would.

The morning of Beryl's dinner party, Kate went out and bought Igor a new Dacron-filled pillow. She arrived home to find Jason and Igor in the kitchen yelling at each other about obligation and betrayal, Jason's references current, Igor's historical. Kate, for the first time, waded in between them.

"Cut it out! Stop it! You two have got to stop screaming and learn to talk to each other."

"How can I talk to a little sneak like this?" Jason's face had taken on a deep red tinge. "At noon he was still in bed, even after what happened yesterday. He's getting worse, not better. At least he used to leave the house and *pretend* he was going to school."

Igor, in contrast to his father, had a deadly pallor and looked on the verge of a swoon. Still, he fought back. "I just overslept. I didn't mean to stay home."

"Cut the crap, Igor. At least you could try to be honest."

"I didn't hear the alarm. I am being honest about that."

"You don't even know what honesty is. You've never encountered it. You've never had to. You've always been allowed to cut corners, sweet talk your way out of a jam, pull the wool—"

"Stop it, Jason," said Kate. "He's being honest with you."

"What are you," said Jason, turning on Kate, "the truth bureau? Capable of detecting integrity where all others fail? Capable of detecting it where it doesn't exist?"

"Oh, for Christ's sake, he was hung over, he didn't hear the alarm, and he overslept—just what he told you." Kate had not meant to refer to Igor's drunken episode and she immediately wished she hadn't.

"Not quite," said Jason. "How did he get hung over?"

"In the usual way, I presume," said Kate, feeling suddenly very tired. "I wasn't there."

"I got hung over by getting drunk and I got drunk by drinking too much." The quaver in Igor's voice, produced by a combination of nerves and the ravages of the alcohol, was mirrored in his body. "I drank everything I could get my hands on so I wouldn't have to think about how nothing I do ever pleases you, about how you wish I was different, more like you and less like my mother, about how you resent me interfering with your life even though you thought you wanted me to come because you felt so guilty for so long. So I just drank and drank, but it didn't help because I kept thinking about all that stuff anyway. I asked her not to tell you because I knew it would just make everything worse, but it doesn't matter anymore because this place sucks. I never should have come in the first place and I'm not going to stay anymore."

As there was no door to slam in the open kitchen area, Igor, as he exited, punctuated his rage by smashing his hand down on the heavy wooden counter, whimpering with pain but not breaking stride.

Jason started to follow, but Kate called him off. "Let him be for now," she said.

"You knew he got loaded and you didn't tell me?"

"I didn't know what to do. I was thinking about it all morning."

"If you hadn't gotten in the middle of this you wouldn't have told me?"

"I don't know."

"Jesus, Kate, whose side are you on?"

"It's not a matter of sides. It's more complicated than that. Everything isn't as black and white as—"

"Spare me the speech, please."

"Jason, let me tell you something." Kate approached where he stood, his back against the six-burner stove set into the counter. She rested her hands lightly on his arms, which crisscrossed his upper body. "He couldn't even tell us that he was allergic to his pillow."

This news did not appear to strike Jason as forcefully as it had Kate the night before.

"Couldn't ... wouldn't ... didn't. He's so goddamn stubborn that once he decides something he's bound to hang on to it."

"Jason, he's been sleeping on a big lump of clothes for months. That's how hard he was trying to be unobtrusive, undemanding. Can't you see that?"

Jason unhooked his arms and pulled Kate tightly against him. She felt his shoulders shudder and knew he was crying though there was no sound and no tears ran from his face onto hers.

"I suppose he's trying," he said finally, "and so am I, but we don't seem to get anywhere."

"He wants so much for you to like him."

"I love him, Kate. You know that. But I've got to take a hard line with him."

"Why?"

The question startled him and he began to bluster through his confusion. "Well, because that's what he needs, that's what he's never had. Look where the soft line got him."

"Natasha's soft line? When she let him do whatever he wanted she wasn't taking him into account any more than you are. She had no expectations, you have too many. It's the same thing and either way Igor gets lost."

"You think it's too much to expect the kid to go to school?" he said derisively.

"That's not what I mean and you know it. Just try to hear him. I'm not saying you have to agree, but don't dismiss him out of hand."

Jason gave a humorless little bleat of a laugh and moved away from Kate. He went to the refrigerator, flung open the door, and pulled out a bottle of seltzer.

"This is great," he muttered to himself, reaching into the cupboard for a glass, "just great." He pushed the nozzle on the bottle and seltzer surged into the glass, up the sides and over the top, puddling on the counter. "She never wanted children, had no interest, practically made me take a pledge that I'd never even mention the subject." He jammed down the nozzle again, and the flood repeated itself, but Jason seemed oblivious. "But she lives with one for a few months, a damaged one at that, and she's a goddamn child-rearing expert."

"Jason, don't make this into a quarrel between the two of us. It's hard enough without that."

She moved toward him and he backed away from her, carrying the seltzer bottle with him. Kate wondered if he might turn it on her, like a firehose sprayed on an advancing dog.

"But it is between us," he said, still circling away from her. "You're making headway and I'm not. He talks to you, not to me. That makes it between us."

"I would think you'd be glad that he and I are managing to get along."

Kate froze as Jason raised the seltzer bottle and pointed it directly at her; finger on the trigger. That he seemed to be unaware of what he was doing made it no less menacing.

"I am," he growled. "I'm delighted. And it hurts like hell." Dropping his weapon to his side, he turned away and fled down the hall to his study.

Kate followed and talked to him through the door. He snarled at her to go away, to leave him alone. Knowing there were certain times when it was impossible for Jason to talk, Kate retreated.

Back in the kitchen, she picked up the pillow she'd bought for Igor and headed toward his room. Her knock was met by silence. She tried a second time and, again, got no response. But the moment Kate opened the door a crack, he screamed out, "Go away. Leave me alone." Kate pulled the door open wider, tossed in the pillow, and quickly pulled it shut again, feeling like a feeder flinging meat into the lion's cage. As she walked away she heard the lock on his door click into place.

In the living room, she sank onto the sofa, feeling Jason in his locked room on one side of her, Igor in his on the other. The two of them were really more alike than they knew, she thought. Perhaps that was cause for hope.

A few hours before Beryl's dinner party was to begin, Igor tried to escape. He had stayed in his room all day, refusing to answer when Kate knocked, ignoring the food she set outside in the hall. Late in the afternoon, Kate was in the kitchen eating corn muffins and strawberry jam (counting on Beryl to have something edible was too risky—what would it be? Pork Punjab? Mackerel Madras?—and, besides, the rigors of the day had left her ravenous) when she heard his door open. Moments later he hove into sight, wearing his GET LOST T-shirt and carrying a suitcase.

"What's up?" said Kate, trying to sound casual, but failing.

Igor glowered at her and kept going.

"Hey," said Kate, moving out of the kitchen and following him toward the elevator, which opened directly into the apartment. "Where are you going?"

He kept his back to her as he stabbed at the elevator button. Someone apparently was holding it on an upper floor and Igor bawled, "Elevator," the desperate squawk causing Jason to rush from his study, where he had been all day, except for two brief appearances during which he'd worn an air of injured chagrin and spoken little.

"Elevator," Igor howled again, and a humming sound indicated that it was on the way.

"Just hang on a minute," said Jason. "Where do you think you're going?"

Igor maintained his silence, his eyes staring straight ahead.

"Igor, I'm talking to you."

The elevator door opened and Igor stepped forward. Jason shot out a hand and grabbed his son's arm, turning him around. Igor strugged to move away, Jason gripped tighter. Igor shoved out a foot to hold the elevator door open, Jason hooked his own over it and pulled Igor's free of the door. As the elevator began to close, Jason reached for Igor's suitcase, Igor clung to it and they tugged it back and forth between them. No one spoke; the only sounds were the grunts occasioned by the scuffle. The suitcase fell. Igor thrust his hand toward the elevator button, Jason reached out and clasped Igor, pinning his arm to his sides. Igor broke the hold and wrapped his arms around Jason, immobilizing him in the same way. With his own leg, Jason pulled one of Igor's out from under him and Igor fell backward. When he landed Jason fell on top of him. Igor bucked him off. Jason quickly scrambled back on top, sitting astride his son, holding his arms against the floor.

Jason's breath was ragged and he took several deep gulps of air before speaking. "I want to ask you just one thing. Wait until tomorrow. Sleep on it. If you still feel you want to leave then, you can go."

Igor made no sign of assent, but when Jason lifted his hands and slid his body off to the side, he lay still.

"I don't want you to go," Jason added.

"Neither do I," said Kate, who had been riveted in place by this primal pantomime.

Igor remained spread-eagle on the burnt ocher bricks that formed the floor of the entryway. Kate, looking down, imagined him springing up, returning to the attack. She imagined him remaining there unmoving hour after hour. Instead, after a few moments, he sat up slowly, rose to his feet, picked up his suitcase, and headed quietly back to his room.

Kate and Jason arrived at Beryl's feeling rather drained.

"I sense low energy," said Beryl when she opened the door on their depleted forms. "We'll have to see what we can do about that."

As it turned out, however, she made no attempt to elevate their energy level. She never appeared, in fact, to notice them again all evening. Her focus on Ram, whom she insisted for the first fifteen minutes of the evening on calling Mr. Samosa (perhaps so that she could tell Kate and Jason that his name meant "turnover," thus making comprehensible her later references to him as various forms of pastry), was uncompromising and steadfast.

He seemed an unlikely object of such vehement attention. Slight, conservatively attired in a light gray business suit, white shirt, and red tie, he had a pleasant enough face, distinctive mainly for its extremely slender mustache that looked penciled on, and skin the color of maple syrup mixed with butter. He seemed to be a man of few words, communicating primarily through inclinations of his head, and slight bows from the waist. Every so often, however, he would utter a slang phrase, its connection with the conversation usually obscure, and follow it with a high-pitched, one-note giggle. The first time it happened, Kate had just remarked, dishonestly, to Beryl that everything looked lovely.

"Far out!" said Ram, trilling directly into Kate's ear.

She jumped, but no one seemed to notice.

"All right!" he piped a short while later.

Kate stayed still this time and she quickly grew accustomed to Ram's purling laugh.

Beryl, who was dressed in some sort of offshoot of the lounging pajama, with enormous raglan sleeves, swooped around Ram like a perfervid bat, brushing against him, plucking at his handkerchief, his tie, emitting little noises all the while. Ram, at the eye of the storm, remained serene and inscrutable.

Beryl had worked very hard to emphasize the Indian theme in every aspect of the evening. Sitar music played

95

softly in the background. Madras spreads had been draped over two of the overweening armchairs. The wine was served in busily engraved brass goblets that must have been bought especially for the occasion. The food, most of it unidentifiable (Beryl, just when it might have been helpful, had given up reciting the menu, Kate noted), was saturated with curry powder and chutney.

During the first half of the evening Kate was acutely aware of the strained conversation, the uncomfortable silences. She attempted to draw out Ram on the subject of his miraculous escape from the village massacre and subsequent journey to America, but she was met almost exclusively by incomprehensible tiltings and swayings of his head. Jason actually assayed a conversation with Beryl about publishing (Kate knew what this cost him and loved him madly for trying to be congenial), but she was so distracted by her attendance upon Ram that even this surefire topic failed to engage her. Eventually Kate, realizing that Beryl and Ram were oblivious to any sense of tension or unease, just relaxed and watched the two of them.

He called Beryl "my little captive courageous." She called him her "trifle," "cream puff," "sweet roll," "pandowdy." (She did once emerge from her fixation long enough to acknowledge Jason's presence, as well as his Hebrew faith, by twinkling significantly at him after she called Ram "my blintz.")

By the end of dinner Kate and Jason were sending each other regular signals about leavetaking, tapping their watches, flashing fingers in the air to enumerate the remaining minutes, yawning conspicuously. Just as Kate was finishing a second cup of coffee and feeling that a reasonably graceful exit might soon be accomplished, Jason turned to

Ram and said, "I understand you're teaching Beryl some Indian dances."

Ram smiled obliquely, his head canting slightly to the
right. Despite close attention all evening, Kate had not been
able to determine if a list to the left meant one thing, a list
to the right another.

Beryl, whom Kate realized had lifted the brass cup to her
lip several times too often, smiled muzzily at Ram and
cooed, "He's very gifted."

"Too much!" crowed Ram, gurgling afterward.

Kate wondered if it was significant that all his idiomatic
explosions were just two words. Perhaps that was all he
could manage at one time?

"I wish we could see your star pupil," said Jason.

Beryl seemed about to demur when Ram leaned forward
from the waist, a definite assent, then made his way to the
stereo and changed the record.

The music that came on was elaborately orchestrated and
decidedly frenzied, but when Beryl moved away from the
table and toward the center of the living room her pace was
sluggish. Once she arrived, she stood absolutely still for
what seemed an interminable period. Kate wondered if the
wine were to blame for her inertia, or if this was a medita-
tive phase that preceded movement. Her question was soon
answered as Beryl broke into violent gyrations, hips crank-
ing, shoulders heaving, head tossing. She careened from one
side of the room to the other, body pitching, arms flailing.
Her eyes closed, then popped open in ecstatic exclamation
as she spun, shimmied, and wheeled about in approximate
time to the music.

"Get down!" cried Ram, his giggle cut short as Beryl
flung herself, face first, onto the floor.

Ram rushed to her, picking her up, explaining, "No, no, my little captive, it is just an expression, not an order."

Beryl, unabashed by her spill, resumed her tempestuous revolutions at once.

Kate was reassured to know that Ram could speak in complete sentences if the occasion called for it, somewhat less sanguine about Beryl's absolute obedience to her master's voice. Was there hidden significance in his calling Beryl his captive? Was their liaison, perhaps, not ludicrous, but sinister?

Finally, Beryl and the evening ground to a halt and Kate and Jason were released into the night, gulping in the exhaust-filled air as though they had been trapped underground and it was sweet, pure oxygen. They stood outside Beryl's building, embracing each other, survivors of a nightmare.

"What possessed you to request the dancing?" Kate asked.

"I just couldn't resist," said Jason. "I felt I had to see it. Was it cruel?"

"Do you care?"

Jason considered for a moment. "I care. I know it was cruel, but I couldn't help myself."

"She didn't know," said Kate. "That's one of the worst things about Beryl. She never knows. I find that unbearable."

"Would it be better if she knew she was making an ass of herself?"

"Yes. I'd prefer it. But, of course, then she wouldn't be Beryl."

They began to walk south on Lexington, arms around each other's waists.

"Do you think she's in his power?" Kate asked.

"No question. My God, wasn't that some dive she took?"

"I mean in some dire, terrible way."

"I wouldn't worry about the Swarr. Don't you know by now that she can take care of herself?"

Kate didn't, but she hated to admit that to Jason.

When they arrived home there was a note from Igor on the kitchen counter saying he had decided to stay, "at least for now," and signed "Iggie," in honor of where they had been that night. The next morning Jason did an impersonation of Ram for Igor, and Kate gave a spirited imitation of Beryl's dance. Igor didn't say much, and he retired to his room soon afterward, but he seemed appreciative of the vaudeville and, for the first time since his arrival, he wore a T-shirt unadorned by any threat or warning.

Kate had agreed with Jason after the dinner party that Beryl was an intolerable presence, that she didn't want her in her life in any way, and that she needn't wait until publication day to excise her from it. She was committed to severe measures to accomplish this (she fantasized about taking out a contract on Beryl, changing her phone number and/or her apartment, leaving a message on Beryl's machine saying Kate never wanted to see her again, moving to another part of the country), but they proved unnecessary as Beryl did not get in touch with her. Day after day the call Kate dreaded didn't come. Had Beryl's terpsichorean abandon so embarrassed her that she was unable to face Kate? Had she sensed Kate's discomfort with their relationship and decided to withdraw herself? Was Ram an even more sinister character than Kate had imagined, one who might bleed Beryl dry financially, bleed her dry literally perhaps, stuff her body in a trunk, and send it back to Harbor View?

All these possibilities seemed unlikely and even the last couldn't motivate Kate to contact Beryl. She was content to live with the mystery, enjoying her freedom from Beryl's daily barrage of calls, wondering why she had put up with it for so long, regretting her lack of moral courage, grateful to Beryl for taking her off the hook.

Just as Kate stopped flinching when the phone rang (it took nearly a month), Beryl surfaced in an early-morning call.

"Kathryn, I'm so sorry I haven't been in touch."

"It's all right."

"I'd certainly understand if you were put out with me."

"Not at all," Kate said firmly. "As a matter of fact—"

Beryl interrupted her. "It's just been one thing after another as publication gets closer. I'm taking a wardrobe course, sending out mailings, working on my comfortability with the cameras."

Where would one enroll for a wardrobe course? Kate wondered. What would it entail? How did one get comfortable before the cameras? Sit in for Jane Pauley on the "Today Show"? What was Beryl mailing out, and to whom?

"How's Ram?" Kate asked.

"Splitsville," Beryl said.

"You're not seeing him anymore?"

"I don't know what else that would mean," Beryl said rather acidly.

Kate felt like hanging up on her, but she was curious to know what had happened.

"His fear of intimacy kept him from meeting my needs," said Beryl. "His nurturing skills were minimal. The truth is, Katherine, he just wasn't ready for someone who could allow him to be a whole person."

He must have dumped her, Kate thought.

"It was a real learning experience," Beryl continued, "but now it's time to move on to other things. No flow, no grow."

"I suppose—"

"At any rate, Melody and Lance are coming next weekend and I thought we could all get together. Melody asked specially to see you. I know they'd like Iggie and I'm sure he'd like them."

"Oh, Beryl, I'm sorry, but we're going to be in the country next weekend."

"The children would probably like that even better. I've actually been a little concerned about having them in the city. It's so urban."

"It's a long trip just for a day—about two and a half hours each way."

"Well, I suppose we could arrange to stay over."

"Jason's mother might be with us. It would be tight in terms of beds."

"Melody and Lance think the biggest treat in the world is to spend the night on the floor in sleeping bags."

"We don't have any."

"Better yet if they get to make their own blanket rolls."

"Will they be in the city next week?"

"They're flying home Monday morning. Stanley won't let me have them for more than three days at a time."

Good for Stanley, thought Kate.

"Melody will be crushed if she doesn't get to see you."

Kate doubted that very much.

"And I'd hate for them to miss meeting Iggie. I've talked so much about him."

Kate gave up. "I guess you'd better come to the country on Saturday."

"I hope you would say, Katherine, if this wasn't convenient for you."

"I'll call you later in the week to make arrangements," said Kate, and hung up.

This was serious, Kate recognized, extremely serious. Once again, Beryl had managed to get her to agree to something she found loathsome. Why did this happen? Why couldn't she turn Beryl down? Generally, in her life, she did not have trouble with this. She thought of the Bozemans, a couple Jason had met at a mystery writers' convention and invited to dinner when they were all back in New York. Mr. and Mrs. Bozeman disagreed continually about everything, contradicting and correcting each other at every turn. And as the evening wore on, the disagreements grew more heated, the voices louder. By eleven-thirty, Mrs. Bozeman, on the verge of losing her voice from screaming at her husband, asked Kate if she might have a cup of tea with lemon and honey to soothe her throat. For a solid year afterward, the Bozemans issued return invitations and Kate turned down every one. Eventually, they stopped calling.

Or what about Liz Weinart, a woman Kate had known in college, who arrived at the Wylies' for dinner so drunk that within five minutes she was on the floor on all fours, pretending to be a cat? The real cats had approached her curiously, circling her body, appearing to listen to her cat noises, but when she rolled onto her back and began twisting and turning, they walked away in disgust. Kate and Jason endured her somewhat longer, but when Liz called the next day to say what a nice evening she'd had, Kate told her that she, herself, had not, and she didn't want to repeat it.

And there were other cases as well: the Randolphs, for instance, who could speak of nothing but food, meals they had cooked, meals that had been served to them, delicacies they'd discovered, delicacies they were stalking; or the Spiegels, who fancied themselves experts on Central American policy after spending five days at an island resort off the coast of Honduras; or Winston Gomez, who was simply innocuous to a fault. (Kate once cleaned up after a dinner party and was about to go to bed when she noticed Winston hadn't left yet.) Kate had had no trouble spurning any of these people.

Had she had a problem with the other people whose books she had written? Jason always accused her of becoming excessively involved with them, but was it true? Estelle Esteban *had* believed for a time that Kate was her dead mother, the one Estelle had dispatched with her own two hands; she had called Kate by her mother's name and begged forgiveness for her bloody deed. Kate had opposed Estelle's efforts to force her into this role, but one day she tired of resistance and simply told the distraught Estelle that she pardoned her. This seemed to free Estelle of her delusion, but she was left with a deep residual attachment to Kate, whom she took to calling Merciful One, then M.O., and finally Mo. Kate still heard from her occasionally and her letters always began "My dearest Mo."

Kate certainly couldn't be accused of overinvolvement with the humming therapist. They lived on different coasts and, in fact, had spent only one week working together in person. During the rest of their association he just fed Kate material (studies contrasting humming and nonhumming patients, interviews with confirmed hummers, diagrams illustrating humming's beneficial physical effects), and she tried to make it interesting and readable, a task at which, she realized early on, she was bound to fail.

The experience with Ulrica Forstman, Kate had to admit,

had been disastrous. Ulrica had not attempted to insinuate herself into Kate's personal life, but she had expected her to be on call twenty-four hours a day to discuss their work. Any boundary line Kate drew, Ulrica violated without awareness or apology. She became utterly dependent on Kate as her mouthpiece, while at the same time denying her importance at every opportunity. Kate remembered the day when Ulrica had looked up from some notes in her lap and spouted at Kate a completely garbled sentence, then gazed at her expectantly. It had taken Kate a moment to realize that Ulrica was waiting for the words to pass through Kate and come out unscrambled. She obliged and Ulrica smiled contentedly and moved on, unaware of what had occurred.

A certain degree of engagement went with the territory of ghost writing, Kate told herself. She gave these people a voice, a public identity. No wonder things got a little symbiotic, a little transferential. But the weekend in the country would be the absolute finale for Beryl, she vowed. And after that she would never be anyone's ghost again.

"I'm not sure I understand exactly how it happened," she said to Jason, "but Beryl and her children are coming out to the country on Saturday and I just want you to know that I certainly don't expect you to be there. Why don't you just stay in town and work on your book? I know you're near the end and anxious to finish. I brought this on myself and I'll deal with it. There's no reason you should be penalized because I can't say no to this . . . person."

She stood over him where he lay sprawled on the flowered chintz sofa in the den, reading the paper. "Are you sure that's the best choice?" he asked.

"Well, of course not," Kate sputtered, voice rising. "It's a perfectly awful choice. I recognize that, Jason. I know it's a problem and I intend to deal with it. But the weekend is on and there's nothing I can do about it."

"I mean 'person.' You called her a person."

"What would you suggest?"

Jason smiled eagerly. "Do you really want to hear?"

"No. No, I don't." Kate slumped down beside him, letting her head fall back on the puffy cushions.

"I'm not even going to ask how it happened."

"Thank you."

"Will the popover be coming along?"

"It's over. He was afraid of intimacy."

"The Swarr wouldn't stand for that, I'm sure."

"I think he dumped her."

Jason mimed astonishment. "No! Really?"

"Anyway, she wants to come to the country so that the kids can meet Iggie."

"I wonder how Ig will feel about that."

"I'll have to see. He'll probably like Melody. She's as surly as they come."

"*Melody? Melody* Swarr?"

"You knew that, Jason. You've just forgotten. She's not a bad kid. She can't help her name."

"Isn't my mother supposed to be going?"

"Yes."

Jason sat up, rubbing his hands together with relish. "Now that's something I'd like to see, Mother and the Swarr head-to-head."

"But you probably won't, right?"

"The draw isn't quite big enough."

"I understand. I do."

Jason slipped his hands onto Kate's shoulders, kneading

them gently, then stretched his fingers up her neck and massaged it.

"Poor Katie," he murmured. "Poor Kate."

Later that night, she cornered Igor in his lair in order to warn him. The room was much tidier than when she'd last seen it, a positive sign. Igor leaned back against his new pillow, *Lupus on Mars* open on his chest. At least he's reading, Kate thought.

In the weeks since Igor had decided to stay, relations between him and Kate and Jason had been civil but tentative. A major underlying assumption had changed: Igor was certain, Kate believed, that he was wanted, and that certainty had eradicated his blatant hostility. But the vacuum left behind had yet to be filled. Kate also knew, because of her revelation of his drunkenness, that she was still on probation.

"I did something really stupid," she said.

Igor looked delighted and invited her to sit down by pointing to the corner of the bed. Who would have dreamed those were the magic words? thought Kate.

"I managed to let Beryl invite herself to the country and she's bringing her two kids with her."

"I thought she wasn't bugging you anymore."

"She wasn't. But now she is."

"Dad must love this." Igor did his eye roll and gave an extra spin for emphasis.

"He thinks I'm hopeless. And he's right. But I told him he didn't have to come."

"How old are the kids?"

"I guess they'd be fourteen and eleven now. A girl and a boy."

"I'm good with younger kids," said Igor.

Kate could have kissed him—for being agreeable, for his

sense of his own great age (he'd turned sixteen two weeks earlier), for offering himself as an ally in the trial ahead. But she still had the feeling that any display of affection would be a terrible intrusion on him. He made her feel that a transparent but impermeable wall, like something out of one of his science fiction novels, surrounded him. Sometimes Kate thought she should attempt to force her way through it; other times she knew it must be allowed to dissolve of its own accord. She contented herself with giving him a big smile.

"They especially want to meet you," Kate said. "Would you like to know their names?"

"Let me guess." He thought for a moment. "Harriet and Ralph."

"Melody and Lance."

"I can handle it," said Igor.

On Friday morning Kate went to get the car from its garage two blocks away. When she pulled up in front of her building to pick up Igor and the bags, Jason was waiting with him.

"For better or for worse," he said, climbing into the passenger seat.

"I guess I don't have to ask which this is," said Kate.

"In sickness and in health." He pulled the seat belt across his torso and buckled it.

"Sickness," she said, edging away from the curb and heading uptown to collect Rose, pleased that Jason had come along.

During the nearly three-hour ride to the end of the North Fork of Long Island, Rose and Igor talked together in the back seat. Kate envied Rose the ability to elicit a side of him that was unconstrained, affable, almost chatty. She had tried once to experiment with the open adoration, blunt candor, and assumption of camaraderie that Rose used to pull Igor out of his taciturnity, but it was hideously false and he had retreated even further.

Kate and Jason had bought their farmhouse the year after they were married, enchanted by its large rooms, wide plank floors, fireplaces, the way the land behind it sloped down to the bay, the giant maple in front that kept it shaded and cool even in summer's deepest heat, the row of gnarled old lilac trees along one side of the property that filled the air in springtime with a haunting fragrance. The house reminded Kate of the one in Maryland, for which she'd sometimes felt a longing strong enough to take her breath away.

The last time she had seen it, she'd gone there to remove Carabel. When Lucius had died, two years earlier, Kate's mother had been cut adrift, and never again managed to find the shore. She remained fogbound, off the coast, her movements random and unavailing. Kate, who had always seen her parents as disparate planets, circling alone in their seldom-intersecting orbits, was astonished by the power of the broken bond. Her mother insisted on staying in the house, so Kate hired a private nurse to reside there with her. But Carabel's continuing erosion finally carried her beyond the reach of a single caretaker, and Kate was forced to consider placing her mother where there was a staff available to look after her.

This turned out to be Quiet Haven on the Maryland shore, an establishment that refused to characterize itself as a "nursing" or "rest" home, but that was, in fact, filled with people waiting out the rest of their lives. True, it was a cut above most such way stations. Every one of the light, airy rooms had a view of Chesapeake Bay, the walls were hung with watercolors from local artists, the staff did not look as though it would practice hidden cruelties. The price for these amenities was high, but Kate didn't care. She spent every penny of the money from the sale of the house on her mother's last few years.

Just as the present cannot supplant the past, the Long Island house never replaced for Kate the house in which she had grown up. But its echoes of the house near Frederick were pleasing to her. The first time she walked through the door, she felt at ease. And that had never changed during the seven years of weekends and summers that she and Jason had spent there. If she was experiencing turmoil, being in the country house reduced it by half. If she was feeling serene, the house sharpened her appreciation of her tranquility.

The azaleas had come into bloom since the previous weekend, their rose and magenta flowers standing out against the background of the house's gray clapboard and smoke-blue trim. Because they hated automobile travel, the cats had been left in the country during the week to be fed by a neighbor. Now they came running to greet Kate and Jason. What a myth feline independence was, Kate thought, as they swirled around her, mewling.

Igor went immediately to his room and got his small transistor radio, carrying it out beneath the giant maple to listen to the Mets game. Rose, who was made uneasy by such country phenomena as bird songs ("It's such a racket!"), ticks ("they could burrow into places you might never know they were"), and open space, tried to insulate herself against these as much as possible by setting up shop in a corner of the living room, surrounding herself with her own things (a piece of embroidery or knitting, a couple of the historical romances she favored, a dish of pistachios that she worked on all day, a heavy wool sweater no matter what the temperature, a stack of mail order catalogues that she perused avidly though Kate had never seen her order anything), basically recreating the atmosphere of her Bronx apartment. She generally left this area only to eat or sleep despite urgings that she get some air, inspect the foliage, or take a walk. ("I walk in the city where there are things to see.") Jason went into the village to pick up the local paper and do the grocery shopping. Kate straightened up the house and set into the earth those few plants she was determined to grow this year.

Beryl, with Melody and Lance in tow, arrived the next day about noon. Kate saw immediately the toll that the breakup with Ram had taken. Beryl appeared to have dropped at least another twenty pounds. Her skin was pulled back over her facial bones as though she were facing into a stiff wind. The flesh of her neck had receded so drastically that the cords stood out in sharp relief. Kate had the illusion that she could have reached out and wrapped her hands around them. Beryl's legs did not appear that much more substantial than the spike heels of her open-toed shoes. So shrunken were her feet that three toes poked through the small aperture. Smoky smudges beneath her eyes bespoke many nights of little sleep.

The blouson look of her wardrobe when Kate had last seen her was gone and she wore a one-piece garment that looked as though it were appliquéd to her skin rather than pulled on over it. Her diminished size did not seem to have reduced her energy, however. She flew down from the train and hurtled toward Kate like a mad greyhound starting a race.

"My God, Beryl," said Kate, unable to suppress her astonishment.

"Doesn't she look great?" said Melody, panting in her mother's wake.

"My God," Kate repeated.

Beryl flicked on her smile, acknowledging what she took to be a compliment. "All it takes is a little time and attention," she said airily.

Obviously, Beryl wasn't crediting romantic disappointment with a role in her emaciation, but Kate would have wagered that it was the fulcrum on which it all turned. In fact, one would never have known that Beryl had recently been in touch with *jiva*, validated as a woman, the performer of a mean Parsee trot. She never mentioned Ram, nor anything that had happened during the time when she'd been seeing him. She seemed to have drawn a madras curtain over the entire period.

Melody, apparently, found Beryl more palatable thin than fat, but Beryl's new body had not entirely muted her daughter's hostility. Within moments of meeting Igor, Melody vilified her mother sufficiently for him to recognize a kindred spirit. He invited her to come down to their dock, which jutted out into the bay, and Lance went along with them.

Less predictable, perhaps, was the way in which Rose and Beryl took to one another. Within an hour of her arrival Beryl was cozied into an armchair in Rose's corner of the living room listening to Rose recount a recent robbery in her building, reciprocating with a story about a young woman who had been assaulted in the sauna of her gym. Rose then upped the ante by telling of the incident several years earlier when she had been mugged on the subway. Beryl ran over the high points of her captivity in the bank. Rose recalled the series of obscene phone calls she had received when she was a young bride. Beryl told how her next door neighbor had exposed himself to her when she was five. They met on the common ground of disaster and rested comfortably there together.

"My own mother," Jason said to Kate in the kitchen. "Firmly entrenched in the enemy camp."

"You should be grateful. If Rose didn't have her, we would."

"I'm grateful, very grateful. And appalled."

His dismay increased later at their dinner cookout down on the shore, when it became apparent that the incipient friendship between Igor and Melody had taken on a romantic cast.

"First my mother, and now my son," Jason muttered to Kate. "I can't believe it."

Igor behaved toward Melody in almost courtly fashion, spreading a towel for her to sit on, cooking her a hot dog exactly the way she wanted it (charred), throwing his sweatshirt over her shoulders when a cool breeze blew in off the bay. And Melody seemed transformed by his attentions into a courteous and winning young woman. Only once during the evening did her darker side reassert itself, and then only briefly. When Beryl called Igor "Iggie," Melody growled at her, "It's *Igor*, Mother." Once corrected by her daughter, Kate noticed that Beryl did not make the mistake again. Was blatant antipathy the only way to reach Beryl? Kate made a note to try it herself.

During dinner Igor and Melody sat slightly apart from the others, drawing an invisible line around themselves, marking their separateness. As soon as dinner was over, they went to sit on the end of the dock, looking out toward the fuchsia and orange sunset. Lance bounded toward them at one point but stayed only a brief time, retreating onto the beach from where he glared at them and, periodically, issued noises of disgust.

Rose and Beryl, sitting at the picnic table on the lawn, swapping tales of ungrateful children (Beryl told of a neighbor whose daughter had refused to wear to the prom the dress her mother had labored over for two months, Rose countered with the story of a healthy, vigorous, but aging friend who had been stuffed into a nursing home by her wretched offspring, and she also mentioned Philip Roth, for good measure), were oblivious to the romance blooming before them. Kate, sitting beside Jason in front of the waning fire, was flooded with memories of adolescent love as she watched Igor's and Melody's silhouettes at the end of the dock, leaning together, falling back, tentative and exploratory at once.

"What are you thinking about?" Jason asked.

"Bobbie Martindale," said Kate.

"Who's he?"

"My eighth-grade boyfriend."

"Oh, I remember. 'Hot Lips' Martindale."

"Kisses of fire."

"To think that tonight, under cover of darkness, our son could be kissing the daughter of the Swarr. It's a thorny concept for me."

Tears welled in Kate's eyes, and she turned her head away.

"But I must admit that the liaison has certainly toned up his act," Jason went on. "He's behaving like the Russian prince Natasha always claimed he was. Of course, I don't suppose he'll retain any of this newfound refinement once Melody's gone. Maybe we should offer to take her in. Adopt her. Offer her asylum. I bet she'd go for that. Wouldn't you?"

Kate was silent.

"Katie?" he said, reaching out to touch her back. "Katie? What is it?"

She turned her face to him, tears visible where they had spilled onto her cheeks.

"You're crying," he said, a note of awe in his voice.

"You don't have to sound quite so reverent," she said, snuffling.

"Why are you crying?"

"You said 'our son'—*our* son might be kissing the daughter of the Swarr. You never said that before."

"No? I guess I didn't think you'd like it. I didn't think it would mean anything to you."

"Neither did I," said Kate. "But it does."

Chapter Six

KATE turned forty that summer. Her gray hair had grown back in almost completely and she thought it looked fine. The self-doubt occasioned by the Tabitha Waxberger episode, which had sent her to the dye pots in the first place, had receded, and even Tabbie's brief reappearance did not provoke so much as a twinge of misgiving.

She turned up one day, with soy scones, saying she was in the neighborhood and thought she'd say hello. The spirit and vivacity so blatantly absent the last time she and Kate met had returned in force and within fifteen minutes of her arrival she was serving tea to Kate on the wide kitchen counter. Proprietary as this seemed, Kate knew it to be completely ingenuous and she couldn't take offense.

Tabitha was now employed by an organization called That's the Rub, doing what she called "body manipulation," a massage technique she offered to demonstrate on Kate "without charge." Kate declined. She felt, Tabitha said, for the first time in her life that she was doing something truly useful—helping people to "encounter" their bodies. (Kate was tempted to note that Tabitha had done some of this in the past as well, notably with Kate's husband, but she resisted the impulse.) Because she was fulfilled in her work, Tabitha believed she placed less emphasis on "the relationship area." She was happy to focus on herself, and to get in touch with her parents and her child.

"I had no idea you had a child, Tabbie," Kate said, thinking how unlikely, even impossible, a candidate for motherhood Tabitha seemed. And where was this child? Where had it been when Tabitha spent evenings with Jason? Where had it been, for that matter, when she'd worked in the daytime for Kate?"

"The child *in* me," Tabitha said, smiling with heavy significance.

"You're pregnant?"

Tabitha's peal of laughter popped a crumb of scone out of her mouth and it clung precariously to her lip. "No, no. We all have a child in us, and a mother, and a father. Right now I'm focusing on my child, the vulnerable, frightened little kid inside who needs lots of attention."

Tabitha stayed for about an hour, leaving just as suddenly as she had arrived, sensing perhaps that Jason was due home and not really eager to see him, although she assured Kate that "the wounds have healed."

"You'll never guess who you just missed," said Kate when Jason came in about half an hour later.

"Tabbie," he said.

"How do you know? You ran into her on the street?"

"No, the timing just seems right. She's been quiet too long."

"She's been getting in touch with her child."

"Tabbie has a kid?"

"Inside her."

"She's pregnant?"

Kate laughed and wrapped her arms around Jason's waist. "I'm glad you're as unacquainted as I with the latest semantic wrinkles brought to us by the human potential movement."

"Oh, God," he groaned, "I see what you mean. She used to talk to her "father" when we were together—out loud."

"What do you mean?"

"She'd tell him he could no longer control her, that she was an adult. Sometimes she'd scream at him; once she went to the door and pulled it open and told him to get out."

"Jason, how could you?" Kate had made this inquiry many times in the past year, with rage, hurt, scorn, exasperation. Now she asked out of pure curiosity.

"I don't know. It's so embarrassing."

She nodded.

"At least you don't have to live the rest of your life knowing you did that."

"No, I have to know *you* did."

"It's better somehow," said Jason.

"I agree," said Kate.

She began thinking that summer of writing a novel about a man and woman who simultaneously delight and disappoint each other for some thirty-odd years of marriage. But it was not until she was just about to begin writing that she realized it was her parents she'd been thinking about, a realization that broke over her one day in the house in the country, as she listened to the Verdi Requiem. The soprano voice entreated "Salva me, fons pietatis," and Kate, quite suddenly, knew that it was the tangled knot of Lucius's and Carabel's sentiments for one another that she was trying to unravel.

She was standing in the middle of the kitchen absorbing this long-delayed insight, when Jason came in from fishing.

"I've been planning to write about my parents," Kate announced.

Jason's look indicated a distinct lack of surprise.

"You knew?" she asked.

"It crossed my mind."

"More than once?"

He nodded. "I promise not to tell Rose. She never has to know that you're just another cannibal, no better than the rest of them."

"She would mind even though my parents are dead?"

"Worse. They can't fight back."

Kate had never conceived of the novel as a therapeutic battleground, a theater of operations where one could thrash out old conflicts, settle scores, lay to rest yesterday's phantoms. Nevertheless, she had had an increasing sense of being imprisoned by her past, rather than enriched by it, and now she found herself planning to dissect her parents' marriage on paper. Was this her way of fighting free? Well, so be it, she decided.

The realization about her parents (this couple she had thought should be childless when she'd begun to imagine them as a fictional entity) was not, as it turned out, a liberating influence. Having become conscious of what she was doing, Kate felt uneasy, scattered rather than focused, eager to find diversions and reasons why it was impossible to begin writing. (She took a great many notes and made a few attempts at a start, but all of these struck her as unsatisfactory.)

The day she found herself paying a visit to Mrs. Karanewski, their new and highly garrulous next door neighbor whom Kate ordinarily tried to avoid, she knew that she was in full flight, a condition she decided she would accept for the moment, calculating that her acceptance would surely cause it to pass.

Beryl had virtually dropped out of sight after her visit with her children to the Wylies' house in the country. And even as she counted her blessings, Kate was curious. What was Beryl up to? She could not have fallen dormant. *Captive Courageous* was to be published in less than two months. Perhaps Beryl was out there doing dry runs of her promotional tour, crisscrossing the country, practicing being an author on the go. Or taking an *advanced* wardrobe course. Or having eye implants that would make her more telegenic (she'd been concerned when she'd heard that brown eyes "read" better on camera than blue). The mystery was solved when Beryl called to tell Kate that she had finally found an agent. Now she had another ear into which she could pour the refuse of her teeming mind.

Securing an agent of her own (Kate's had negotiated the book contract for both of them) had been a priority of Beryl's ever since she'd arrived in New York, but she hadn't been willing, as she put it to Kate, "to take just any old hack listed in the Yellow Pages." She'd added, "Plenty of people would like to hitch their wagon to this star." The anointed party, as it turned out, was a woman named Esther Heilbrun, herself a creation of the media, familiar to Kate as the subject of a television documentary about her impending death from bone cancer, who had undergone a confounding reversal of her disease, a complete recovery, and then written a book about the miracle that had served as the springboard into a partnership in a literary agency. When Beryl reported that she and Esther were on "the exact same wavelength," Kate believed her.

Esther was known in the publishing business for her success with such books as *Cat Cuisine, The Dictionary of Ethnic Slurs,* the memoirs of a motel magnate ("surprisingly lively and engrossing," according to *Playboy*), something called *The Thirty-Second Wife,* and *Run for Your Life,* a book that proposed jogging as a cure for cancer and a series of lesser ailments.

This last brought Esther a certain amount of notoriety when questions were raised about the ethics of promoting such a thesis. The publisher bore the brunt of the inquiries, but Esther also came in for a certain amount of abuse, which she neatly deflected by saying that "to give hope in any way, shape, or form to a cancer patient cannot be bad. Believe me, I know." And everyone recognized that Esther knew whereof she spoke because, after all, for six weeks running they had seen her dying on television.

Kate was delighted that Beryl and Esther had found each other and that they were working in tandem to get *C.C.* off the ground. And indeed, in her occasional calls to Kate, Beryl sounded rather like a jet thundering down the runway toward takeoff. With each call she seemed to pick up speed. If she got Kate, she managed to speak in complete sentences, but they were clipped and hastily uttered. ("Book-of-the-Month looks good." "Dalton wants me at headquarters.") Messages on the machine were never more than terse fragments. ("L.A. distributor 8,000." " 'Good Morning, America' definite." "Warner option pending.") Kate pictured Beryl's study like a war room, filled with charts, graphs, and maps plotting the campaign. Beryl was gathering such speed that she could no longer manage even to say good-bye at the end of phone conversations. "Nice day," she'd blurt, dropping "have a" in the interests of expedition. And Kate had to admit, as she received these bulletins, that the signs pointed toward C.C. achieving at least a modest success.

But it was not only the imminent publication of their joint effort that caused Kate and Beryl's lives to intersect. They were also brought together by the romance between Igor and Melody, begun during the country weekend in June and still flourishing.

Initially, it was fed by a prodigious exchange of letters, at least two or three a day arriving at the Wylies' New York apartment, a comparable number presumably finding their way to the Swarr home in Harbor View. Igor, once again, had retreated to the seclusion of his room, emerging every few hours for a brief trip out of the house, repairing immediately to his lair when he returned. Kate assumed he was writing letters and going out to mail them; it was the least offensive activity she could imagine that fit with his pattern of movement.

Jason was disturbed by his son's recidivism and more than a little dismayed that the cause of it should be Beryl's daughter. His latest Theobold was completed and he had looked forward to spending a free summer with his son, cultivating the understanding that had begun to spring up between them in the late spring. Instead, Igor was more inaccessible than ever, locked away in his room, mooning over the young woman Jason called the Swarrette.

Kate also felt thwarted by Melody's powerful effect on

Igor and she was astonished and hurt when he turned down her invitation to a Mets game in order to compose what she reckoned was his fourth letter of the day. What could they possibly say to each other at such incredible length? she wondered, wishing that she could ask Igor, knowing it would be an unforgivable mistake.

The only time Kate and Jason actually spent with Igor these days was in the car, traveling to the country and back again. During these trips, he slouched in the back seat, sealed off by his Walkman headphones, vacant-eyed and slack-jawed.

"Ain't love grand?" Jason muttered to Kate, glimpsing the uninspiring figure of his son in the car's rearview mirror.

When, in midsummer, Igor made a foray from his cave in order to ask if Melody might come for a visit, they quickly consented, remembering the weekend when it had all begun, when he'd been so gallant, she so genial. Perhaps if Melody were here, they reasoned, Igor would rejoin the human race.

This hope proved groundless, for when they arrived in the country where they were planning to be for the duration of Melody's visit, she and Igor repaired immediately to his room and closed the door.

"We know they're not in there writing letters to each other," said Kate after several hours had passed. "What are the other possibilities?"

"Let's just give them a little time to get reacquainted," said Jason. "I'm sure they're not doing anything major."

"How do you know?"

"It's just a feeling. Igor would be scared to death, I think."

"And Melody?"

"She's fourteen years old, for Christ's sake."

"That means nothing today."

"I guess we need to have some ground rules."

"Right," said Kate.

That night at dinner, for which Igor and Melody appeared looking reassuringly unrumpled, Kate and Jason laid down the guidelines: separate bedrooms, of course, regular meals, a few daily chores apiece. Igor and Melody readily agreed (Kate and Jason checked to make certain the separate bedroom edict was being observed), but their compliance did nothing to relieve their intense sequestration. What was it they did in Igor's room, Kate wondered, that made them, when they emerged, so excessively courteous but completely detached. She, along with Jason, believed there was no need to fear the commission of advanced sexual acts, but she began to wish sex *were* the problem.

By the end of the first week of Melody's visit, Kate was still baffled and Jason's nerves were ragged.

"They are really starting to give me the creeps," he said one night after Igor and Melody had washed the dinner dishes and retired to their inner sanctum.

"They're not really *doing* anything," said Kate, feeling an inexplicable need to defend them.

"Nothing you can put your finger on. They live in his room and every once in a while they come out and prowl around."

"They don't *prowl*, Jason."

"That's what it feels like to me. They're so goddamn quiet you never hear them coming up behind you. They prowl around and have food and water and they smile and nod and answer questions monosyllabically and do their assigned tasks and then slink back in there. It's really starting to give me the creeps."

"You make it sound awfully sinister."

"I had a dream last night that the two of them were standing over me, staring down, and wearing matching T-shirts that said KILL THE PIG."

Kate couldn't help laughing. "But they haven't been hostile," she pointed out.

"Not directly. I wish they would be. I find myself longing for a return to surliness and rancor. It's easier to deal with."

"I suppose it could be worse," said Kate, still struggling to put the best possible face on a dismal situation.

"How?" Jason challenged her. "How the hell could it be worse?"

"They could be on drugs."

"And we know they're not because their pupils aren't dilated and they never leave the house to score."

"They could be connected to a cult."

"And we know they're not because they never leave the house to get brainwashed."

"Well, wouldn't those things be worse?"

"At least you can sink your teeth into them—go to a drug program, call in Ted Patrick. There's a clear-cut problem and a choice of solutions. But this—I don't even know what to call it."

"I know you'd feel better if you could give it a name."

"Don't start, Katie. Don't give me a speech about how I have to label things."

"I wasn't going to do that."

"Yes, you were."

"Yes, I was. But I won't."

"So what the hell is it? What is going on?"

"Jason, I think we just have to accept that there is some terrible teen toxin running loose in their systems that we can't control or eradicate. It will probably play itself out and there's not much we can do but wait."

Despite her strong laissez-faire statement, Kate that evening called Beryl to see if she might have an explanation for her daughter's part in the *folie à deux* being played out in the bedroom at the head of the stairs. It took several minutes to nudge Beryl out of the role of soon-to-be-best-selling author and into the role of mother (Kate felt she was on the verge of asking "Who?" when Kate raised Melody's name), and even then she was not especially helpful.

"Melody doesn't speak to me for months at a time," said Beryl, "so I wouldn't be too concerned if she's been a little tight-lipped for the last week or so."

"This isn't just normal adolescent reticence, Beryl. She and Igor are . . . remote. Even when they're present, they're absent, if you see what I mean."

"Sounds like drugs to me," said Beryl briskly but without undue concern.

"No, we're quite sure that's not the problem."

"Igor's from California, isn't he? They start young out there."

"This doesn't seem like drugs, Beryl."

"Tom Brokaw said the other night that 65 percent of all young people will have had some drug experience by the time they're fourteen."

"This has a different sort of quality to it."

"Melody just turned fourteen, of course."

"We feel drugs aren't involved."

"I wouldn't worry if she were in Harbor View. But you can't tell now that she's been exposed to an urban environment."

"Beryl," Kate said sharply, interrupting the fugue state

Beryl seemed to have slipped into, "it's not drugs."

"Well, that's certainly a relief, although Tom Brokaw said there are some wonderful programs today to deal with young addicts."

Kate got the feeling that Beryl might not have minded her daughter being enrolled in a drug rehabilitation program that had been mentioned by Tom Brokaw on the evening news.

"I suppose it could be S-E-X," Beryl said.

Why was she spelling it? Kate wondered. "No, we don't think so. Has Stanley said anything lately about a change in Melody's behavior? Have you noticed anything when you've seen her?"

"She did go through a born-again thing a little while ago. She kept telling me that she would pray for my salvation."

"What's been going on here doesn't have a Christian tinge to it," Kate said.

"Melody's not a very nice little girl, you know," said Beryl. "I don't know why that is, but I'm afraid it's true."

Kate felt a momentary pang of sympathy for Beryl, that melting mixture of pity and concern that had so often disarmed her in the past. Quickly, Beryl undercut it.

"Well, whatever it is I'm sure you'll handle it just fine, Katherine," she said. "Let me know if there's anything else I can do to help."

"Thanks a lot, Beryl," said Kate, with an irony lost on her listener. "It's been great talking to you."

What had she expected, after all? Kate chastised herself when she hung up. It had been a pointless call; she deserved exactly what she got.

The second, and final, week of Melody's visit differed from the first only in its intensity. Igor and Melody's aloofness was even more extreme, if that were possible. Jason's aggravation was more acute. Kate's bafflement deepened.

Kate and Jason fought more about the situation as the tension wore them down, taking refuge in recriminations ("If you hadn't brought the Swarr into our life this would never have happened. I'd be spending a nice summer with my son, getting to know him, establishing an understanding between us, undoing all the years of neglect." "If you hadn't slept with Tabitha, I would never have done the Swarr's book"), lashing out at each other instead of at the impervious, obdurate pair lurking in the bedroom overhead.

One night at dinner, however, unable to contain himself, Jason did direct his fire at the proper target. Unwilling to concede that the toxic teens were living in another dimension, Kate made an apple walnut cake for dessert, a favorite of Igor's and, she hoped, a wedge that might be driven through his defenses. She set the cake and a large bowl of whipped cream in front of Igor.

"Why don't you cut it?" she asked. "That way you can take as much as you like."

Kate swore she saw the ghost of a smile pass over his face, like the sun briefly glimpsed through thick cloud cover. Then he raised his eyes to Melody's and something passed between them. Igor cut two pieces of cake, one for Kate, one for Jason, and put down the knife, lowering his hands to his lap.

Jason slammed his fork onto his plate. "Just what the hell is it with you two?" he hollered, swiveling his head back and forth between them. "I've tried very hard not to ask, to leave you alone, to give you room to do whatever you pleased. But I feel now that I have the right to know just what the hell is going on. What is it? You can't eat certain things without

checking with each other? You can't speak unless you're
spoken to? You can't go outside because if sunlight hits you
you'll disappear? Are those the rules? Who made them up?
Just what the hell is going on?"

"If it bothers you, Dad," Igor said quietly, "I'll be happy
to eat a piece of cake. So will Melody."

"Certainly, Mr. Wylie. I'd be glad to."

"It's not the goddamn cake," said Jason.

"I thought you said—"

"I know what I said. I also know what you said. And the
words are meaningless. What I'm talking about is what's
underneath the words."

"If you could explain what you mean—"

"Forget it." Jason cut him off. "There's no use talking to
a zombie. Why don't you two just excuse yourselves and return to the fort."

Igor and Melody, unspeaking, rose as one and left. Kate
went to Jason's end of the table, putting her arms around his
slumped shoulders, kissing the top of his bent head. Had she
discerned a triumphant glint in Melody's eye as she'd glided
out of the room? Or did she want to believe Melody was the
malign influence so that she could absolve Igor?

"Only two more days to go," she whispered against
Jason's cheek.

"I'm afraid she won't leave," Jason murmured in a broken
voice. "I'm afraid we'll be locked in this house with them
for the rest of our lives."

"No, we won't, darling," said Kate. "If I have to knock
her out, throw her in a sack, and ship her back to Harbor
View, she'll leave on Monday."

Sunday evening, with an eye to making good on her
promise, Kate decided to be certain that all was in readiness

for Melody's departure. She approached Igor's room and rapped sharply on the door. When she got no response, she knocked again and called out their names. Met again by silence, she launched into an appeal.

"I know your privacy is very important to you and I'm sure you'll agree that we have respected it. But tonight I need to talk to you. We have to leave early in the morning to get to the airport and I want everything to be set to go."

Kate stopped and awaited a sound from within.

"We have been cooperative and understanding with you," she continued when stillness greeted her, "and I'm sure if you think about it you'll want to return the favor."

As the silence persisted, Kate felt herself becoming angry. "All right, we don't even have to talk, but could you knock on the goddamn wall if you hear me and if you understand that you have to be up and packed and ready to go at seven tomorrow morning?"

She waited a moment, but heard nothing. "This is ridiculous, you little creeps," she muttered, as she drew back her right leg and shot her foot forward toward the door. It gave easily, Kate's leg went out from under her and she spilled clumsily into the room. It was empty.

Dazed by this, and by her violent landing, she sat, unmoving, for some time. Then she picked herself up, looked around the room, and made her way down the stairs and out onto the porch where Jason was sunk in the hammock, rehearsing the relaxation he would enjoy when the Swarrette had taken her leave.

"They're gone," said Kate.

"What do you mean?" he asked.

"They're not here. The room is empty."

"They're gone?"

"That's what I said, Jason."

"Maybe he decided to show her a big night on the town before she left, general store, post office, the works."

"Would she take her suitcase for that?"

Jason swung his legs over the hammock's edge and sat up. "I thought I felt something different in the air as I was lying here," he said, "an absence of poison, a kind of peace."

"What are we going to do?" Kate asked.

"Lie back down and enjoy it." He took hold of Kate's hands and pulled her toward him.

"Be serious," she said, resisting his efforts.

"I was never more so." He flipped his legs back into the hammock and managed to get Kate positioned on the edge.

"We can't let them just vanish—just disappear."

"You wanna bet?" he asked, hauling her into the hammock beside him.

"You're not thinking straight."

"For two weeks our house has been inhabited by the walking dead. Now they are gone, and I am happy. That's all I know." Jason stroked Kate's hair, he took hold of her hands and kissed her fingertips, one by one, he drew her on top of him and held her tightly.

She let herself be caressed, she felt her body meld into his. Eventually, she lifted her head and looked into Jason's dark eyes.

"One of the living dead is your son," she said.

"I'm a lousy father, Katie, and that surprises me. I thought I would be better at it. I thought I could make up for the first betrayal, and what I've ended up doing is adding another one to it."

"You've just been learning as you go along. We both have."

"Even you do it better than I."

"That's not true."

"At least sometimes you get through to him."

"Well, no one could these last few weeks. You're not responsible for that."

"If he and I had established some sort of relationship, it wouldn't have happened. He wouldn't have fallen under the Swarrette's spell the way he did."

"You were trying, Jason. And you'll try again—after we find him."

They drove into the village, through its empty streets. They went to the neighboring town, large by comparison, and checked the train station. They traveled the entire length of the North Fork, looking for hitchhikers alongside the road. They arrived back home about midnight still ignorant of Igor's and Melody's whereabouts.

They phoned the apartment in New York, although they knew that if Igor and Melody were there they would be unlikely to answer. They phoned neighbors in the building to ask them to check whether or not the apartment was occupied, but it was the end of an August weekend and no one was home. They even phoned Beryl, who announced tartly to Kate that her news "impacted on me very negatively" and, hinting darkly at abduction, ransom demands, and possible terrorism, suggested they call the police immediately. Kate allowed as how there was very little terrorist activity out their way and told Beryl she'd call her first thing in the morning. Then she and Jason drove into New York, finding no evidence in the apartment that Igor and Melody had been there.

After sleeping for a few hours, they went at dawn to Kennedy Airport, from which Melody was scheduled to depart at nine-thirty, and stationed themselves so that they could see the American Airlines check-in desk, but not automatically be seen themselves by approaching passengers. And there they waited.

About nine-fifteen, the unkempt figures of Igor and Melody came into view, slithering toward American's counter, eyes darting furtively about the terminal.

"Don't jump all over him," said Kate as they rose. "It will be humiliating in front of her and, besides, it won't do any good."

"Isn't this a situation that calls for a little humiliation?" Jason asked.

Igor looked startled as he saw them approaching, but Melody's chilly audacity steadied him.

"Good morning, Mrs. Wylie, Mr. Wylie," she said. "If you'll excuse me I have to check in now or I'll be late."

Kate could feel Jason trembling with rage beside her, but Melody moved out of range, and Igor followed her. When her ticket was processed, she turned back to the Wylies.

"Thank you very much for everything," she said. "I had a very nice time."

"Oh, not at all, Melody," said Jason acidly, inclining toward her in a bow. "It was our pleasure . . . loved having you . . . had a grand time . . . all those talks by the campfire, long walks on the beach, cookouts, swimming, boating—"

Kate cut in. "You'd better get going or you'll miss your plane."

Melody, who had been backing away as Jason's words pelted her, now turned and ran toward her gate, Igor following, giving her a quick, fumbling hug before she vanished into the crowd in the long passageway. Unbuttressed by Melody, Igor's self-assurance began to disintegrate as he made his way back to Kate and Jason. It fell away from him visibly: his shoulders sagged, his head drooped, his gait foundered.

"I'm sorry if you were worried," he muttered when he reached them, chin resting on his chest.

Words gargled in Jason's throat. Igor breathed rapidly, awaiting the explosion.

"Let's go home," said Kate.

And they headed out of the terminal, Jason on one side, Igor on the other, Kate between them, where she hadn't wanted to be.

Chapter Seven

*I*T took several weeks for the full story of Melody's sorcery to emerge. But Kate eventually came to understand that Igor had at first recognized in Melody a kindred spirit, one who had as much trouble with the adult world as he did. Even when she was being pleasant to her mother in person, she said perfectly vile things about her behind her back, and Igor was impressed by her fierce hostility. He would never, he told Kate, have been able to articulate such scurrilous thoughts; he would never have been able to *think* them. But they flowed freely and vividly from Melody's lips and there was something compelling about her incontinence. Igor felt himself bound by endless constraints. Melody's abandon exhilarated him.

During the course of their letter writing Melody stressed her need for Igor. If she had him, she wrote, she didn't need anyone or anything else, sentiments that Igor found more than a little heady. If he could be everything to someone, he reasoned, he must possess more substance than he had thought. Unless she heard from him often, Melody wrote, she would sink into despair. Igor took his responsibility as a lifeline very seriously and wrote her several times a day.

When Melody arrived for her visit she immediately apprised Igor of the need for solidarity against the outside world. Together, they were a complete universe, she told him. But other people wouldn't understand that; they would try to drive them apart. The two of them must be vigilant against such attempts and the best way to do that, she counseled, was to be agreeable and polite.

"Don't give them anything to hang on to," she told him, "because if you do they'll grab it and tear you away from me."

To reinforce their united front, Melody had devised a chant that she required them to intone at regular intervals: "We are one, one is all, all is we, we are one, one is all, all is we," over and over again, especially before and after meals when they had to be with the Others, as Melody insisted they call Kate and Jason.

As the end of her visit loomed, Melody began to talk about the need to avoid their impending separation. Once put asunder, they might never get together again if the Others had anything to say about it (and they would: it was in the nature of Others to have something to say about everything), a prospect that was not without its appeal to Igor at this point, although he was fearful of resisting Melody outright. He went along when she suggested they flee the night before her departure. But when they arrived at the airport at six A.M. that Monday morning (Melody intended to turn in her air ticket and use the funds for bus tickets for them both, destination unknown: "The journey, not its end, is what matters," she argued), Igor drew the line.

He hated to relinquish the sense of strength and power with which Melody's need had endowed him, however temporarily. He didn't have the heart to tell her that he'd begun to doubt the efficacy of their cause. What he did say was that running off together would play into the Others' hands, making the two of them candidates for permanent separation when they were found, as they surely would be. Melody ultimately saw the wisdom of this and they huddled in an empty departure area chanting their unity mantra until it was time for her plane.

Kate was moved by this story, which she received from Igor piecemeal, moved by its revelation of his extreme vulnerability and of his probity. She knew Igor still wrote to Melody (no longer several times a day but perhaps several times a week), although she suspected he now considered this something of a chore, rather than a privilege. And she admired the air of responsibility this conveyed.

Jason saw it all in another light. He had managed to hold his tongue during the drive from the airport to Long Island on the day Melody flew home. But when they arrived at the farmhouse, he announced that he and Igor were going to have a talk. They were closeted in Jason's study for nearly an hour and during that time Igor, apparently, did not move much beyond his simple apology for causing them worry. Jason was looking for answers; Igor hadn't any. Once again, they were at an impasse.

Jason continued manfully to struggle with his fatherhood as though it were an entity separate and apart from him, one determined to lay him low. But whatever his intentions when he approached Igor, as soon as they began to talk Jason's notions of the proper framework between father and son (based on lifelong fantasies of the behavior his own father would have manifested had he not chosen, instead, to leave before Jason was three years old) asserted themselves. He could neither accept Igor on his terms nor bend him to his own. And as Jason, in his powerlessness, became more rigid, Igor, who had during Melody's visit witnessed adult impotence in the face of adolescent resolve, grew more defiant. Jason also began again to resent Kate's ability to reach Igor when he could not. And Kate started to retreat into work, just as she had when Igor first arrived.

Actually, what happened in her study could not accurately be called work. When she entered it each day, closing the door behind her, she felt she stepped out of present reality, into the past. Two figures, whom Kate had thought she understood, governed this territory. But when she came to write them, to alchemize them into characters, their lines of definition grew quavery, their motives blurred. They disintegrated in her hands like the pages of an old family album, brittle with age and disuse.

Why, really, had Lucius been obsessed with a bloody war that ended more than fifty years before he was born? What had been the meaning of his inventions, fashioned during those long, mysterious hours in the barn? Why had he cut himself off from his family so completely? Were they really all so detestable, every one of them? What would have become of Carabel if she hadn't spent sixteen hours of each day reading? Why had she chosen that way of losing herself? Why had she had to insist on that loss? Why had both Kate's parents been so unlike other people?

She had planned to begin her novel with the wedding of her two main characters. When she found it difficult to envision, or justify, their coming together, she decided to open instead with their death, accomplished with one stroke when she placed them in an airplane that crashed and burned in the mountains of Peru. (Lucius always said he regretted missing South America during his youthful travels, so Kate, despite the unfortunate outcome, felt pleased that she had at least gotten him there.) Perhaps starting at the end, and looking back, the secrets of this marriage, of its two partners, would reveal themselves. But that did not occur. Instead for days Kate felt submerged in grief at the loss she had inflicted on herself.

Then she took a stab at each of them in childhood— begin at the beginning, that made sense—but this proved fruitless as well. She even tried giving them a child who, as an adult, would tell their story. And that was worst of all. Day after day, she sat facing the page in her typewriter, never able to move beyond the first sentence or two.

She began to think that perhaps she should give up altogether. Maybe this wasn't the time for her to write a novel after all, at least not this one. If God had intended her to write this, wouldn't he have made it easier?

Her agent called regularly with prospective ghost projects (the story of the first woman to cross the Atlantic Ocean in a canoe; Anastasia's two years in hiding after her family's massacre, related by the woman who claimed her family had sheltered the Tsar's daughter; something called *Silicone and You*; the biography of a writer of romances), and Kate began to talk herself into considering them. She needn't get involved with the person whose book it was: Beryl had taught her that lesson for all time. The work itself was so much less taxing than writing fiction. One didn't really have to generate anything. It was just a matter of organizing a structure and putting together sentences. That came easily to Kate. Of course it wasn't very satisfying, but how much satisfaction had she gained from wrestling with the ghosts of her parents the past few months? These rationalizations, left to root in the dark fertile soil of her own mind, shielded from the outside scrutiny that might have nipped them in the bud, flourished and grew. She was just considering revealing them to Jason (she knew what his objections would be and had her arguments prepared) when she received a letter that saved her from herself and also made her realize there was something to be said for deus ex machina.

The mail that day contained some bills, a letter to Igor from his sister, Ludmilla, who'd been lobbying to join him in New York (Kate and Jason had received several tearful calls from Natasha begging them not to strip from her the last thing that gave life any meaning and they were able to assure her that that was the farthest thing from their minds), nothing from Melody, Kate was happy to see, but a flyer from Beryl announcing the imminent publication of *Captive Courageous* (who was footing the bill for all these costly little extras? Kate wondered), and several of Jason's trade publications, magazines, pamphlets, newsletters that addressed every aspect of the mystery genre and its practitioners (Jason had been featured recently in one of the less obscure of these, conducting a tour of some of the neighborhoods in which Theobold stalked his nefarious prey). It was from the pages of one of the periodicals that the pale blue envelope dropped. Kate could distinguish her own name, though the script was shaky. The return address read only: "Aikenfield, Lindenville, New York."

She read:

I am writing to you because I am an old woman filled with regrets and I wish to avoid adding one more

139

*to my store. Perhaps it is too late, perhaps not. That
will be up to you.*

*While there is no way to change the past, I con-
tinue to hope there are ways to redeem it. If we could
see each other, I would be grateful. If not, I would understand.*

Ceilia Cadwalader
(your father's mother)

Despite the letter's rather forbidding tone, Kate knew immediately that she wanted to go, and feelings of disloyalty
surged through her. She recalled a conversation with her father, driving up to Gettysburg on one of those piercing autumn days when everything was clean and distinct. The
edges of the clouds were clearly etched against the deep blue
sky. Each color on the trees—orange, red, gold—stood out
sharply. Kate remembered the sound and feel of her teeth
biting into one of the crisp apples they'd bought at a cider
mill on the way. She must have been eleven years old.

"We're supposed to write papers about our families for
social studies," she'd said to Lucius.

"I hope you'll treat me kindly," he answered, reaching
over to Kate and running a finger down her cheek as if he
were making a mark on a blackboard, a characteristic gesture of his.

"Not you," she said. "Not parents."

"Oh?"

"Cousins, aunts and uncles, grandparents—all that
stuff."

"What about kids who don't have all that stuff, or any of
it?"

"You mean like me?" Kate hadn't been able to keep a
note of accusation from her voice.

"Well, it's not strictly true that you don't have relatives."

"It may as well be. I never see them." Kate suddenly felt quite desolate about this deficit although, in fact, she had never thought about it much before her current school assignment and this conversation.

"You saw Mr. Langford, your mother's father. He came to visit once."

"Before I was old enough to remember," said Kate, rejecting this crumb.

"He was a fine gentleman," said Lucius. "You liked him very much."

"I'll have to take your word for it," she replied. "Why didn't he ever come back?"

"He didn't like to move around much—just like his daughter."

"We could have gone to see him."

Lucius was silent for a moment. "He died, Kate, when you were about six."

She had known this, of course, but in the car with her father that day, on their way to remember the Confederate and Union dead, she felt nearly overcome with the bleakness of it.

"Well, what about you?" she asked, angry at Mr. Langford's untimely death (would she have had to call him that if he'd lived? she wondered), and at her father's schism with his family that deprived her of the company of cousins, aunts, uncles, grandparents, as well as material for her social studies paper. ("We don't see them," was all she knew about this bunch, and it had come from her mother.) "All of them aren't dead, are they?"

"Oh, I very much doubt it."

"Well?" Kate challenged him.

Lucius seemed to sense her urgency and seriousness. She remembered how he had shifted his body behind the wheel, moved his hands up to the top of the steering wheel as if he were gripping a podium, perhaps even cleared his throat.

"I never fit with them," said Lucius. "I don't know why. I don't even know whose fault it was. But I knew if I stayed there rubbing off corners to fit their mold, I'd just gradually disappear without a trace." He took one hand off the wheel and blew a good-bye kiss from his fingertips into the air.

This stark statement dissipated Kate's anger and made her feel excessively solemn.

"Didn't you ever miss them?" she asked.

Lucius didn't reply right away. He appeared to be considering her question, and Kate, who believed she detected sorrow in the tilt of his head and downward cast of his eye, was certain he would answer, "Yes, terribly." But then a grin cracked across his face and his glorious laugh, which she loved, filled the car.

"Not enough, I guess," he said.

That was the only conversation Kate ever had with her father about his family. She knew that he had tried to answer her and, as unsatisfactory as she found it, that he had probably done the best he could.

Carabel wasn't much help either. She once told Kate, as if it were a comprehensive explanation, that Lucius had been forced to call his mother Ceilia, rather than Mother. This seemed curious to Kate, and perhaps a bit austere, but also inadequate as grounds for a lifetime exile.

Neither of her parents ever unraveled the mystery any further, Carabel because she couldn't (she, after all, had had her own curiosity stifled quite unequivocally soon after her marriage), Lucius because he wouldn't. But Kate never

142

stopped wondering about the Cadwaladers, while at the same time accepting her father's judgment that they were to be avoided at all costs.

And now this woman, who had insisted that her son call her by her proper name, had written to Kate, wanting to see her. Would Lucius really have minded? Would he himself have been able to resist a letter such as Kate had received? She murmured a small prayer to him, asking to be forgiven, and sat down to answer her grandmother's letter.

Ten days later she was driving up the Hudson, heading for the bottom of Saranac Lake and Aikenfield, which was not, as it turned out, the Cadwalader Adirondack retreat, but a "custodial facility," although Ceilia had assured Kate that she needn't anticipate confronting "a dim and dusty shadow. I'm not what I once was," she had written, "but the lights haven't gone out yet." If for no other reason, Kate felt she would be able to warm to her grandmother for her turn of phrase.

Kate's last acquaintance with a nursing home had been during the final years of her mother's life and memories of that time inundated her as she pulled into the Aikenfield parking lot. Carabel's disjointed chatter about unfamiliar characters, delivered in a deep Mississippi drawl that she had lost almost completely in her years "up North," as she had always considered Maryland. Her requests that Kate read to her, a reversal of the configuration from Kate's childhood that invariably made her feel like crying. Carabel's eyes, larger, more protuberant, as her face receded from them, asking Kate an urgent question she couldn't begin to answer. The day her mother had not known her at all. Kate sat in the car for several minutes, waiting for the images to recede.

When she presented herself at the front desk, she was told that Mrs. Cadwalader liked to "receive" people in the sun room, and she was shown there to wait. She scrutinized carefully each person who entered, searching for some familiar aspect of mind or body, convincing herself she had found it, then watching the person pass her by. But when Ceilia came in, Kate knew instantly that this was the woman she had come to see.

She rose as her grandmother approached, leaning slightly on the walking stick in her right hand, her keen blue eyes holding Kate's firmly. She was tall, graceful despite the stick, and Kate recognized each of her features, the absolutely straight nose, sharp cheekbones, the wide but thin-lipped mouth. How could a son who had resembled her so closely have found her so alien? Kate wondered. She also wondered what her grandmother was doing here. She did not appear in the least to need looking after.

Arriving in front of Kate, she shifted the stick to her left hand and extended her right. "Thank you for coming," she said.

"I wanted to," said Kate, as she touched the cool, dry flesh of her grandmother's hand, emblem of the history that had been denied her.

If Kate's view of their meeting was romantic, even mystical, Ceilia's seemed decidedly down-to-earth. She led Kate to a corner of the bright, airy room, settled herself in a chair whose cover was splashed with blue and purple flowers, and plunged not into an explanation or recapitulation of the past, but a vigorous inquiry into Kate's present. Was she married? Did she have children? Why not? What sort of work did she do? What kind of books did she write? Were they successful? What kind of books did her husband write? Was he well known?

While fielding this barrage of questions, Kate tried once or twice to turn her grandmother's mind backward, but Ceilia would have none of it. She just acted as if Kate hadn't spoken and continued interrogating her. While they talked, other Aikenfield residents drifted, wheeled, or were pushed by, the sentient ones greeting Ceilia in some fashion, she responding in kind.

The most boisterous greeting came from a tiny woman who stopped directly in front of them, shouted, "Hiya, Seal," and then began to bark, clap her hands together like flippers, and toddle round in a circle with heels together, toes splayed, simulating a performer in a circus marine show.

Ceilia gave the woman her attention, nodding along with her barks, smiling, waving good-bye when the display ended.

"I'm afraid she's got my name spelled wrong," she murmured, as the woman sauntered away with a perfectly normal gait.

Kate was struck forcefully by the discrepancy between her grandmother and her fellow residents. Those whose minds appeared sound suffered from obvious physical decrepitude; the majority seemed to have experienced a dimming of both their physical and mental lights. But Ceilia, so far as Kate could determine, seemed fit in both respects.

"Why are you here?" Kate asked her grandmother. "You surely wouldn't have to be."

Kate thought Ceilia might, again, ignore her curiosity, but she did not.

"I just wanted to get away from them all," she said. "That must have been how Lucius felt."

It was the first time she had spoken his name and it brought all Kate's stifled questions rushing back. But she sensed she should not ask them. It was obviously important

Linda Crawford

to Ceilia that their meeting be conducted on her terms, and
Kate wasn't willing to challenge that.

"But there must have been another way, some other
place—"

"I like it here," Ceilia said. "It suits me fine."

"You don't find it depressing?"

She seemed surprised. "No. Should I?"

"I think I would," said Kate, feeling on uncertain ground,
a little frightened of this formidable woman, eager to have
her approval. "I mean if I were fine, which you certainly
seem to be, I think it might disturb me to be surrounded by
so many people who weren't."

Her grandmother laughed, Lucius's laugh, a sound Kate
loved. "Oh, my dear," she said, "after the Cadwaladers, this
is a picnic. Some of the people here are a bit eccentric, the
seal lady, for instance, or my next door neighbor, who re-
fuses to eat unless she's in the altogether, and there are
others who aren't as well as they might be, but they're all
basically decent and well meaning."

"And the Cadwaladers aren't?" Kate asked.

An indecipherable noise rumbled in Ceilia's throat, but
she swallowed it before it could emerge. Then, disregarding
the query, she asked Kate about her mother, another barri-
cade of questions that put her effectively beyond reach.

Because of her grandmother's letter, with its mention of
regret and redemption, Kate had anticipated that they
might discuss those subjects. And that such discussion
might answer the questions, fill in the gaps, present Kate
with her missing history. But Ceilia was no more forthcom-
ing than her son had been. If anything, she deepened the
mystery.

After wringing from Kate a full chronicle of Carabel,

Ceilia said, "I'm so glad to have seen you," signaling that their meeting was at an end.

Didn't she want to know something about the last nearly fifty years of her son's life? Kate wondered. Was she too proud to ask? Too stubborn? Was this to be their only meeting? "I'm so glad to have seen you" sounded final somehow, the description of an occasion with distinct boundaries.

Ceilia rose and Kate stood with her. "I'd like to come again sometime," she said.

Ceilia neither agreed nor declined. She just gazed at Kate, her eyes seeming to look through her and beyond.

"I missed him every single day that he was gone," she said finally, turning away to hide the effect of this utterance on her face, leaving the room the same way she had entered.

That evening, at home, when Kate described to Jason her visit to Aikenfield, she omitted Ceilia's final line. She did not make a conscious decision to leave it out. She found she simply couldn't repeat it. It had been her grandmother's secret all these years; now Kate felt it had become hers.

The statement's air of loss and desolation, the effort it must have taken Ceilia to make it, had shaken Kate deeply. It was frightening to contemplate how fragile and how indestructible human connections were, and how easily abused and squandered. She supposed she ought to share it with Jason, as a cautionary tale, if nothing else: this is what happens when parent and child give up on trying to reach an understanding with each other. But she felt she had to hoard it, to keep it to herself.

While she took her grandmother's appearance in her life as a signal that she probably ought to write the novel she'd been attempting, rather than escaping into the relative

147

safety of, say, *Have I Got a Gal for You*, reminiscences of a
San Francisco madam (Kate's agent had called last week to
offer this), it didn't speed her on her way. Her grandmother
had raised questions, not answered them, and Kate took to
pondering these as she sat at her desk each day, listening to
the Requiem, writing not a word.

The publication date of *Captive Courageous* was set for
mid-October and in the few preceding weeks Beryl called
frequently to tell Kate of yet another promotional appearance that had been added to her already heavy schedule, her
relentless harassment of the Waverly Press publicity depart-
ment having apparently paid off.

"The ball is really rolling," she reported in one of these
bulletins. (They could not be said to be conversations, as
Kate rarely contributed more than the occasional mutter or
hum of encouragement.) "We've got the big markets sewed
up: New York, L.A., Dallas–Fort Worth, print and radio-
TV."

"Mmmmm," said Kate.

"So now we're going after some of the smaller ones. Just
pinned down 'Good Morning, Duluth,' and 'Bangor Book
Beat.' "

"Great," said Kate.

"Katherine, let me just put on my other hat for a moment," Beryl said, turning exceedingly earnest.

"Of course," said Kate, wondering what hat it was Beryl
had been wearing before the switch.

"I think C.C. is going to impact very positively on some
of the smaller areas. These people will identify with me,
with my background, with my struggle to break free of hostagehood in all areas of my life. C.C. isn't just going to be a
big book, Katherine, it's going to be an important one."

"Hostagehood?" said Kate. She hadn't used that word in the book, had she? Thank God she didn't put her name on these things. And to think that recently she'd been considering doing another.

"All those things that keep us from being fully ourselves, those daily imprisonments where we're our own jailers, those self-constructed barriers that get between you and you."

"Me?"

Now Beryl tossed aside her cap of viscous sanctimony. "This book is *hot!*" she said, spitting the word into the phone so that it popped in Kate's ear. "H-O-T hot!"

"Yes, well—"

"More later. Nice day," said Beryl, and she hung up.

When Kate felt aggravated by these calls, she comforted herself with the fact that in a matter of days now, Beryl would belong to the world, and no longer, in any way, to her. If the book did as well as Beryl anticipated, she would believe she had written it and cease to remember Kate's existence. If Beryl's expectations were not met, she would blame Kate and never again want to have anything to do with her.

The occasion, more than any other, that Kate had begun to think of as marking her liberation from Beryl, was Beryl's appearance on the "Dave Duncan Show." This was set to air in New York on publication day and, in the subsequent few weeks, virtually everywhere else in the country. Kate stationed herself in front of the television just before air time, relieved to be alone (she was taping the show so that Jason and Igor could see it later). She felt that this broadcast, which millions of people would see, was essentially a private matter for her.

149

Linda Crawford

The theme music sounded and Dave Duncan, a wiry little man with a mop of dark curly hair and a toothy smile, appeared, holding aloft a copy of *Captive Courageous*, advising his audience, "This is some kinda story, folks, some kinda story." Then, in a series of staccato phrases notable for their lurid and alliterative language ("hair-raising horror," "grit and guts," "dazzling and daring denouement"), he outlined Beryl's ordeal in People's Bank & Trust, and wound up with an introduction:

"Folks, please welcome the heroine of this story, the woman who lived it and then wrote it (Kate winced involuntarily), Beryl Swarr."

Standing before a chair on a raised platform, Beryl faced fearlessly into the camera, perhaps experiencing a renewed sense of her own courage, perhaps moved by Dave's description of it. She was wearing a yellow wool outfit with heavily padded shoulders, deeply nipped waist, what Kate believed was a peplum (though she hadn't seen one for many years), and a sharply flared skirt that reached to mid-calf. The severe angles of this garment, in combination with her perpendicular shafts of hair, gave Beryl a dimension that seemed closer to science fiction than to the realistic drama Dave had described. (Kate searched for a trace of the little teller to whom these events had happened but found none.) Nevertheless, the audience greeted her warmly and Beryl responded by flashing her transitory smile.

"Okay," said Dave, pacing up and down in front of the platform where Beryl was now seated, tossing the microphone back and forth between his hands, "he shoots your fellow teller in the back, guns down two other people in cold blood, he looks like a walking ammunition depot, for God's sake. In your own words, Mrs. Swarr, what do you feel when you realize you're alone in the bank with this insane and dangerous man?"

The words were Kate's, of course, as Beryl responded by quoting a chunk of manuscript. "I felt as though time had stopped. Everything inside me went very still. In that moment I felt completely powerless. I no longer possessed my own life. It was in someone else's hands and I could only wait to see what he would do with it."

Not bad, Kate thought. A little melodramatic perhaps, but not bad.

"Life and death," said Dave. "That's what it's all about."

Was he talking about the book? Or had Beryl's recitation triggered in him the need to share a bit of personal philosophy?

"But you didn't feel powerless for long, did you, Mrs. Swarr?"

"No, Dave. I began to realize that there were things I could do about my hostagehood."

Kate winced again. Obviously that word was here to stay.

"And you sure did them, little lady. Boy, oh, boy, did you ever!"

Dave now ticked off the actions Beryl had taken in her own behalf—her insistence on certain housekeeping standards, her masterful stance at her press conferences, her negotiation of the final settlement—the audience greeting each with longer, more enthusiastic bursts of applause, Beryl attempting a show of modesty by lowering her eyelids and inclining her head to the side as her feats were announced. When Dave finished, he was slightly breathless.

"Where did you find the nerve, the fortitude, the sheer *chutzpah* to go one-on-one with this maniac?" he asked.

"Inside, Dave," Beryl replied, tapping herself on the

chest with one very long, brightly painted nail, lest there be any doubt about inside what.

Kate wondered whatever had happened to the "greater power," the "something larger" to whom Beryl had orginally ascribed so much of her courage. Apparently, it had bitten the dust along with Harbor View, Stanley and the children, and God knew what else.

"I was alone in my nightmare," said Beryl. "I was the only one who could wake myself up and make it go away."

The words, Kate had to concede, were dangerously florid, at least as rendered by Beryl. Kate remembered them sounding less sensational on the printed page.

Dave was rooted to the spot for a few admiring beats, gazing at the paragon before him. Then, managing to break the spell Beryl's bravery had cast on him, he turned back to the audience.

"Powerful stuff," he said, causing the audience to applaud. "Incredibly powerful."

The camera showed Beryl trying, without much success, to look diffident.

Dave walked to a table where he had earlier set down *Captive Courageous* and picked it up again, appearing to study it thoughtfully, weighing it in his hand as if to assess its heft.

"Why a book, Beryl?" he asked. "I hope I can call you Beryl. You come so alive in these pages, and now seeing you here, I guess I feel I know you."

"Yes, you may, Dave." Her smile was coquettish.

"I mean, this hadda have been one hell of a painful thing to relive the whole nightmare in order to get it down on paper."

"Well, Dave, I was reluctant at first to do a book, although people were urging me to do so. But when I began to see that sharing my experience might be helpful to others, that's when I made the commitment to go ahead."

"And it musta been hell to put yourself through the ordeal all over again."

"It was very painful, Dave, but let me tell you something: nothing produces as much insight as putting those words down on that page. Doing the book became part of the process of making this a self-validating experience for me."

"And a real catharsis, I bet."

"That too."

"How can the book help the rest of us, Beryl? Probably not too many of us are gonna be locked in a bank with a looney-tunes killer for ten days. At least we hope not." Several members of the audience joined in with Dave's mildly hysterical laughter.

Beryl waited for quiet. "I'm glad you asked me that, Dave. You see, I think my experience was really a metaphor for something that occurs in everyone's life. We're all captives, in a sense. We're all held hostage by one thing or another. And I think, if we're shown how to tap into it, we're all capable of being courageous. In ten days I worked my way from powerlessness to freedom. So can you."

"All right!" said Dave. "This is one gutsy lady. Let's hear it for her."

As the applause faded into a commercial break, Kate let her head fall back onto the soft cushion of the sofa. This was how Frankenstein must have felt when his monster was on the loose: horrified by his own craftsmanship—out of control—ashamed. Kate let the sounds of laundry detergent, pain medication, and sanitary napkins being hawked wash over her. Then Dave Duncan's theme music sounded again

Linda Crawford

and she raised her head to see him bounding up an aisle and thrusting the mike toward the mouth of an audience member.

"Weren't you horribly afraid?" asked a plump, middle-aged woman with a round, open countenance and spectacles that exactly replicated her facial shape. "And, if so, just how exactly did you get over it?"

If Beryl had been slightly subdued when Dave Duncan was her interrogator, this question from one of the common herd seemed to galvanize her. She rose, grasped a microphone resting in a stand beside her chair, and moved to the front of the platform, whipping the mike cord behind her in a manner reminiscent of a Vegas headliner. For one mad moment, Kate expected to hear her belt out a show tune (perhaps something from *Gypsy* or *42nd Street*).

"I was looking down the barrel of a gun at death," said Beryl, feet planted shoulder distance apart. "Wouldn't you be afraid?" she asked, causing the round woman to nod vigorously, while others in the audience murmured their assent.

"So what did I do?" she continued, timing impeccable, when the whispers died. "I turned my gaze inside. And what did I find? A kind of self-energy I had never imagined was there. And what did I say to myself?" Beryl paused just long enough to allow suspense to build. "I said, 'Take charge, Beryl.' And from that moment on that's just what I did."

Dave was already scampering toward another woman who had risen near the front of the audience, stretching the mike toward her over several other bodies.

"Do you think a person such as myself could get over fear just in my regular life by reading your book?"

Beryl swept across the stage toward her questioner, mike

154

cord snaking in her wake like a quivering cobra. "I was just an ordinary person when this ordeal happened, just like you, and circumstances forced me to get pretty brave pretty fast. I *had* to discover my inner self-resources in a hurry. If I hadn't—" Beryl paused, drew a finger across her neck and made a screeching noise that sounded like a nail on glass. Then she laughed rather giddily, perhaps actually recalling the moment. "But this same kind of self-energy is available to you, if you'll just get in there and dig for it and take charge!"

The woman, looking bewildered but hopeful, sat down as Dave shifted the microphone to a man at the end of the row.

"What exactly do you mean when you say, 'Take charge?' " he asked.

"I was hoping someone would ask me that," Beryl replied. "When I say, 'Take charge!' I am talking about total self-command. Be in charge of your mind, your actions, your environment. Harness that inner self-energy and use it to do whatever you want. Anything is possible. Anything."

Beryl began now to move back and forth across the stage in full inspirational flight, the slithering cord occasionally threatening to entwine her ankles and bring her down like a roped steer. It made Kate nervous, but Beryl's performance was mesmerizing.

"I was held hostage for ten days, locked in a bank with a man who had killed before and could kill again, locked in with the bodies of his victims, reminders of what he was capable of, and I not only survived that ordeal, I came out a winner! And why? Because I looked inside myself and I found self-energy and I said—"

"Take charge!" The high-pitched cry came from a rather servile looking woman in the front row, moved by Beryl's hortatory harangue to rise up, scream out, and fling her fist in the air.

Beryl looked startled, but pleased, and she moved to extend her hand over the edge of the stage toward the oppressed figure who appeared to have terrified herself with her own zeal. The woman fell back leadenly into her seat and would have pulled Beryl from the platform if she hadn't wrenched her hand away just in the nick of time.

"You've got 'em goin' now," Dave remarked as he hurried the microphone to another prospective questioner.

"You said that you were in there ten days," said a stocky man with a gray crew cut and heavily pocked skin.

"Right," said Beryl.

"And you said there were bodies in there with you of the people who were shot."

"Right," she replied again.

"Well, I just wondered what that was like."

Beryl stared at him, uncomprehending.

"I've been in a war and I know what can happen to a body in ten days."

Dave, sensing this was not a productive direction, barked, "Here's a young lady with something on her mind," as he shoved the mike into the face of an elderly woman.

"What if you find yourself in a situation that you just can't do anything about?"

"No such animal," Beryl responded, hitting each word sharply and underlining it further with a sharp jab of her red-taloned finger.

"Well," said the small but spirited woman, "I'm thinking of plenty of times when I could've said to myself, 'Ethel, take charge,' but if my husband was around it wouldn't do me a damn bit of good."

A wave of sympathetic laughter greeted Ethel's remark, prompting her to continue.

"I've lived for quite a long time, a lot longer than you have," she said to Beryl, "and I know that sometimes life hands you situations that are beyond your control, no matter how much energy you have."

Kate, alone in her den, applauded.

"And I also have observed," said Ethel, warming to the task of the devil's advocate, "that some people can do some things, and other people can't. Everybody can't do everything. What works for one person may be useless for another. Somebody else could've been in that bank like you were and looked inside themselves and found nothing and got herself shot." She sat down abruptly, crossing her arms over her chest as though to fend off attack.

The audience began to clap and Kate sensed that it was torn between subscribing to Beryl's appealing panacea and Ethel's solid common sense. Beryl also recognized that Ethel had struck a responsive chord and decided wisely not to argue with her, at least not immediately.

"Ethel," she said, "I want you to have a copy of *Captive Courageous,* an autographed copy, and let's see if we can't make a believer out of you."

The audience cheered the gesture and ended up right back in the palm of Beryl's hand. Even Ethel, obviously flattered, was smiling.

"You make sure you see me after the show," said Beryl, and Ethel, dropping her arms from their defensive position, flashed a thumbs-up signal with both hands.

"All right!" said Dave. "Didn't I promise you this was gonna be some kinda show today?"

The audience applauded heartily.

"Didn't I?" he asked again.

The clapping was louder still, and mixed with whistles and shouts of enthusiasm.

Beryl, sensing that a tide was running, rushed to meet it. "Ethel felt that my message was not for her," she said, "but I beg to differ."

My God, thought Kate, now she's actually calling it a *message*.

"Everyone is capable of finding self-courage," Beryl asserted, "every single person, no matter what age, or sex, or color, or creed. Everyone is capable of refusing to be held hostage, whether your jailer is an idea, a situation, another person, anything that is imprisoning, anything that gets between you and you."

As Beryl approached her peroration, Kate could feel her intensity increasing.

"Everyone is capable of looking inside, of finding self-energy, that force that tells you you can do anything. Everyone is capable of looking inside and saying, 'Take charge!' "

The audience shouted the final two words in unison with Beryl, impelling her to greater heights.

"We can do anything if we just—"

"Take charge!" the audience cried.

"Look inside and just—"

"Take charge!"

Beryl prowled the stage, punching her fist aloft with each audience roar.

"Let's all get together and—"

"Take charge!"

"Nothing's beyond our control if we just—"

"Take charge!"

Kate would not have been surprised if Beryl had cartwheeled across the stage, dropped to one knee (siss-boom-bah) before flinging herself, arms and legs spread wide, into the air, or maybe even exhorted the audience to give her a B, give her an E, give her an R-Y-L. But instead, as if to say, "Need I say more?" she simply replaced the microphone in its stand, pirouetted a half-turn, and sank into her chair as the audience's acclaim flooded toward her. It was, indisputably, a propitious beginning to what, even Kate now had to admit, might be a very long journey.

Chapter Eight

ATE was both fascinated and horrified by Beryl's progress, which, on some occasions, she followed of her own volition, on others not. When she knew Beryl was going to be on a television or radio show available to her, she invariably debated whether or not to ignore it and, just as regularly, tuned in. There was something irresistible about the repugnance Beryl excited in her and, time after time, she gave herself over to an antipathetic wallow as she listened or watched, frequently crying out at Beryl's language (as Beryl went along it became increasingly her own, less and less Kate's), throwing her body about on the couch in whorls of outrage. Jason claimed he knew Beryl was on the air when the noises coming from the den sounded like pain experiments in an animal lab.

The fact, increasingly clear, that *Captive Courageous* might very well bring Kate permanent financial independence (she and Beryl split all revenues fifty-fifty) did nothing to diminish her abhorrence of Beryl's performance. It may, in fact, have increased it. For Kate had to live not only with the knowledge that she had had a hand in generating this spectacle, but that she was also profiting from it. ("Think how much worse it would be if you were getting less," Jason said matter-of-factly.)

She encountered Beryl involuntarily nearly every time she opened the newspaper. At first there were the ads on the book page, heralding *C.C.* as "quintessentially human," "a powerful story from the woman who lived it," "a book that shows us how to release ourselves from captivity," and Beryl herself as someone who "emerged from this searing event with a compelling vision."

Then there were the stories in the entertainment section about casting the film version of the book, rights to which had been sold shortly after the book was published. Beryl was quoted extensively in these as giving what she called her "dream list" of candidates, which included Jane Fonda in the title role ("I think she has the depth and experience necessary for this demanding part, plus a physical resemblance that would make her a good choice"), Robert Redford as Rodney Flint ("He might be a little old but I think he could bring it off"), Linda Blair as Lana Van den Haag ("She's been a favorite of mine ever since *The Exorcist* and this might give her a chance to get her career back on track"). When it was pointed out that Lana's part was an exceedingly small one and unlikely to be filled by a "name" of any sort, however reduced in stature, Beryl noted rather unnecessarily that Lana, after all, was the cause of the whole thing, adding that she hoped the filmmakers would not show disrespect for Lana's memory by having her played by an unknown. The Van den Haag family, she added, had suffered enough.

Linda Crawford

Next Beryl turned up in the news section in stories about
Rodney Flint's trial, which ended with a verdict of not
guilty by reason of insanity. Beryl was quoted as saying that
she thought the verdict was a fair one even though "Rodney
never behaved like he was crazy with me, but of course I
wouldn't have allowed it," and that she was pleased he
would now get the help he needed and perhaps one day be
returned, rehabilitated, to society. Wasn't she bitter? she
was asked. Didn't she hold him responsible for the scars her
ordeal must have left?

"Certainly not," Beryl replied. "If that were the case, I'd
still be his hostage, wouldn't I?"

(At least she had the good grace, Kate noted, not to
express her gratitude to Rodney for her new career, although
he had in a sense, launched it.)

It had not been so easy for Norma Van den Haag, mother
of Lana (nor, Kate assumed, for the survivors of the other
victims of Rodney's madness) to move beyond the unpleas-
ant consequences of Rodney's actions in People's Bank &
Trust. Asked her reaction to the verdict in the Flint trial,
Norma had been unable to speak for some moments,
choked, it eventually became clear, by a vituperative rage
that cause her face to turn "the color of eggplant," according to a reporter, and her entire body to shake with visible
tremors.

"He should be shot in the back, like my Lana," she finally
said, "and Swarr along with him. Line them up and gun
them down." Then she broke into hysterical sobbing that
obscured portions of her continuing tirade, leaving audible
only such fragments as "getting rich," "all over TV," and,
most intriguingly, "cannibalizing my baby's death."

Asked, for purposes of clarification, if she was charging

that Mrs. Swarr was as guilty as Mr. Flint, Norma attempted to answer (in the affirmative, Kate imagined) but was so overcome that she collapsed and had to be carried into her house.

Finally, Kate came across Beryl in the life-style section of the newspaper in an article headlined SWEAT CENTER TO OPEN SOON, accompanied by a picture of Beryl standing outside a building that looked familiar to Kate. Briefly, she wondered what a SWEAT center was and why Beryl was being photographed outside its prospective home, and then, with a sick certainty, she knew.

Kate had been aware, as she monitored Beryl's appearances and perused her press clippings (Waverly Press, in a fit of conscientiousness unparalleled in Kate's publishing experience, made sure Kate received reviews, articles, interviews from all over the country, up-to-date copies of Beryl's promotional schedule, tapes of particularly dynamic performances Kate may have missed), that Beryl's message was being purified and crystallized and that it had moved far beyond C.C.'s confining parameters. It was not uncommon now for Beryl to give barely a passing nod to her days of confinement in the bank and to move on quickly to what she had begun calling her "program for growth." (Her marketing instincts had not grown dull, however, and she took pains to mention the book title frequently, even as she began to ignore the book's substance.) But Kate had not thought it so refined that it deserved a name and dissemination through a center. Yet here it was, in black and white. SWEAT, the article said, stood for Swarr Energy Awareness Training. The center, a building Kate finally recognized as a former bakery just two blocks from her home, would offer SWEAT when it opened next week.

Linda Crawford

Beryl, interviewed for the article, outlined the elements of the SWEAT program, which promised nothing less than a complete metamorphosis of one's life in a period slightly longer than a week. ("My life was transformed in ten days. Why not yours?" Beryl said to the reporter, a remark that had obvious possibilities as a motto.) These included something that Beryl called "body function," unspecified save for its purpose of "putting you in touch with those energy meridians" (Kate, who had no idea what these might be, wondered if Beryl might have based this aspect of the program on her brush with Indian dancing); journal writing ("There is no substitute for getting those words down on paper"); nutrition ("Eat all you want during your training period; remember, you are stoking the fires of selfhood. Kate heard here the echoes of all those take-out orders Beryl had placed during her incarceration); self-confrontation (Beryl suggested that writing out one's life story was the best avenue to accomplishing this so Kate supposed that it tied in with the journal-writing element); meditation (would the influence of Mr. Samosa show itself again here?); and last, and most crucial, what Beryl called Lock-up, the simulation of a hostage situation in which the trainee is held prisoner by an instructor until such time as the trainee is ready to give voice and life to SWEAT's rallying cry: "Take charge!"

How long might the simulation phase last? Beryl was asked. That would depend, she replied portentously. On what? On the judgment of the instructor holding the trainee hostage. Presumably these instructors would be well trained? Indeed they would, said Beryl, and until she was certain that they had all reached the desired level of competence she herself would determine the length of every single Lock-up. Yes, she agreed, it would mean a great deal of time and effort on her part, but she felt she owed her public no less than that. They had been good to her. Should she not return the favor?

Kate, after reading this and a follow-up article the next day about Beryl's hopes for a nationwide network of SWEAT centers, went into a decline that kept her mooning about the house, unable to get out of her pajamas until noon, or to prepare anything to eat besides ham and cheese sandwiches, or to read anything more challenging than news magazines, which she combed eagerly for any mention of *Captive Courageous* or SWEAT. Her mind crawled with images of Beryl on the promotional circuit, sounds of Beryl gleaned from the airwaves of the printed page. ("Humanistic synergy" drummed in Kate's mind more often than any other phrase, and she asked herself, repeatedly and unsuccessfully, what it meant.)

"What have I done?" she wailed to Jason one evening.

"Nothing," he said rather curtly, adding his perpetual reminder: "And if you hadn't, someone else would have."

"That's not very reassuring."

"It's the best I can do right now."

Kate knew he was exasperated with her, preoccupied with his ongoing struggle with Igor, who had, at Jason's insistence, looked for a job and ended up as a busboy in Little Italy, bringing him into contact with what Jason feared was a disreputable crowd (last week Igor had told Jason he was thinking of getting his own apartment from which he might launch himself into what he called "free enterprise"), and more than ever disgusted by the Swarr. Still, she couldn't pull herself out of the malaise into which Beryl's ubiquity had plunged her.

"Look, Katie—"

"Don't say look . . . please."

"Listen—"

"That's no different."

"Would you stop picking at my language and hear what I have to say? The woman is a sewer. She was a private sewer, I'm sure, before she met you and now she's a public sewer. And you helped her to become public. That's true. But you can't keep torturing yourself about it. It's something you just have to accept and move on."

"You're absolutely right."

"So you'll snap out of it?"

"I'll try."

Kate's refusal to make a stronger commitment fed Jason's aggravation.

"You know what I think?" he asked angrily. "I think this whole thing is a dodge, a way to keep from getting to your own work."

"You're probably right."

"So you'll get to it?"

"I'll try."

His reproof, and the truth it contained, did energize Kate, if not enough to propel her to begin writing, at least enough to get her out of the house, where she had been ever since she'd read that Beryl had invaded her neighborhood. Even an article in that morning's science section about something called Hostages Anonymous, which had been set up by the Beryl Swarr Foundation, did not stop Kate. It was high time she did a little shackle breaking of her own, she told herself, and she sallied forth.

She had no conscious intention of heading for the center. Indeed, she first walked in the opposite direction, visiting her green grocer, the gourmet emporium with its dazzling display of exotic foodstuffs, the newsstand that carried only foreign publications at exorbitant prices, a gallery that could be counted on to display inexplicable objects, all these sights greeting her eye as though she were a traveler returning to her native land after a long absence. How long was I in there? Kate wondered as she relished her reacquaintance with the world.

As her passage through the neighborhood continued she wound her way back toward the former site of Petrucci's Bakery and eventually, instinctively, found herself standing outside the SWEAT center's doors. Unthinking, seduced by her need to know just how far Beryl had gone in her quest to extend her allotted fifteen minutes of celebrity into something rather longer, she went inside.

As she entered, Kate imagined that the aroma of freshly baked bread still clung to the walls and drifted on the air. But what, in fact, assailed her nostrils and ears was the smell of incense and the sound of rhythmic chanting. Beryl's little Indian popover of days gone by had evidently left his mark.

A reception desk near the entrance was empty, although a cup of steaming liquid on its surface indicated that the occupant would return soon. Kate glided past, drawn by the beat of the unintelligible mantra, toward the first door that opened off the hallway bisecting the building. She cracked it and peered in.

Several bodies in the lotus position dotted the room's small floor and Kate could now decipher the words: "Feel the force, touch the power. Feel the force, touch the power." This must be the meditation phase of the training, and it was practiced just about on the spot where heavily mustached old Mama Petrucci used to sit in her armchair, announcing to each new customer what had just come out of the oven. "Round wheat," she'd whisper, as if she were uttering a secret password. Or: "White braid." Or: "Split roll." Kate felt a sense of loss and desecration come over her and she quickly shut the door.

As she did the chanting died and she started guiltily, fearing she'd been discovered. But no SWEATee rushed out to accost her and she deduced that the meditation had just slipped into a quieter mode. In the silence Kate heard some muffled, but minatory, noises, heavy thuds followed by high-pitched whines, coming from the back of the building. Lock-up, no doubt. Surely journal writing or nutrition wouldn't produce such sounds. The Lock-up area must be back where the ovens used to be. Might Beryl be *using* the ovens for this aspect of the training? Kate's contemplation of this disturbing possibility was interrupted by a voice from behind her.

"May I help you?" it chirped.

She turned to confront a compact young woman with a fixed and forceful smile and a bristling energy.

"I was just sort of looking around," Kate said weakly. "I live in the neighborhood."

"I'm Roxanne and I'd be happy to show you our facilities and introduce you to the program."

"Oh, I'm not—"

"No problem at all. Just follow me." Roxanne turned smartly and, to Kate's disappointment, headed back toward the front of the building, away from what Kate was now convinced were ovens stuffed with the bodies of unsuspecting trainees.

"I heard some rather alarming noises," she said, trailing the spry step of her guide.

Roxanne tossed a cryptic little laugh over her shoulder.

"Simulation can get pretty vigorous," she said, flinging open a door directly behind the reception desk, stepping aside for Kate to enter.

Kate could tell that Roxanne was definitely someone who had taken charge! A SWEAT graduate, no doubt. Probably, one of the first.

In the doorway, Kate froze. Facing her, on the far wall, was a display of *Captive Courageous*, half of them facing outward, screaming the title, the other half turned to the wall in order to show the photo of Beryl that adorned the back of the jacket. The volumes showing title and photo were commingled, creating a kaleidoscopic and, to Kate, nightmarish effect.

Roxanne's kinetic little form sped past her. "Our founder," she said, snapping her fingers and shooting one out toward the picture of Beryl. "Our bible." Another crack sounded and she pointed at a jacket showing the title.

Kate, still unmoving, uttered a little moan, which Roxanne appeared not to notice as she hurled herself into the swivel chair behind a small desk, spinning two complete revolutions before stopping and beckoning Kate toward the chair opposite her.

"Don't be shy," Roxanne ordered.

"It's not that," said Kate, inching her way, against her will, into the room.

"I know all about indecision. Used to be filled with it."

She pulled from a desk drawer a packet of papers, which, with the single sweeping motion of the casino dealer, she spread fanlike on top of the desk.

"I heard the chanting," said Kate, standing behind her designated chair, clutching its back. "I wondered what the force and the power were."

Roxanne's unwavering smile gleamed at Kate even as displeasure flickered in her eyes at this impromptu inquiry. Orientation, as the sheaf of papers indicated, doubtless had a prescribed order, which Roxanne disliked breaking. Kate felt she might refuse to answer. But then Roxanne held up an index finger, turned it toward herself, and thumped her chest with it several times in a manner reminiscent of Beryl's breast rapping on the "Dave Duncan Show."

"Self-energy?" said Kate.

"You got it," said Roxanne, giving a broad wink that was also redolent of Beryl.

Were SWEATees required to adopt the founder's mannerisms as well as her ideas?

These evocations of Beryl made Kate realize how strong was the possibility of running into her, and how devoutly she wished not to. In an effort to extricate herself from the insistent Roxanne she began to back toward the door, prepared to make a run for it if necessary.

"I really am just from the neighborhood and I wandered in to see what had happened to the old bakery."

"Motives don't matter," Roxanne said brightly. "The important thing is that you're here."

"But I won't be," said Kate, continuing to move doorward. "That is, I'm not a candidate—"

"Trainee," Roxanne corrected her.

"Yes. I'm not. I'll just find my own way out."

Roxanne shot up from her chair, the prelude, Kate feared, to attempting to restrain her bodily from leaving. For a beat Kate hesitated. But as Roxanne stepped out from behind the desk, Kate whirled about, headed for the door, and ran directly into Beryl, who was entering at a trot, calling Roxanne's name. Their collision choked off the sound, turning it into a rather nasty squawk, whether from the impact or from astonishment, Kate was not sure.

Her first thought, as she and Beryl drew back from each other, was that now she would be revealed to Roxanne as an impostor, no mere wanderer from the neighborhood but, in fact, a participant in C.C.'s genesis, practically, by guilty association, a cofounder of SWEAT itself. She needn't have worried. Beryl, a hunted look in her eye, obviously fearful of being revealed as anything less than the absolute creator of this glorious undertaking in which she and Roxanne were joined, treated Kate as if she were indeed someone she had encountered once or twice in the neighborhood streets.

"Katherine?" she said, a distinct question mark in her voice.

Kate, scrutinizing Beryl, noticed that she looked more sweaty and disheveled here in the shop than she did in her television appearances. Perhaps she'd been in Lock-up, evaluating whether or not some neophyte was ready to emerge from the oven and take charge! That sort of heavy responsibility could cause a person to sweat.

"Beryl," Kate stated, omitting the interrogatory tone.

Roxanne, anxious lest she be accused of mishandling the boss's acquaintance, began pouring forth a torrent of explanation. "She said she was from the neighborhood and she was just looking around, but I found her down the hall near the meditation room so I brought her back here and I was—"

Beryl stemmed the flood with a sharp, chopping motion of her hand and an explosively uttered "Rox!"

Yet another human being, Kate noted, whom Beryl was able to call by a nickname, even as she refused in Kate's case. Would she ever know why?

"Get down to body function and take a look at the new instructor," Beryl commanded her minion. "He may need a little more seasoning. Let me know what you think."

Roxanne practically goose-stepped out of the room, closing the door behind her.

If Kate expected Beryl's guard to drop once Roxanne was out of the room, she had reckoned wrong.

"When you try to get something like this off the ground in a hurry," she said, sweeping past Kate, deftly putting the barrier of the desk between them, "sometimes you bring people along a little too rapidly. But I can't do it all myself. The demand is just too great."

"You could have waited a bit, taken more time to get organized," Kate said with what she thought was good common sense and a hint of judgment.

"I thought it was extremely important to capitalize on the Mo that was produced by the tour," Beryl replied.

"Big or little?"

"I beg your pardon?"

"The Mo."

"Big Mo, Katherine. Extremely big."

"How will you season the instructor further, if you find he needs it?" Kate asked.

"I hope you realize that I am under absolutely no obligation to discuss with you anything that goes on here."

"Of course you're not," said Kate, taken aback by Beryl's severe tone. "I was just curious."

Despite a mote of suspicion still glinting in her eye, Beryl answered. "He might need a night or two in Lock-up to straighten out the kinks."

"I guess you have to run a pretty tight ship," said Kate.

"That's exactly right."

"Are you enjoying yourself at all?"

Beryl's eyebrows, which had been removed and then redrawn to match her hair, shot up in dismay. "Look, Katherine, this is hard work I'm engaged in here, not some joy ride, not something I'm in for the *fun* of it, for the *enjoyment*. So you can just put those thoughts right out of your mind."

Kate was puzzled by Beryl's overwrought manner and uncertain how to defuse it. "I hadn't had those thoughts actually—"

"I work sixteen hours a day to see that the center is running smoothly, that HA groups have the literature and guidance they need, that my personal appearance obligations are met. On a day when I'm training a new instructor or inaugurating a new HA chapter I may log as many as eighteen or twenty hours. Sometimes the only thing I eat all day is the cookie and cup of coffee I have at a HA meeting. There simply isn't time for anything else."

Kate wondered about the derisive little tic Beryl had developed and then realized that she was referring to Hostages Anonymous. "I thought you looked thinner than ever."

Beryl leapt on her words. "Oh, no, you don't! That old trick's not going to work. Just because I'm working my fingers to the bone, don't think you can come in here and say, 'She's so tired, she's so run down.'"

They were directing words at each other, but Kate felt that she and Beryl were involved in separate conversations. "I didn't come here to say that," she said in a conciliatory tone.

The color in Beryl's face deepened, her hair, if that were possible, stood up even straighter than usual, her mouth worked furiously though no sound emerged.

"I really didn't," she added, concerned by Beryl's appearance.

"Say it," Beryl croaked. "Say what you came for."

"I really was just walking by. I read about the center in the paper and I thought—"

Beryl slammed both hands onto the desk and shot her words at Kate through teeth bared by a vicious curl of her lip. "Just because you had a hand in the book it doesn't mean that you're entitled to any part of this. Not one single part. So don't think you can come in here and put the squeeze on. I've checked it all out and SWEAT belongs to me, nobody else."

Finally understanding, Kate said, "Beryl, I don't want any part of this. Believe me."

Her obvious sincerity apparently reached Beryl, who quickly retreated into generalities. "Well, you wouldn't believe the people who come out of the woodwork when you're in the public eye, all of them wanting something, looking for a free ride."

"Rest assured, I'm not one of them."

Beryl looked at her closely, searching for the mark of the parasite. "No, I suppose not," she said finally.

Was it her imagination, Kate wondered, or did a shadow of disappointment pass over Beryl's face? Would she rather Kate had tried to cut herself in on SWEAT? At least then she would have known how to deal with her.

"I really don't want anything to do with you," Kate said quietly, secure in the knowledge that Beryl would fail to apprehend the personal and all-inclusive nature of her announcement, needing, for her own sake, to hear aloud this declaration.

"Well, that's a relief," said Beryl, giving a tight little laugh. "Do you know even members of my family have tried to ring themselves in on this?"

"Not Stanley surely?"

Beryl looked at her blankly for a moment, as though trying to place the name. "No, it's a couple of the Wease cousins. When we go nationwide they want to open boutiques
called SWEAT SHOPS that would carry a line of products
to enhance training."

Had the unfortunate connotations of the name put her
off? Kate wondered. Or was there another reason for Beryl's
negative reaction?

"It's not a bad idea, and the name's cute," Beryl continued, "but we'd have to map out franchise arrangements and
fee schedules. They didn't like it when they heard that.
They thought I'd just give them the name." She shook her
head at the covetousness loose in the world.

"You certainly have your hands full," Kate remarked.

Beryl flicked on her smile in appreciation of Kate's understanding. It still stopped well short of her eyes. "I'm not so
busy that I can't show an old friend around."

As Beryl began to rise, Kate rushed to demur. Half an
hour ago she'd been longing for a glimpse of the center's secret recesses. Now she just wanted to escape.

"No, no," she said. "I really have to be getting along."

Beryl seemed about to insist, then thought better of it.
"Well, you must take these." She scooped up the papers
Roxanne had spread out on the desk and tamped them into
a tidy pile. "They could be a real eye opener for you, Katherine."

"I'll bet," said Kate, reaching for the proffered papers.

Beryl seemed to change her mind, pulling them away
from Kate's grasp and placing them back on the desk. Kate
thought she had, at last, offended her.

Beryl riffled through them, extracted a large, glossy pho-
tograph of herself and scrawled her name on a slant across
one of the bottom corners. "I don't do that for everyone,"

she said, winking and handing the packet back to Kate.

"I'm speechless," said Kate.

Beryl looked pleased. "Maybe we'll see you back here one day as a trainee."

"I really must go. Don't bother to see me out. I'm sure you have things to do."

The phone rang, cutting off any protest Beryl might have made.

"I really shouldn't answer this," she said. "It's Roxanne's job but—"

"Go ahead. I'm leaving."

As the phone continued to ring, Beryl crossed the room, took the packet from Kate again, set it on a table by the door, and grasped both Kate's hands, crossing her wrists over each other in a pantomime of restraint. She clasped the joined wrists in her own hands, raised them up to chest level, then flung them downward, splitting the wrists apart. Kate couldn't help flinching as her hands slapped against her thighs, although she supposed that this rather violent intrusion upon her was some sort of arcane blessing, the equivalent of a secret handshake. Beryl, oblivious to having inflicted discomfort or surprise, shoved the packet back into Kate's hand and turned away toward the phone; Kate hurried out into the street.

She began to walk rapidly toward home, unaware for at least a block that she was clutching the sheaf of papers against her. When she realized this, she halted and looked down at Beryl's photo, which lay atop the pile. "Very freely yours, Beryl Swarr," the message read.

Fortuitously enough, there was a trash basket on the corner where Kate had stopped and, piece by piece, she dealt Beryl's picture and the other material into it. Then she resumed her journey home with a considerably lightened step.

Chapter Nine

KATE'S sense of emancipation from Beryl produced in her a euphoria that made her believe she could do almost anything. She decided to go alone to the country for a few weeks and try again to begin the novel about her parents that had been eluding her for so long. Jason, who would be left alone in the city with Igor, said he didn't mind. He said, in fact, that perhaps it would be good for the two of them to be alone. This was one situation they hadn't tried. Nothing else had worked. Why not give this a chance to fail also?

Faced with his gloom, Kate offered to change her plans.

"No," Jason said, "if you're not here maybe he'll turn to me."

"If that's your hope, I think you're bound to be disappointed."

"You mean I'm not even a candidate for last resort?"

"He doesn't turn to me either, Jason."

"But if he had to he might."

"I'm not so sure. He's not at the 'turning to' age. He's too busy establishing his independence."

"Is that what he's doing? I thought he was shunning me."

During the time he had lived with them Igor had found one way after another to thwart Jason's need to play the long-neglected role of father. He had been sullen and defiant, compliant but cool, lost in the mists of the obsessive relationship with Melody, and now he was employing a kind of extravagant and splashy self-reliance to keep his father at a distance.

Igor had, for instance, for those occasional meals when he was at home, taken to buying his own food, which he consumed conspicuously in front of Kate and Jason.

"What's the matter with our food?" Jason asked bitterly, the third or fourth time Igor did this. (He had endured the first few occasions in silence, suffering kicks from Kate beneath the table.)

"Just want to pull my own weight, Dad," Igor said.

"Well, that's fine," said Jason, his voice tight with the struggle for control, "an admirable principle, but don't you think you're carrying it a little too far?"

"A principle's a principle," Igor replied. "That's how I see it."

"Do you?" said Jason, still managing to keep himself in check.

"Anything worth doing is worth doing all the way."

"Where did you pick that up?" he asked. "From the *capo* you work for?"

Igor, refusing to be baited, said, "Take it easy, Dad. It's just a little food."

The patronizing tone sent Jason over the edge. "It is not

just 'a little food.' It's the fact that it's ours and that you refuse to eat it, for Christ's sake!"

Igor also flaunted his autonomy by refusing money when Jason offered it ("Thanks, Dad, but I've got my own now." "What's wrong with a little extra?" "I've got enough . . . really"), proposing, when Jason forbade him to get his own apartment, to pay rent to Jason and Kate ("Are you out of your goddamn mind?" Jason fumed), getting his own telephone line installed in his room ("That's so we can call to make an appointment to see him," his father said), even making a fetish of doing his own laundry, hauling large, heavy sacs of it down the street to the laundromat rather than using the washer and dryer in the loft (Jason offered to meter the machine so that Igor could pay his own way but Igor declined). When Kate told Igor she was going to be away for a few weeks, he asked if there were things he should know about "looking after" Jason. Kate told him she thought he could manage on his own.

Jason was having enough trouble being denied the role of father. What would happen if Igor tried to play parent to him? Kate didn't wait around to see. Rationalizing that they'd do better without her, she got out of town.

Driving to the country, there were just enough leaves of dazzling color left on the trees to make Kate melancholy, as though she were actually witnessing the death of the season. She could feel her sense of confidence and resolution begin to dissipate as she observed autumn's last gasp and imagined the barrenness to come. Quite suddenly, getting free of Beryl seemed not a miracle of self-restoration, but merely a long overdue manifestation of good common sense. The air of new beginnings and fresh possibilities that had possessed her seemed premature and presumptuous. Her impending novel loomed unpropitiously. By the time she reached the house, she wished she hadn't come.

Inside, drinking a cup of coffee at the kitchen table, Kate thought about her present mood, how unacceptable it was, how unexpected, how she must do something to dislodge it. Give the house a good cleaning, perhaps. Clear out the dense undergrowth and prune the trees in the thickets on either side of the property. Paint the upstairs bathroom that had been peeling badly for the past year. Mulling over possible projects, she wandered through the house, eventually making her way upstairs to the bedroom, where, confronted by the appealing quilted expanse of the high brass bed, she lay down and sank almost immediately into unconsciousness.

When she awakened, annoyed in her dream by Rose, who had taken over Kate's kitchen and was noisily beating cutlets with a mallet on the counter, it was dark. Kate realized then that the pounding was outside, on her front door, to be exact. She flicked on the bedside lamp, looked at her watch, and saw that it was nine-thirty. She had slept for nearly six hours.

Running her fingers through her hair and her hands over her rumpled clothes, she made her way downstairs, calling out her approach, which had no effect whatsoever on the steady banging. Turning on the porch light, pulling open the door, Kate saw standing in the yellow glow Dorothy Karanewski, a widow of some years' standing who, insofar as Kate had been able to determine in the several months she'd lived next door, devoted her life to three things: keeping her house and yard so meticulously groomed that they constituted a perpetual rebuke to Kate (Jason claimed he had once seen her sweeping her lawn); butting, indiscriminately, into other people's business; and talking incessantly.

"I'm so relieved it's you," she said to Kate, panting from her characteristic shortness of breath, the result, Kate assumed, of her excessive girth and unceasing industry.

"Is something wrong?" Kate asked.

"When the house was dark I began to worry."

"But you saw my car."

"Exactly. The car and then the dark house. I didn't wake you, did I?"

"No," said Kate, knowing it was a ridiculous denial, given her undoubtedly telltale face and the darkened house.

"There was a break-in just last week at a boathouse down the beach," Mrs. Karanewski said.

Kate suspected this was offered to justify her barging in on Kate, though the connection was tenuous at best.

"They took a couple of motors, a tool kit, one of those fancy ice coolers . . ."

Kate knew she would be given the exact location of the boathouse, its history, and a description of the items that had *not* been stolen if she did not intervene.

"I'm going to be here for a few weeks, Dorothy—"

"I wish you'd call me Dot."

Kate had a hard enough time calling her Dorothy, but Dot seemed quite impossible. It was a ridiculously diminutive sound to apply to such a large woman. It also seemed another step in the direction of an intimacy Kate wanted to avoid. Was there any connection between these feelings of hers and those that had kept Beryl calling her Katherine? How curious that she'd never thought of it before.

"So you'll see me coming and going," Kate said. And leave me alone, I hope, she added silently.

"Mr. Wylie's not here?"

"No, he's in the city. I'm going to be doing some work here."

"I noticed the other day that the east side was starting to peel. It always goes first where the sun hits it."

I knew it! Kate thought. She had always suspected that Mrs. Karanewski regularly reviewed the Wylies' house and grounds and found them wanting. Now it was confirmed.

"I'm going to be doing some writing actually," she said.

Mrs. Karanewski didn't even have the good grace to be discomfited by her misunderstanding. "Another ghost story?" she asked.

Kate rued the day she had revealed this aspect of her career to her neighbor.

"No," she replied, digging in her heels.

"I saw your husband's latest at the library the other day," said Mrs. Karanewski, undaunted by Kate's stinginess. "It seems to be doing very well. Sixteen people had it out in just eight weeks."

Had she actually counted?

"That's two a week," Mrs. Karanewski added.

"Right."

"I haven't gotten to it yet, but I will."

"All in good time," said Kate, a meaningless phrase but one that she hoped had a valedictory ring to it.

"You should enjoy the peace and quiet out here."

You, and God, willing, Kate thought. "Yes," she said.

"Well," Mrs. Karanewski said, "I'll let you get back to what you were doing." Her tone made clear that she knew what the activity was and what she thought of people who did it early in the evening.

Kate remained silent, anxious not to upset the delicate balance that had at last swung in her favor.

"Enjoy your stay."

As if she wouldn't be seeing her again, Kate thought. Who was she kidding?

"I hope it will be a pleasant and productive one."

To thank her would be to risk reopening the floodgates.

"Good night," said Mrs. Karanewski, turning away, crossing the porch, heading down the three steps.

Only when the woman's foot hit the ground, did Kate speak. "Good night," she said, as warmly as possible. Then she quickly shut the front door against any renewal of hope on her neighbor's part and turned off the porch light. These seemed stern measures, but Kate had known Mrs. Karanewski to rebound from a position halfway down the stairs and return to the door for another fifteen minutes. Tonight she took no chances.

Kate thought of going directly back to bed, but then realized that she was hungry. In the kitchen she cut a couple of slices from the Italian whole wheat loaf she'd brought from the city. (She still missed Petrucci's bread, but she supposed she'd get over it, just as she had gotten over punishing herself for the forces now desecrating Petrucci's bakery.) She warmed the slices in the oven, spread them with fresh goat cheese that had been drizzled in oil and sprinkled with herbs, and ate them standing at the counter. Then she turned on the kettle, placed an Earl Grey tea bag in a blue and white willow mug, and sat down to wait for the water to boil. Before it did, Jason called.

"What are you doing?" he asked, sounding wistful.

"Just having something to eat," Kate replied.

"It's a little late, isn't it?"

"Oh . . ."

"Knowing you, you've been to town, shopped for two weeks, spent all day getting organized, settling in. I hope you'll take it easy out there and not waste your time on a lot of projects."

"I won't."

"You know, you don't have to rearrange the pantry shelves and paint the upstairs bathroom before you can begin writing."

"I know. Sweetheart, let me get the kettle."

Uneasy with the drift of the conversation and with her lie of omission, Kate welcomed the whistle. Why hadn't she told Jason that she'd slipped into a six-hour coma almost immediately upon her arrival? She poured the water and felt the smoky smell permeate her nostrils.

"How about you?" she asked, returning to the phone. "How are things there?"

"The Russian prince stopped in for a few minutes after school, just long enough to tell me he thought I had a lot of hangups."

"Oh, Jason, I'm sorry." That's why she hadn't told him. She felt guilty because he'd been suffering in the city while she'd been blissfully sleeping in the country. It didn't seem fair.

"I'm baiting the trap for tomorrow night."

"How so?"

"Getting Rose down here for dinner. He said he'd come. He also said he'd eat my food. 'I'd be happy to be your guest, Dad,' is actually what he said."

"Try to be patient. He'll pass through this."

"Maybe I should have her come and live with us."

"Rose?"

"It would give him a reason to come home once in a while."

"And me a reason to stay away indefinitely."

"Just kidding."

"And you a reason to move out and leave Igor and Rose there together, defeating your purpose."

"Just kidding!"

"Jason, sixteen people have taken *The A Capella Gang* out of the library in the last eight weeks."

"You counted? Katie, that's so sweet."

Kate considered letting it go. It pleased Jason to think she'd been thinking of him. And of course she had, even though she hadn't done the tally at the library. She thought of him all the time, rather like breathing. Perhaps even when she was sleeping he was in some sense on her mind. Who could say? So it might not be so shabby just to let his assumption stand. On the other hand, this conversation had already had its share of evasions.

Jason read her silence perfectly.

"Mrs. Karanewski came by."

"Right."

"That's two a week," he said.

"Exactly what she said."

"Do you find us alike in other ways as well?"

"Jason, if I'd thought of it, and thought it would cheer you up, I *would* have gone to the library and counted."

"I know you would have, Katie. I know."

The discouragement in his voice pained her. She wished he were near so that she could touch him, reach out with her fingers and erase the lines of weariness and worry on his forehead.

"You know that if you want me to come back I will," she said.

"Don't be silly. Go get some sleep now."

A sharp stab of guilt ran through her.

"Get up tomorrow and have a great writing day," he said.

"I will. I love you."

"Me too."

Linda Crawford

Kate added milk and a spoonful of honey to her tea and carried it up the stairs. In the bedroom, she pulled a mystery from the bookshelves and set it on her bedside table next to the tea, turned back the covers (during her earlier seizure she'd slept atop the quilt), and propped two pillows against the bedstead in reading position. Then she peeled off her clothes, tossing them onto the overstuffed armchair that sat near the fireplace, and crawled into bed. When she let her head fall back against the pillows, she immediately fell asleep, leaving book and tea untouched.

Kate was surprised when she slept past noon the next day, but she decided her body must need the rest and willed herself to be grateful, not guilty. It was also surprising, she supposed, that she didn't awaken to find Mrs. Karanewski by the bed, holding a mirror beneath her nostrils to see if she was breathing.

She went downstairs and flipped on the kitchen radio, which was tuned to a station that broadcast popular music of the past, and sang aloud with the haunting melody: "Do I love you, do I? Does July need a sky of blue?"

Kate had always been somewhat ashamed of her excessively emotional response to popular songs, good and bad, old or new, but today she didn't hold back. The windows were closed. Mrs. Karanewski couldn't hear her, for God's sake.

"If the sun should desert the day, what would life be?"

She made coffee and warmed a bran muffin in the oven. She could work this afternoon. She wasn't used to that, but neither was she used to being alone, having the house to herself, doing whatever she pleased on no one's schedule but her own. She thought of Jason and Igor, the battle of wills raging in the city, and sang a little louder to drown out her guilt.

Ghost of a Chance

"Will I worship you forever? Isn't heaven forevermore?"

After dressing, she went into her study, set up her typewriter, unpacked the bag filled with paper, notes, pieces of opening paragraphs that she carried around to remind herself that she had, in fact, tried to begin this novel several times. When she had things arranged, and saw that it was already two-thirty, she decided it was rather late in the day to start.

She considered going outside to attack those places where the rank growth of weeds was most noticeable, and the contrast with Mrs. Karanewski's manicured yard most glaring. But this was likely to bring her into contact with Mrs. Karanewski and besides, she reminded herself, winter was coming and would do the job without any help from her. Next spring, perhaps, she would manage to stay on top of things a little better.

Deciding that the most productive thing she could do with the rest of the day was to get her grocery shopping done, she went out to the car, backed down the driveway, made the turn onto the road, and there was flagged down by Mrs. Karanewski.

"I just wanted to let you know I have some extra squash, acorn and butternut, so don't buy a lot of vegetables," she panted at Kate when she rolled down the window.

"Thanks very much. Just set it on the front porch, would you?"

"Lovely day for work, so crisp and clear."

Did Kate imagine it or was Mrs. Karanewski's tongue conspicuously in her cheek?

"The kind of weather that makes you feel creative, I'll bet," she went on.

Kate felt certain now that her neighbor knew she hadn't done a lick of work that day.

"I always get twice as much done on a day like this, don't you?" Mrs. Karanewski asked.

Kate gave a noncomittal grunt, thanked her neighbor again for the squash and quickly pulled away before Mrs. Karanewski assayed another gambit.

When Kate returned from town she fairly sped past her neighbor's house, making a perilous turn into her own driveway with wheels squealing noisily. When the car shuddered to a halt, she leapt out, grabbed her bag of groceries, hurried to the porch, snatched up the squash, and made it inside safely.

Jason called in the late afternoon, in the midst of cooking dinner for Igor and Rose, neither of whom had arrived yet.

"I'm sure you'll be going to bed early so I thought I'd get you now," he said.

Early, late, midnight, noon, you're apt to catch me in bed almost anytime, Kate thought.

"The evening here will probably be such a success . . . God knows when it might end," Jason said.

"It really might be nice, you know."

"Want to give me odds?"

"Do you want me to come back, sweetheart?"

"Are you going to ask me that every time we talk?"

"Have I?"

"Two out of two. How'd the work go today?"

"Oh, you know what it's like the first day." Not really a lie, Kate thought, but certainly not the truth either.

"It'll get better."

"I hope so." What if it doesn't? The thought skidded across her mind, then vanished.

"There's the bell. Gotta go. I love you."

"Me too."

Kate unpacked the groceries: oranges, broccoli, pasta, a can of crab meat, a loaf of pumpernickel bread. What was Jason cooking tonight? She hadn't even asked. He'd probably spent all afternoon on it. He liked to go out and shop at lunchtime, then come home and putter in the kitchen for hours, all this after having written in the morning. Just think of what he'd accomplished today. And, she couldn't help adding, what she hadn't.

Kate told herself that she was going upstairs to change her clothes, that she didn't need to be in three heavy layers if she was going to sit in the kitchen and have dinner in front of the wood stove. But once in the bedroom, she felt herself irresistibly drawn to the bed and, abandoning all pretense of wardrobe change, she lay down on it and fell into a deep sleep.

When she awoke near noon the next day after sleeping seventeen hours, she told herself that she was adjusting to the presence of country air and the absence of city stress. The thing to do was to take it in stride, wait it out, and not panic. Tomorrow she'd probably be at her desk by nine, writing fluently, this heavy somnolence a thing of the past. Today she would work outdoors and that, at least, would give her a much-needed sense of accomplishment.

Kate had always questioned her ability to grow things. The simple tending of a houseplant could hover over her as a problem and a puzzle: how much water, sun, shade, how often, when to pinch, when to ignore. The prescriptions of friends always seemed hopelessly vague: they were instinctive gardeners and did not understand Kate's need for rigid specificity. When she tried to find answers in a book, she seemed constitutionally incapable of absorbing the information in any useful way. Nevertheless, this past summer she had attempted a few simple crops on a very small scale.

Near the weed-infested thicket that separated her from Mrs. Karanewski she had turned over a patch of earth and laid out a row of tomato plants, a row of lettuce, and a row of radishes. ("Be sure to put radishes in because anybody can grow them anywhere," Rose had told her, revealing what she thought of Kate, horticulturally speaking.) All had failed. The tomato plants never got beyond the spindly stage (when Kate saw the heavy red fruit dangling from Mrs. Karanewski's robust stalks she felt like the mother of a retarded child, viewing someone else's healthy offspring); the lettuce, during its brief life, was inedibly acrid; the radishes, despite Rose's assertion, never even broke through the ground.

Kate first attacked this pathetic plot that had been an eyesore all season long. Mindful of the obvious symbolism, but indifferent to it, she tore out the tomato plants by their roots, feeling a burst of satisfaction as each scrawny skeleton ripped free of the soil. With a trowel, she dug out the withered plugs of lettuce that had been nibbled to the nub by rabbits. She broke up the earth where the radish seeds had been sown, searching for some trace of a red globe below ground, finding none.

After removing this evidence of her incompetence, she turned to the thicket, which had suffered from sheer neglect. Just as she had difficulty deciphering the instructions for the care and feeding of houseplants, so Kate had trouble with the proper procedures for cutting back shrubs and trees. She tried to read columns on the subject when they appeared in the paper and had even, a few years back, gone so far as to consult a gardening book in the local library. But she remained fuzzy about which nodes represented proper pruning points and usually fell into generalized hacking and slashing when she attempted to thin out overgrown areas.

This day, for some reason, knowing that she was most likely being observed by Mrs. Karanewski did not inhibit Kate but spurred her on. Working furiously, she reached hitherto unscaled heights of destruction, dismembering trees, carving up bushes, flaying the weeds with her scythe.

That evening she managed to eat dinner, talk to Jason, and read three pages of the mystery on her bedside table before falling asleep. But, once again, she slept profoundly and long, not waking until close to noon the next day. Recognizing now that her sleeping represented more than an adjustment to country life, she rose in determined fashion, dressed quickly, and went downstairs to make coffee. When it was ready, she carried a cup into her study and rolled a piece of paper into the typewriter. Her study was on the side of the house facing Mrs. Karanewski's and through the window near her desk she could see the decimation she had wrought the day before and, beyond that, her neighbor's ponderous figure beating a series of rugs strung along a line.

She sat at her desk for two hours, sometimes, when she felt Mrs. Karanewski's eyes on her, rapping out a meaningless sentence, the rest of the time gazing absently at the warm colors of the primitive painting above her desk, counting the caramel-colored streaks in the gray fieldstone surrounding the fireplace across the room, reading the titles of the books in the bookcase and, in her mind, arranging each shelf in alphabetical order. Utterly drained by two o'clock, she dragged herself out to the kitchen, where she ate a slice of pumpernickel bread spread with apple butter, then crept upstairs to take a nap. Jason's call at five-thirty awakened her.

"You weren't sleeping, were you?" he asked.

"No," said Kate, "I just haven't spoken to anyone today so my voice sounds funny."

"Getting a lot done?"

"It's never enough. You know that feeling."

"The important thing is that you're getting started."

"How about you?" Kate asked. "You said Igor was sweet when Rose came to dinner."

"Sweet?" Jason yelped. "Sweet?"

"You said the evening was pleasant."

"He managed not to choke on my food, he stayed until Rose went home, he was very attentive to her—sweet, I guess."

"But—?"

"But then he went out and bought her that tiny little TV she's been wanting."

"Well, that's thoughtful."

"Bought it and delivered it to her, a little errand that caused him to miss school, but so what? After all, as he told me, he's 'into people' and he thinks that giving his grandmother a little pleasure is a lot more important than passing 'some crummy geometry test.' "

"What did you say?"

"I suggested he get 'into school' and give *me* a little pleasure once in a while."

"Still, it was a thoughtful thing for him to do."

"I concede that. I don't know what the hell she needs another TV for. She's already got two, but she says she wanted this one to take in bed with her. Can you tell me why she'd want to do that?"

"No, I can't, darling."

"She says it will help her sleep."

Just the mention of the word made Kate cringe with guilt.

"Why would it help to have the sound coming from the next pillow?"

"I don't know," said Kate. "Do you want me to come home?" Did she want him to say yes? To rescue her from her lethargy?

"Kate, for God's sake, stop with that question."

"I didn't ask you yesterday."

"A day off does not entitle you to start asking again. What is it? Don't you want to be there? Jesus, I'd give anything for two weeks of peace and quiet."

"Of course I want to be here—getting started on the book." Once having committed herself to the deceit, Kate couldn't stop. "It feels great to get going after ducking it for so long. And I do work better here, there's no question about that. There simply aren't any distractions."

"Mrs. Karanewski?"

"Oh, she's manageable if you handle her right."

"Well, you just stay put and get a lot done."

"I will, Jason."

"I love you."

"Me too."

Kate made her way downstairs, nearly staggering under the weight of the guilt produced by the phone conversation. She had never lied to Jason before this week and now she did it automatically, every time they spoke. It was as though she were having an affair, and the brass bed, not another man, was her illicit partner. In the kitchen she turned on the radio and sang along with the ballad that issued into the early-evening dusk.

By the fifth day Kate had begun to accept her languor and to give in to it. It must be serving some purpose, she told herself. But, unwilling to have Mrs. Karanewski become aware of her shiftlessness, she took to setting her alarm each morning, going downstairs to her study, pulling down the shade by her desk and turning on the light, then going back to bed. When she began truly to *live* in her bed, and to keep a fire going in the bedroom fireplace, she made sure a morning fire blazed in her study fireplace so that smoke would issue from its chimney as well and indicate Kate's hardworking presence within.

Despite these precautions, however, there was a day when Mrs. Karanewski, who had obviously been reading the smoke signals as avidly as a Roman citizen waiting for the announcement of a new pope, did beard Kate in her den, but Kate was able to send her away quickly and, she thought, reassured about Kate's well-being.

During her time in bed (she estimated that she was only out of it some two to three hours a day) Kate read, dozed, slept deeply, and puzzled over her peculiar state. Was she unable to work because she no longer had a financial motive? (*Captive Courageous* was currently number one on the *New York Times* best-seller list.) But she'd never planned to make money with a novel. She'd written her first because nothing gave her such a sense of pleasure and competence as the construction of a well-turned sentence. She'd written it because her earliest, best way of giving herself an illusion of control was to create characters who would respond to her direction. Didn't these needs still exist?

Or was she unable to work because she understood so little of the past she wanted to explore in her novel? When she thought of her parents, she felt herself immersed in murky currents that allowed no light to penetrate. Or had she simply written someone else's book once too often? Had the experience with Beryl made her phobic about writing anything?

Floating in her soporific state, Kate reached no conclusions but returned to these questions over and over again. She dreamed once that she and Beryl got married, another time that she was rushing to get home to her parents, but when she arrived she found two skeletons sitting side by side on the flowered sofa.

One day in the second week, she managed to get up and dress and drive into the village to buy milk, fruit, and a loaf of bread. She also picked up a newspaper and, when she got home, read every article carefully, as though she were studying the workings of an alien culture. So complete was her absorption that she even read the financial page, which she ordinarily skipped, and there she encountered the news that SWEAT was going to be franchised nationwide, a bulletin that brought her reading to a halt and sent her creeping back into bed.

Her conversations with Jason during this period followed the pattern they had established at the outset of Kate's time in the country. She lied about her work and accepted his encouragement; he worried about Igor, whom he now called Ivan the Terrible, and welcomed her sympathy.

Kate herself talked to Igor one night and he suggested she think about coming home.

"Dad really doesn't do well without you," he told her, at which point Jason grabbed the phone from him and said, to Kate's great relief, that she mustn't even consider returning.

She had stopped offering and lived in fear that Jason might request it anyway. It was impossible to contemplate getting behind the wheel of a car and staying awake long enough to get back to town. And once she got there? What then? Someone was bound to notice that she was sleeping roughly twenty hours a day.

As it turned out, Kate had Mrs. Karanewski to thank for prodding her into leaving on schedule. The day before her time was up, a day Kate spent contemplating telling Jason that she needed to stay for another week, Mrs. Karanewski cornered her (Kate thought of ignoring the knock but she knew her neighbor was capable of calling the police and Kate didn't want the local constable to discover her sleeping in the middle of the day) and announced that the following day she was going to be making and preserving the apple butter Kate had once admired. She wouldn't take no for an answer: Kate must come and watch how it was made and have a bite of lunch and make a day of it.

"Oh, I am sorry," Kate said, trying to sound disappointed, "I'm leaving tomorrow to go back to town." So dazed did Mrs. Karanewski look that Kate added, "I'll have to take a rain check."

She knew immediately that that was a mistake, but she consoled herself by thinking that next year at this time either she or Mrs. Karanewski could be dead. Anything could happen. And she was glad to see hope replace despair on her neighbor's broad face. It made her feel less guilty.

"I'll put a jar aside for you anyway," said Mrs. Karanewski, never one to hold a grudge.

"That would be lovely," said Kate.

"You can just pick it up next time you're out."

"Yes."

"Of course, people don't come as often now that the weather's getting cold."

"No."

"Once the leaves are gone you never see a tourist in town."

"No."

"Do you know the village collected more than three thousand dollars just from the parking meters in July and August?"

"Mmmmm."

"I like the autumn best myself."

"Yes."

"The harvest, canning, burrowing in for the winter . . ." She wriggled her burly body in illustration.

"Well, I'd better be off. Things to do . . ." She began her retreat slowly, but when she realized that Kate was not going to interrupt it, she picked up speed and moved off toward her own yard.

Now Kate had two choices. She could leave tomorrow, or she could hide the car, live with the lights off and the fires extinguished, and crawl around on her belly below window level. She decided that she would go back to town.

Chapter Ten

KATE'S somnolence began to recede once she was back at home. The rhythm of the city and the need to relate in some fashion to Jason and Igor pushed it aside, but it didn't disappear entirely. She explained the nagging residue by ascribing it to her work, about which she continued to lie.

"You know I'm always a little peculiar when I'm starting something," she would say as she drifted off to take an afternoon nap, or to go to bed at eight-thirty or nine o'clock at night. Jason, who was willing to blame virtually any unusual behavior on the beginning of a new book, would smile fondly and give her a rather abstracted pat or a kiss. He was glad she was back, but his problems with Igor continued to absorb most of his energy and attention. Kate's guilt increased when she admitted to herself that she was, in some small way at least, grateful for the father-son impasse. It shifted the focus away from her.

She had never, in fact, seen Jason quite so preoccupied.

He began every day with a new resolution: he would be more relaxed with Igor, he would exert more authority, he would suspend judgment, he would set standards, he would be more demanding, less rigid, more flexible, less permissive, less of a father, more of a pal, more like Kate, less like himself, less black, more white. No resolve ever survived for twenty-four hours. Many were dead by the time breakfast, which Jason required Igor to eat with them (out of respect for Kate, he said), was over. When he was not formulating resolutions Jason was brooding, alternately, over his own failures as a father and Igor's inadequacies as a son.

Igor, in direct contrast to his haunted father, appeared to be thriving. Kate saw in him few traces of the boy who had arrived nearly a year before, clad in his insolent T-shirts, practically sublingual, holed up in his room like a jittery animal, shifty-eyed, restive. He now wore an air of assurance that was reflected in his direct gaze, his easy conversation, the way his clothes hung on his still angular but increasingly sturdy frame. He had a job, friends, a satisfactory, if not stellar, record in school.

"Stop berating yourself and him," Kate said to Jason during one of their frequent middle-of-the-night conversations that she considered her penance for lying and oversleeping. (This time Jason, to be companionable, had waited up for Igor, only to become enraged when he arrived home very late.) "Can't you see how much he's improved? You must be doing something right."

"All I do is provide a target, something to rebel against." Jason shoved his pillows up against the wall and settled back into them, his hands behind his head, his body stretched out in the bed.

It was obvious that he was prepared for a discussion, not

just a quick, fuzzy exchange. Kate, who had already been asleep for seven hours, arranged herself in a sitting position and tried to look alert.

"Maybe that's what he needs to grow up," she said. "He seems to be doing it."

"You call that growing up? He's too smart-ass for his own good, thinks he has all the answers. I liked him better when he was cowering in his cave."

"No, you didn't. You've forgotten."

"At least then he had a little humility, a sense of his own limitations."

"Too much so." Kate yawned widely.

"You could talk to him."

"No, you couldn't. He was either too frightened, or too surly."

"What's wrong with surly and frightened?"

Kate could feel her lids, like window shades, rolling down to cover her eyes.

"At least it can pass for respect," said Jason. "But now he's got this attitude that he doesn't have to answer to anyone . . ."

Kate heard no more. When Jason poked her awake she spoke to the last idea she remembered.

"Respect isn't necessarily the most important thing," she said.

"That was a long time ago," said Jason. "If you hadn't been sleeping—"

"I was just resting my eyes."

"You were snoring."

"Just breathing heavily."

"And what's more important than respect?"

Kate felt herself slipping away once more. "Could we discuss these things in daylight sometime?" she managed to murmur before toppling over on her side, sound asleep.

Jason did not wake her up again that night, and on the other nights when he did Kate did not object too strenuously. As Jason pointed out, she'd always had at least several hours of sleep before he propped her up and made her try to talk. And, he also noted, it's not as though she had any trouble going back to sleep. But no matter when they discussed Igor, they always disagreed. Those qualities that gave Jason the most trouble were the same ones that Kate took to be signs of his incipient maturity.

These were fully on display during the evening when Igor took Kate out to dinner. He issued the invitation at breakfast one morning when he heard Jason remind Kate that that night he would be attending a gathering of the Mystery Writers of America.

"I'm off tonight," said Igor, scraping a spoon around the bottom and sides of a yogurt container labeled in Magic Marker with a large black I. "Why don't I take you out for something to eat?"

"That would be lovely," said Kate.

"There's a place down in my neighborhood," Igor said, eating the last of the yogurt, crumpling the container in his hand. "I think you'd like it."

"Great," said Kate.

"You don't get out enough." Igor flipped the flattened container into the garbage receptacle, as though he were shooting a basket, and shrugged into his New York Mets jacket.

"Oh, I don't know about that. But I'll look forward to tonight."

"Seven o'clock?" said Igor, punching the elevator button.

"Fine," said Kate.

"See you then." The elevator opened and Igor stepped in. "Bye, Pop," he added as the doors began to close, nearly swallowing his words.

Jason stalked about the kitchen, wordless but managing to create a great deal of noise. He slammed the kettle onto the burner, flung open the refrigerator door to get the milk, banged about in the pantry extracting his cereal.

"This is exactly what I've been talking about," he said finally, splashing some milk onto his cereal and taking a large bite. "And if you can't see it—" He shook his head and wolfed down two more spoonfuls of cereal.

"Then what?" Kate asked.

Jason looked at her blankly.

"What if I can't see it?" she said.

He literally brushed the question aside, flinging out his arm and toppling a pot of marmalade into the butter. "He's just got to play the big shot. 'Why don't *I* take *you*,' he says. He's got to be in charge. Why couldn't he just say 'let's have something to eat'? I'll tell you why. Because then it wouldn't be clear who's calling the signals."

Jason rammed a piece of bread into the toaster and shoved the lever downward. He yanked the whistling kettle off the stove and poured water on the tea bag in his mug, sloshing it over the edge. Kate followed him silently with her eyes.

" 'There's a place in *my* neighborhood,' he says. '*My* neighborhood,' for Christ's sake. As if he doesn't even live here."

Jason grabbed the piece of toast from the toaster, slapped butter and jam on it, and ripped off a large piece with his teeth. Kate hoped he would stop talking until it was chewed. She was afraid he might choke.

"Oh," he said, and visibly swallowed some of the toast. "Oh." The rest went down. "And how about the crushing of the carton! What the hell was that supposed to be? A display of strength? It's not as if it were a beer can."

He threw himself onto a stool at the counter and began savagely shoveling cereal into his mouth, slurping great gulps of tea, gobbling up the rest of the toast. Gradually, his pace slowed and by the time the food was gone he seemed almost eerily calm.

"Do you wish he hadn't asked me?" said Kate, reaching out with her hand to cover one of Jason's, which lay limply on the counter.

He shook his head and Kate thought perhaps he was too drained to speak.

"No," he said after several moments, "at least one of us counts with him. That's better than none."

"You count, Jason. But right now he's busy trying to prove you don't. I'm acceptable because I'm irrelevant, in a sense."

The forlorn look on Jason's face told Kate he was not convinced.

"Really," she said, sliding off her stool and wrapping her arms around him. "You'll see."

At seven that evening, when Kate emerged from her bedroom, Igor was waiting in the living room, wearing a broad-shouldered, loose-fitting, one-button gray tweed jacket with the sleeves pushed up, a red sweatshirt beneath it, tan pleated pants that fell loosely over his gray leather boots, looking something like Kate's idea of a rock star.

"You look great," she said.

"So do you," he said, pleasing Kate even though she felt rather matronly and staid next to him.

The night was mild for December, allowing Igor not to

Linda Crawford

spoil the effect of his outfit by covering it up with a heavy coat, and Kate suggested they walk down to Little Italy.

"I've got money for a cab," he protested.

"It's not that," said Kate.

"You're sure?"

"I just feel like walking."

"We'll take a cab home," he said.

On the walk downtown, Igor told Kate he was thinking of trying out for the role of George in a production of *Who's Afraid of Virginia Woolf?* being done at school, asked her opinion of the relative merits of savings accounts and money market funds, gave a cogent synopsis and critical overview of the work of J. D. Salinger, a part of which he had just completed reading, and looked back wryly on his bondage to Melody Swarr. ("I was so desperate to feel important to someone that I went a little overboard.") Kate felt that she was out with an older man.

When they passed by Donatello's, where Igor worked, he made an excuse to go inside and there introduced Kate to his coworkers, whom he called "my boys," though it was obvious that some of them were several years older than he. They treated Igor with a kind of regard and he accepted it gracefully, assuring one that he would mediate a dispute with the boss, working out scheduling difficulties between two others. Kate realized that Igor, who functioned here as a sort of benevolent, baby godfather, had wanted her to see him in this setting, and she understood why. It was his stage and he absolutely shone. Jason should see this, Kate thought: Igor's impudence transformed into leadership.

The restaurant where they ate dinner turned out not to be the modest little trattoria that Kate had expected but an ele-

gant spot where the maitre d' addressed Igor as Signor
Wylie and treated him with a degree of familiarity that indicated Igor had passed this way before.

When Kate had examined the heavy linen, the sparkling
crystal, the menu with the obscure Italian and the very
expensive prices, she asked Igor, "Is this a hangout of
yours?"

Her astonishment obviously delighted him, but he strug-
gled to stay suave. "I've been here a few times. I think you'll
like the food."

"You know I would have been satisfied with the Neapoli-
tan Café," said Kate, referring to a place in the lower Village that went in strictly for pasta and parmigiana.

"I wouldn't take you to a dive like that," he said.

"Can you afford this?" she asked, realizing immediately
that the question was bound to offend.

His withering look, the first he'd directed at her in quite
some time, caused Kate to retreat behind the menu, which
remained almost indecipherable no matter how long she
stared.

Igor seemed to have no trouble, however, and he ended
up ordering for both of them and choosing a wine as well.

"Do you think Dad would like this place?" he asked.

"Oh, yes, I think so," said Kate.

"I'll have to bring him in sometime."

Could she explain to Igor why that was the wrong approach to take with Jason? Could she explain that all Jason
really wanted was a chance to give on his own terms to his
son? That if he had the chance he would most likely pass on
quickly to another stage and accept Igor on *his* terms?

"You know, Igor," she began, "your father's a little sensi-
tive about certain things—"

"Tell me about it," he said. "All he wants is to play Big Daddy, and when he can't he goes bananas."

In a certain sense, Kate had to admit, that wasn't a bad description of Jason recently. But he had his reasons.

"He missed a lot of years of being a father," she said.

"That's not my fault," Igor said defensively, as though Kate had accused him of something.

"No, of course not."

"Those two could've held things together if they'd tried."

"I guess they didn't think so."

"They just gave up." The distress in his eyes and the bitterness in his voice were as fresh as if his parents' failure had been yesterday. "And don't tell me I'll understand better when I'm older."

"I wouldn't—"

"Even though I probably will," he added softly.

The food arrived and they shifted onto more comfortable ground, Igor again playing the urbane host, Kate his appreciative audience. His success at camouflaging his rancor and hurt concerned her, but she was also relieved not to have to confront them.

At the end of a magnificent meal, Igor rejected Kate's offer to split what must have been a massive check and paid it without hesitation. ("Where do you get your money?" she asked, "and don't tell me tips because I won't believe you." "I'm a spectacular poker player," he answered, deadpan.) He took Kate's suggestion that they walk home as another attempt to spare him expense, but when she assured him that she just wanted to enjoy the night air, he easily fell into step beside her.

Kate looped her arm through his, amazed at her sense of comfort, at the solid affection she felt for this young man who only a year ago had seemed a burden, an obligation she was bound to assume out of wifely duty.

"Do you know when you first came to live with us I was afraid of you?" she said.

"You?" Igor gave a hoot of laughter. "I don't believe it."

"My throat used to close when I tried to talk to you."

"I thought you were terrifying."

"Me? How come?"

"I don't know, you just seemed so . . . perfect. You were always in control, you never raised your voice."

"Because my throat was closed."

"I was used to my mother screaming and crying and carrying on. Everything is very dramatic with her. You were so low-key."

"It's just a facade."

"It's a really good one," Igor said, his voice full of admiration.

They walked in silence for a block or so, their tandem footsteps ringing against the nearly deserted sidewalk.

"You must have hated that I was coming to live with you," Igor said.

"I guess I did in a way . . . because I was frightened. I didn't think I'd be very good at it."

"Me either. But I really wanted to come."

"I didn't feel that way for long, Igor. I hope you know that."

Kate took his silence for acquiescence.

"You've been very good for me," she said, knowing it was true but uncertain just exactly how, hoping he wouldn't ask her.

"Yeah?" He grinned, pleased, and content to take her statement on face value.

Again they fell silent, wrapped in the unusual warmth of the soft December air that seemed a reflection of the thaw that had occurred between them.

"How come you and Dad never had children?" Igor asked, as they turned uptown.

"He already had you and your sister."

"What about you?"

"Do you want to hear what I used to think or what I think now?"

"Both."

"I used to think that my parents should never have had a child, that they just weren't cut out for it. I didn't want to make the same mistake."

"And now?"

"Now I think I was wrong about them. It's true that they didn't give me some of the conventional things parents are expected to give their kids, but they gave me so much else." Kate felt suddenly quite overwhelmed by the richness of Lucius's and Carabel's legacy, filled with regret at her long denial of it. A scrim of tears covered her eyes, making the streetlights quiver.

"Anyone who used to take you to see the Orioles couldn't be all that bad," said Igor.

Kate laughed softly and blinked back tears. "They weren't all bad—far from it."

When they arrived at their building Igor announced that he wasn't coming upstairs.

"There's a game on tonight," he said. "I'll be home in a few hours."

"I hope you get lucky enough to cover dinner," said Kate. "Next time it's on me."

"Don't tell Dad about the poker, okay?"

Kate appeared to consider his request. "Would you do something for me?" she asked.

A crafty gleam, absent all evening, came into Igor's eyes. "You mean I scratch your back, you scratch mine?"

"No, I'm not trying to strike a deal. I just want to ask you a favor."

"No harm in asking," he said, although it was evident he didn't really believe it.

"Would you try to compromise with your father a little bit, just in one area?"

Igor's body tensed with suspicion and he stepped backward as though to move off the rug that he feared was about to be pulled from beneath him. "I've got to be true to myself," he said fiercely.

"Of course you do," said Kate. "I understand that. All I'm asking for is a gesture of good faith, something that tells your father that your behavior has to do with being true to yourself, not with rejecting him."

"And if I do it you won't tell about the poker?"

It was hard to believe that the agitated young man bargaining with her here on the sidewalk was the same one who had swept Kate through the earlier part of the evening in such polished fashion. Talk of his father, keeping secrets from him, striking compromises with him had, it seemed, unmanned him.

"I won't say anything about that in any case," said Kate.

"You mean no matter what I do?"

She nodded.

Relief softened the jut of Igor's chin and removed the rigid angles from his body. Kate could see him making the decision to be magnanimous.

"What do you want me to do?" he asked.

"Just let him buy your goddamn food."

Kate wasn't sure whether Igor's surprise was due to the request or her vehemence. Had it never occurred to him that Jason considered his insistence on separate food a slap in the face?

"That's all?" He could hardly believe his good fortune.

"That's all."

"No problem," he said. "Consider it done."

"Thank you."

Now Igor seemed restored to his earlier state of self-possession, all traces of the nervous, hesitant boy gone. It was a little like being with a werewolf, Kate thought, as she took hold of his arms and gave him a kiss on the cheek.

Igor allowed himself to give Kate's arms an answering squeeze.

"This was a lovely evening," she said. "Thank you for asking me."

A broad smile broke over Igor's face and reflected upward into his eyes. "You know what I was saying earlier about Mom and Dad?"

"Yes."

"Well, it's sort of a good news/bad news thing."

"What do you mean?"

"The bad news is that they didn't stay together. The good news is that I got to know you." He turned away quickly and headed down the block, calling out "see you later," and waving over his shoulder.

Kate, verging on tears for the second time that night, was grateful for his swift departure, but stood watching until he reached the end of the block.

Upstairs, discovering that Jason was not yet home, she decided that she would wait up for him, changed into a nightgown and robe, and settled down in front of the television set, which seemed more likely to keep her awake than a book. Her nighttime reading lately seldom exceeded five or six paragraphs.

The news seemed always the same, she thought: a horrifying story of custodians preying sexually upon children in their care, a medical miracle story (frozen embryos and implants and transplants figured heavily in these), something about cocaine, the Middle East, and Central American civil wars. It lulled Kate and she might have missed the big story had she not, moments before, fallen asleep, her head plunging forward, then jerking back, pitching her glasses off her nose and onto the floor, awakening her. Anxious that Jason not find her comatose, she picked up her glasses, righted herself, and gave the television her full attention just as the picture of a devastated storefront came on the screen.

A voice intoned, "A bomb exploded early this evening in Kalamazoo, Michigan, in a building occupied by SWEAT, the organization responsible for the new mental fitness craze sweeping the nation."

At first, the bomb seemed less significant to Kate than the fact that SWEAT had reached Kalamazoo, and that it was being described as "sweeping the nation."

"No one was hurt in the blast, which occurred after the center was closed for the day," the reporter continued, "but the building was destroyed."

Kate was surprised to hear there was a closing time. She would have thought Beryl would have insisted on round-the-clock operations. And what of the SWEATees who had reached Lock-up, the hostage-simulation phase? Did their captivity now run only from nine to five, with a break for dinner and an overnight visit at home? Kate supposed there must necessarily be some sacrifice of purity when a program became as widespread as SWEAT apparently had, but this seemed a major breach of principle.

"Kalamazoo police say they have received no calls taking responsibility for the bombing, nor are there any suspects at the present time. In New York, at SWEAT headquarters, Beryl Swarr, the organization's founder, met with reporters just moments ago."

Beryl's face filled the screen, microphones poking toward it like the lances of a horde of picadors. She gazed out with steely eyes, unfazed by the commotion. This is where she had come in, after all. She was in her element.

"I have no idea who was responsible for this act of terrorism," Beryl said, "but you may be sure that whoever it was will be apprehended and brought to justice. You may be just as sure that we will not be intimidated and that SWEAT's work will go forward. The Kalamazoo center will be rebuilt with the help of volunteers from all over the country. We expect to reopen within two weeks."

"Who might do something like this, Mrs. Swarr?" a reporter called out.

"I have no idea," Beryl replied, "but I can tell you that it will take a lot more than just one little bomb to stop this movement."

My God, thought Kate, now it's a movement.

"Is that what this is about?" someone else hollered. "Is somebody trying to bring down SWEAT?"

Beryl's chin rose to an indomitable tilt. "If so, they are doomed to fail. We've been under the gun before," she said, slipping simultaneously into the royal "we" and a mixed metaphor, "and we're perfectly capable of taking the heat."

"Any message for your members, Mrs. Swarr?" a voice shouted.

Beryl hesitated just a split second before, in Nixonian fashion, thrusting her arms upward and waggled victory signs on each hand. The camera froze her in that position for a few seconds, the icon of the hour, before cutting away to a commercial.

Kate, soon after, fell asleep again and dreamed of a bomb blowing Beryl to bits, each fragment then turning into an exact replica of the original in a nightmare of regeneration. Jason found her on the sofa when he came in and carried her in to bed without her ever‚waking up.

The next morning she awoke earlier than usual, feeling curiously refreshed; Igor helped himself to some of Jason's cereal; Jason noted this approvingly and made a point of telling Igor that a fellow mystery writer had mentioned the night before how much he liked Donatello's. Kate wasn't about to declare a breakthrough on any front, but she did feel more hopeful than usual as she approached her study with something resembling a spring in her step. She wouldn't go overboard and attempt actually to *write* today, she told herself, but she might at least allow herself to *think* about writing. She'd given up even that the last few weeks, practicing diversions as varied as reading the English-Italian section of her dictionary and looking through a stack of old maps she'd found on her study shelves. Only yesterday, in fact, she had been marveling over the wonderful sounds of the towns of Canada's Gaspé Peninsula: Anse-au-Griffon, Riviere-la-Madeleine, Petite-Pabos.

She approached her desk, settled into her leather swivel chair, and was just beginning to sort through the papers she'd let pile up on her desk (third-class mail, the folder containing the false starts she'd committed on her novel, notes she'd written to herself during recent stuporous days: "Shop Jason birthday." "What is wrong with you,

Katherine Wylie?" "Socks in dryer.") when the phone rang.

"Beryl Swarr here," she heard when she picked it up.

"Hello, Beryl," Kate said cautiously.

"I need to see you."

"Really? Can't we talk on the phone?"

"This matter demands a direct interface," said Beryl.

"I see."

"I can be there within the hour."

"Well, I'm not sure—"

"I'm talking urgent, Katherine, with a capital U."

Kate supposed one really couldn't turn away someone who had been bombed the night before. Besides, she was immune to Beryl now. What harm could it do?

"All right, Beryl," she said. "Come on down."

"Nice day," Beryl snapped and slammed down the phone.

When she arrived forty-five minutes later, she flew out of the elevator, casting glances backward at the empty car, shifting her eyes from side to side as she moved toward Kate's study. Once inside, she threw off the cape she'd been wearing, revealing a purple wool jumpsuit that itself had a small cape attached to its shoulders (Kate was curious about the motif but not enough to ask its significance) and lowered herself into the corner of the couch where Kate had lately passed so many languid hours.

"We've got a real crisis on our hands," said Beryl who, despite her cool disclaimer of the previous evening, was looking extremely threatened. "Kalamazoo was bombed last night."

If she had not seen the news, Kate would have assumed the entire city had been flattened.

"We don't know yet if it's a one-shot or just the beginning of an attempt to strike at the heart of the Movement."

Kate heard the capital letter and tried to look mildly respectful.

"In case anything should happen to me, it's more important than ever to push forward with the Work."

"Oh, come on, Beryl," Kate said, unable to stop herself. "Are you telling me that someone is out to get you?"

Having said it, Kate realized the idea was not really so impossible. Hadn't she herself had fantasies of expunging Beryl? Perhaps someone out there was bent on just such a course.

"All I am saying, Katherine, is that these are dangerous times."

"Do you know anyone with a grudge against you?"

Was it her imagination or did Beryl's eyes glint momentarily with suspicion as she looked at Kate?

"Anyone in a position of prominence is bound to have detractors," Beryl said.

"I suppose—"

"And any public figure, anyone whose success is visible, can become a magnet for a lot of sickies and weirdos. Why do you think presidents get assassinated?"

Kate let that one pass while Beryl hastened on.

"The point is the Work, get it done, get it out there, go for it."

Kate was beginning to discern a shape taking form amidst the fog of Beryl's verbiage. It was rectangular, about an inch thick, and it looked like a book.

"Waverly has been pressing me for some time," Beryl said. "They're very high on a sequel. I see it taking up where C.C. left off, opening in the green room of the 'Dave Duncan Show,' and telling everything that's happened to me since."

"You feel there's an audience for that?"

"People are hungry for it, Katherine, with a capital H."

"Well, Beryl, I wish you lots of luck," Kate said.

Beryl rose and approached Kate's desk, gripping its edge, leaning in toward Kate with a grin. "Did you think I'd leave you out?" she asked. "What kind of person do you think I am?"

"I'm not going to answer that," Kate murmured.

"I want you to be as much a part of this as you were of C.C."

"No, Beryl," Kate said quietly.

"I'd consider it a full collaboration, even though the book is virtually written and really just needs to be pulled together."

"No."

Beryl appeared not to hear Kate and to be picking up steam, rather than losing it. "The material is all there. I taped every day I was on the road, every day that we were setting up SWEAT, all during the early days at the center—"

"No." It was a little like talking to Mrs. Karanewski, Kate thought, though Beryl was proving harder to arrest.

"When you think of how C.C. impacted, you can imagine what this will do. And people are out there waiting for it. It will be extremely big."

"No."

"Esther has authorized me to offer a fifty-fifty split, the same arrangement as we had before, so you're looking at top dollar as well as the opportunity to be part of a great challenge."

"No."

"A breakthrough."

"No."

Beryl was exhausted from hurling herself at the barrier of Kate's refusals and the effort had taken its toll. Her face gleamed with a sweaty film; her arms, still stretched out toward the edges of Kate's desk, shook violently.

"Why not?" Beryl asked.

Should she answer honestly? Kate wondered. Tell Beryl what she thought of SWEAT, of *Captive Courageous*, of the regret she felt for her part in it, of the notion that more of the same might be perpetrated? Tell Beryl what she thought of her? Staring at the face before her, makeup muddy, brows drawn upward at an impossible tilt, bones jutting out where the flesh had fallen away, thinking of what Beryl had been and what she had become, Kate decided there would be no point.

"I have my own work." Although that was not, at this moment, strictly true, Kate felt certain that it would be. This meeting with Beryl had only strengthened her resolve.

Beryl pushed off from the desk and spun around its corner, coming to a halt directly over Kate. "This is no time to sit on the sidelines," she said, poking a finger into Kate's face.

"I don't consider my work the sidelines."

Beryl gave a dismissive little laugh and whirled round again, revolving into the center of the room where she began to pace up and down.

"I'm not sure you understand what you're turning down here, Katherine. I'm offering you a chance to reach millions of people. Millions! A chance to touch lives and change them." Beryl's hands worked avidly in the air as though she

Linda Crawford

were, even now, shaping the clay that was her readers. "How many copies would a novel of yours sell? Three thousand? Five? How many?"

Well, Kate thought, if she wants to fight dirty, I can do that too.

"Why don't you write the sequel yourself?" she asked.

When Beryl stopped dead in her tracks, Kate thought she had scored a hit. Beryl must know that she would be hard pressed to write a cogent paragraph, let alone a complete book. She could not really believe that Kate had just pulled *C.C.* together.

"Are you kidding?" said Beryl. "Do you have any idea what my schedule's like, what kind of demands I have on my time? I eat my meals in meetings, I make phone calls from my car."

Kate was glad she had been spared seeing Beryl in her car with her phone.

"Do you know what I think?" Beryl said, beginning again to shuttle back and forth before the desk. "Do you?"

Wanting to be certain she had Kate's attention, she waited for an answer.

"I can't imagine," Kate said finally.

"I think that you have a problem with success." Beryl flung one purple arm upward to emphasize her observation and the little cape hanging down her back billowed outward. "I think you have a problem with successful, dynamic people." Now her other arm rose, causing the cape to heave and fall again.

Kate watched, fascinated.

"It's threatening to you to be around too much positive energy. I am a successful, dynamic person who is filled with positive energy, so you are threatened by me. I want you to sleep on this, Katherine. I'm going to give you a second chance to get on board. Think over what I've said and I'll get back to you."

Beryl grabbed her outer cape from the couch, hauled open the study door, and exited, seemingly all in one motion.

Kate thought of following her, telling her not to call. She thought of rushing to the window and dropping something heavy from it as Beryl passed by below. She thought of calling in a bomb threat to the SWEAT center down the street. But she did none of those things. Nor did she creep over to the couch and curl into a sleeping ball, as she almost certainly would have a few days ago.

Instead, she removed the cover from her typewriter and sat down before it. Had Beryl galvanized her in some mysterious way? she wondered. Or had last night's conversation with Igor illuminated the dark place where she'd been holed up, making it impossible to go on hiding? Maybe the cumulative weight of her lies to Jason about her work had finally become insupportable. Maybe all of those things had conspired to make her feel that she could commit words to paper. Her only certainty was that she felt free of her recent affliction.

She rolled a piece of paper into the machine, intending to begin the novel about her parents and their marriage that had eluded her for so long. Instead, she found herself writing:

Dear Ceilia,
When we met there were many questions I wanted to ask, but I felt I would be intruding on you. I wish now I had been more forceful for I realize how impor-

tant your memories are to me. Your existence in the present is important to me also and I wish I had insisted that we meet again.

I've spent a great part of my life running from the idea of family, thinking I wanted no part of it. I thought my parents and I led too odd an existence for the word family *to apply to us (a failure of imagination, I see now). When I grew up and considered establishing my own, I felt I was, by virtue of my experience, ill-equipped (another failure of same).*

In the past year, through no effort of my own and, in one case, against my will, I've been presented with a grandmother and a teenage son, pieces of the past and the future, and I see what I have been missing: a sense of history and a promise of continuity. I think now my life would be rather empty without these things.

You and I have lost a lot of time with each other, but we needn't lose any more. I don't know whether or not the past can be redeemed, but it can certainly be remembered and built upon. I hope you may feel the same way as I. If you don't, I'll try to understand.

Love,
Kate

Chapter Eleven

*O*N the days that followed, it appeared that the SWEAT Bomber, so dubbed by the media, had taken Beryl's statement in the wake of the Kalamazoo explosion ("it will take more than just one little bomb to stop this movement") as a challenge and decided to see if two, three or four, each bigger than the one before, would do the trick. Kate learned of the second blast from Beryl herself, picking up the phone two days after their meeting to hear: "They've hit Toledo. Do you still want to stay on the fence?"

Despite Beryl's making her appeal sound roughly on a par with a summons to the Republican barricades in the Spanish Civil War, Kate held firm.

"I'm not on the fence, Beryl."

"This is the time to stand up and be counted, Katherine," Beryl said.

"Count me out," said Kate.

Explosions in Cleveland and Youngstown resulted in similar calls-to-arms from Beryl, whose pitch became more strident as each successive detonation proved ever more conclusively that an organized campaign of destruction was under way. No longer was there talk of the devastation being random, tied to local issues, the work of a copycat. It was clear that SWEAT was the target. And when a note arrived at a local newspaper after a blast in Pittsburgh destroyed the SWEAT center and an adjacent dry-cleaning establishment, the bomber's quarry was defined even more specifically.

"Swarr must be stopped," it said, in letters cut from the glossy spreads of magazine advertisements.

"It's me they're after," Beryl shrieked at Kate over the phone immediately upon hearing this. "Me!"

"I'm very sorry, Beryl. I really am." Was she? Kate wondered.

"Surely now you can see the importance of the sequel. We've got to *move* on this. *Move*, do you hear me?"

"I understand your position," said Kate, "but it doesn't change mine."

"The Movement is under seige," Beryl rasped. "I am under seige. And still you refuse?"

"I do."

The rumbling at the other end of the line sounded as though Beryl might be going to take a run at a major denunciation, something iniquitous in content, operatic in style. But all that emerged was a croak: "You'll regret this," followed by the line going dead.

Kate felt the squawk was Beryl's swan song with her, a hunch confirmed a few days later when the police arrived to question Kate about the bombings, Beryl having supplied Kate's name as a possible grudge harborer. If Beryl was willing to sic the police on her, Kate assumed she must have given up on the idea of Kate's writing her book. ("Did Mrs. Swarr say what my grudge might be?" Kate inquired of the detectives interviewing her. "She said you'd helped out with her book and you might be sore she was getting all the attention," said one. "Helped out?" said Kate. "Is that what she said?" "Organizing and shaping, I think that was it," replied the other.)

In the press conferences she held after each bombing, Beryl resembled not at all the virago who had lately been assaulting Kate with panic, hysteria, and threats in their phone conversations. The cameras and microphones had their usual soothing effect on her. And never did she have herself more firmly in hand than during her meeting with the press after the disaster in Pittsburgh. In her opening statement she was the very vision of the cool commander.

"To those forces who are attempting to bring us down, I would say this: you will fail. Every center that is destroyed will be rebuilt. If you persist on this dangerous course, look over your shoulder. The SWEAT network will never be far behind. We will not be held hostage to your negative energy."

Beryl hit every beat of this last sentence sharply, eliciting raucous cries of approval from the SWEATees in her audience. (SWEAT had set up a hot line that members could call to get the latest news on the bombings, and it announced as well the time and place of Beryl's appearances so that the troops could turn out in force to support her; also Beryl never went anywhere these days without a cordon of members, called Swarrguards, surrounding her.)

"How do you feel about the fact that they've named you as their target?" a reporter hollered.

Linda Crawford

Obviously cognizant of the opportunities inherent in martyrdom, Beryl replied, "Let them strike directly at me." Angry shouts rose from her supporters. "The movement will go on." The shouts turned to cheers.

"Are you daring them to come after you?" someone else asked.

Beryl relaxed her ramrod posture and leaned companionably on the lectern behind which she stood. (Because Beryl liked to get around to as many different neighborhoods as possible, today's press conference was being held in Hostages Anonymous headquarters on the Upper West Side.)

"Look, gentlemen," she said, ignoring the fact that there were several women among the reporters, "I'd like nothing better than to be working for SWEAT, and for hostages everywhere," she added, mindful of her surroundings even though they were nonprofit, "without distractions. But as the song says—"

Beryl hesitated, milking the pause for a beat or two. Kate shuddered, afraid she knew what was coming.

"Que sera, sera. Whatever will be, will be," said Beryl.

The roar that rose from her supporters was deafening and accompanied by heavy foot stamping and ear piercing whistles. Kate wondered how "que sera, sera" could be reconciled with "take charge," SWEAT's rallying cry. Obviously, it was not a discrepancy that bothered anyone in the hall.

Kate flicked off the television, unable to watch more. But she discovered it was very hard to avoid Beryl these days. There was an interview with her in the *Times*, alongside the story of the Pittsburgh bombing. Her picture filled the *Post*'s front page. The *Daily News* head ran: BERYL TO BOMBER: YOU WILL FAIL.

That evening when Kate, despite Jason's absence, turned

224

on the one television program the two of them watched faithfully, a detective series about which they argued weekly (Jason claimed the investigative procedures portrayed were shoddy, Kate said it didn't matter because the hero was so charming), she was appalled to find it preempted by a recap of Beryl's career, beginning with the seige at People's Bank & Trust, showing excerpts from her promotional appearances, the ribbon-cutting ceremony at the original SWEAT center, the recent press conferences. Angrily twisting the dial away from this, Kate was astonished to find similar specials on Beryl and the Bomber on the other networks as well. Eventually, she went back to the original and watched it until the end.

Afterward, feeling vaguely unclean, Kate decided to go outside and walk in the snow that had begun falling in the late afternoon, casting a hush over the city. She dressed warmly, pulled on boots with waterproof coverings up to the knee, and tugged a watch cap down tightly over her ears. Stepping outside into the muffled night, she found she was alone except for a cross-country skier moving by her door and a young man pulling a little girl along on a sled. The streets were empty of traffic. It could have been a winter evening at the turn of the century, before Beryl, and SWEAT, the Bomber, television, promotional tours, self-help books. Before Kate, before Lucius and Carabel. It was soothing to imagine herself in a time wiped clean of everything and everyone she knew. She felt mercifully empty as she moved through the heavy flakes, walking north toward the park.

Two young boys ran by, throwing snowballs at each other. A couple moved along the opposite side of the street, holding hands. Kate thought at one point she sensed someone behind her, thought she heard the soft whoosh of a footfall at her back, but when she turned around there was no one there. She walked the last block to the park alone, comforted, not frightened, by the thought that she had the city entirely to herself.

In the park she headed toward the huge evergreen tree at the bottom of Fifth Avenue, which still bore the lights of Christmas past. Midway there, she again had the sensation that someone was following in her wake. She whirled around quickly this time. Had she caught sight of motion in the corner of her eye? Was there a space behind her still vibrating from the swift departure of its occupant? Surely the pushers didn't come out peddling in the snow, hissing "smoke, smoke, hash, blow." And if they did, they would approach and hiss, not run and hide. Kate convinced herself that the wind and snow were playing tricks and she moved on through the park, then up Fifth Avenue to Tenth Street, across Tenth, where the snow-covered town houses added to her nineteenth-century reverie, to Sixth Avenue, where she began to head downtown again, passing by the large newsstand filled with papers blaring news of the bombings and bringing her visit to another time zone to an abrupt end.

By the next day, the pure white snow that had covered the city so gently the night before had already, with the help of a bright sun and a brigade of salt trucks, begun to turn into a menacing gray slush, spewing up from automobile wheels, eddying in the gutters at ankle level, drawing salt lines on the leather of people's boots. Kate judged this a day for a hearty winter soup and set out to get the ingredients.

On the way to the butcher's to pick up some bones, a block-and-a-half walk, she felt a shadow behind her, just as she had the night before. It's ridiculous, she told herself. I will not turn around. And she kept to her resolution until she turned into the butcher shop, shooting a sharp glance to her rear as she entered, seeing nothing.

Waiting for the bones to be wrapped, she stared out the front windows, but no face peered through the glass, no figure darted by, no one stood across the street staring into a window to catch her reflection, as the tails always did in Jason's novels.

Between the butcher and the vegetable market she felt the back of her scalp prickling, but she told herself that she, no one else, was creating the impression that someone was breathing down her neck. Between the vegetable market and the bakery, no longer swayed by her own arguments, she stopped abruptly and wrenched her body into a 180 degree turn, nearly colliding with a tiny, ancient Italian gentleman who apologized profusely in his native tongue. The other people behind her, none of whom she recognized, were a young man in shorts and T-shirt who jogged by looking unbearably single-minded and self-righteous; a vacuous-faced young woman in a brief skirt and stilt heels, also apparently oblivious to the temperature and the slush; a woman who looked like a cross between a bag lady and a clown, her bulky body clad in dark, worn garments, bright red curls atop her head casting an orange glow over her stark white skin—obviously, Kate thought, someone recently and inappropriately spilled out of an institution, onto the streets; and a heavyset man who was talking to himself, a conversation that appeared to have nothing to do with Kate. They all, in fact, passed by her without missing a beat.

On the way to the liquor store for a bottle of wine, after selecting a round loaf of whole wheat bread at the bakery, Kate passed by the SWEAT center. She might have missed it, so preoccupied was she, had not a banner recently hung over its front door snapped sharply in the wind and caused her to look upward. WE SHALL OVERCOME, it read. Similar sentiments filled the front windows. HANG TOUGH, STAND TALL, SWARR WILL EMERGE AGAIN TRIUMPHANT read the hand-lettered signs. Pictures of Beryl were scattered among the printed material.

Kate hurried on to the liquor store and, for the first time in her life, considered buying something to drink right away, on the way home perhaps, or the moment she got inside the apartment at the very latest, something she could just open and pour down her throat, something sweet and fruity and intoxicating that would make her forget that Beryl existed. Just as she was reaching for a pint of blackberry brandy, the spell passed and she let her hand fall, quivering, to her side. She left the liquor store with a single bottle of wine and an absolute determination to reroute her movements around the neighborhood so that she would not have to pass by the SWEAT building.

That night, with the soup, and the bread, and the wine, she told Jason and Igor (he realized his pledge to Kate had to apply to more than the occasional bowl of cereal so he showed up now for one or two dinners a week) about her feeling of being followed.

"I'm sure it's ridiculous," she said. "There's no reason why anyone would follow me."

"Unless that creep got the cops all involved again," said Igor.

No one had to ask who "the creep" was.

"I think I should have some of my boys patrol the neighborhood and get a few others for escort duty," he added.

"I think what's going on is that you're guilty as hell and you're dragging it around behind you," Jason said to Kate. (She had confessed a few days earlier to her long writing drought; Jason said he'd suspected all along and figured Kate would tell him when she could.) "It makes you feel that there's someone hanging over your shoulder."

"You're the mystery writer and you don't even recognize a case when it's right under your nose," Igor taunted his father.

"Maybe because I am a mystery writer I'm able to recognize when something is being created by psychological conflict and anxiety, and when something is actual."

Kate knew Jason was fighting to keep his condescension from showing, but he was not altogether successful.

"Or maybe," said Igor, "just because I believe it's real, and I'm interested in getting involved in it, you have to shoot it full of holes."

"Maybe you can tell me who might be doing the following, and why," Jason said.

"How should I know? It could be a lot of different things."

"Well, how about sharing one of them with me. Just one of your theories. That's all I'm asking."

"I don't know," said Igor, looking a little desperate. "Maybe it's the same people who are bombing the Swarr."

"And why would they be following Kate?"

"Maybe they found out she wrote that piece of shit."

Kate felt a momentary, but sharp, sense of injury, even though she concurred in Igor's judgment.

"Maybe they figure she's also responsible for SWEAT because of that," he added.

This had never occurred to Kate, but she had to admit there might be something to it, an idea that made her distinctly uncomfortable. She saw that Jason was also considering the possibility for the first time.

"The note said they were after the Swarr," he said.

"Sure it did. Everybody knows her. Nobody knows who Kate is. Sorry, Kate." Igor extended a hand in Kate's direction; she stretched out her own and gave his a squeeze. "I mean, the Swarr's the one who's out front on this. She's the logical target. It wouldn't mean much if they went around bombing all these SWEAT centers and then sent a note saying they were after Kate Wylie, would it?"

"Let's say your theory's right," said Jason, "though I don't for a minute believe it is. But let's just say it is, okay?"

"Yeah, let's." Igor was trying to tamp down his belligerence, but failing.

"I don't think the answer is to have some punks follow Kate around wherever she goes."

"Well, what would you do?" Igor said, rising. "Call in Theobold, master sleuth? Give the case to old Gerard?"

"Gerald," Jason corrected.

"At least my boys know a little something about this kind of work, about the neighborhood. They're used to looking after their own people, on the streets, not just on paper."

Now Jason rose as well. "Oh, I get it. The men of action, right? The tough guys. Real men don't write books. Is that what you're talking about?"

"They're not punks, but how would you know that? You've never taken the trouble to find out anything about them."

Igor slammed his chair in against the table and walked away, heading for the door to the stairwell, unwilling to wait for the elevator. When he reached the door, he opened it and disappeared.

Immediately Jason began to berate himself. Why had he let Igor provoke him? Why couldn't he maintain any distance, any perspective, when the two of them tangled? Things had just begun to get better. Why had he made them worse?

"Nothing has changed but the date," Jason lamented. "I just can't deal with this kid."

Kate couldn't contradict him. He did let Igor provoke him unnecessarily. The atmosphere between them had been easing but now it seemed that they had taken a giant leap backward.

Later that evening, as they watched the account of another SWEAT bombing (this one had leveled the Harrisburg, Pennsylvania, center), Jason again debunked Igor's notion that the same forces might be trailing Kate. She didn't put much stock in it herself but, nevertheless, when she went out the next day to do an errand at the post office and found two of Igor's cronies posted by her front door, she felt rather relieved.

They fell into step on either side of her, introducing themselves as Angelo and Carmine. They were the day shift. Dino and Anthony would be on duty at night. Igor had told them to tell her that there was no reason for Mr. Wylie to know about them. Angelo assured Kate that she could "rely on his discretion," which he pronounced to rhyme with "excretion."

They entered the post office with her, stationing themselves by the door while she stood in line, scanning the room and the entering patrons with the sharp eagerness of ferrets. It was obvious that they took their work very seriously.

In the late afternoon when Kate went out again to pick up some dry cleaning, they gave her a full report on the day's activity outside her building, while they accompanied her to the cleaners and back. The only recurring faces were the

red-headed, white-faced bag lady, obviously a new addition
to the neighborhood; a fellow pushing a shopping cart laden
with the refuse of his possessions up and down the block
(Kate assured them that he, too, was a fixture, residing
across the street beneath the overhang of an abandoned
loading dock); a short, bullet-bodied young woman with
close-cropped hair who passed by the building once or twice
each hour (Kate thought she recognized in their description
a clerk from the health food store whom she had often noticed tearing down the block to the sleazy little deli on the
corner and emerging eating some unwhole, unnatural food);
the UPS delivery man who came through the neighborhood
once in the morning and again in the afternoon (Angelo and
Carmine felt this was somewhat unusual and said they
would check it out); and one possible suspect: an extremely
nervous, middle-aged man who approached the building
several times during the day but always turned away at the
last moment, retreating to a doorway across the street from
which he continued to stare at the building's entrance. Kate
hated to tell them this sounded like a patient of the psycho-
analyst on the sixth floor. After watching him for months she
had finally figured out that he arrived hours early for his appointment at six o'clock in the evening and rehearsed his arrival all day long, obviously a man with a threshold problem.

Carmine could not disguise his disappointment.

"I thought this hadda be the guy," he said, pounding his
fist dramatically into the palm of his hand. "He just looked
like such a creep."

"I'm sure he is a creep," said Kate, trying to console him.

"Yeah, but not the one we're after," said Angelo. "Not
our creep."

"It's possible I'm not even being followed, you know,"

she said, disliking deflating their sense of mission, but feeling that they ought to know.

"We got all the bases covered," said Angelo.

"Don't worry about a thing," Carmine added.

They simply didn't believe her, Kate realized. "Okay, fellas," she said. "Thanks for your help."

That night, she and Jason walked several blocks downtown in the bitter cold to have dinner with his agent at a new Senegalese restaurant. ("Funny, I was just feeling like Senegalese food," Kate had remarked when Jason told her where they were going.) She felt his tension through the several layers of clothing that separated them.

"Don't turn around, he whispered to her somewhere in the middle of the third block.

"I wasn't planning to," she said.

"Sssssshhhh. Don't."

"Don't what?"

"Don't say anything."

"I wasn't until you started hissing at me."

"Just keep walking."

"What else would I do in this cold?"

"Just act natural."

"What about you?"

He yanked at her arm as though it were a lead on a dog, issuing a command for silence.

"I think you may have been right about being followed," he said softly. "I think there's someone behind us right now."

Oh, God, thought Kate. Dino and Anthony. "I don't think so, Jason. And I'd be the one to feel it. They'd be following me."

"We're going to cross the street now." He was talking out

of the side of his mouth, beginning to steer her toward the curb. "See if they stick with us."

"There's more than one?"

"Sssshhh! Just follow my lead."

"We're going out of our way, Jason. It's too damn cold for that."

"Whatever you do, don't look back."

Jason guided Kate across the street, gradually picking up their pace. When they reached the end of the block, he swerved swiftly around the corner, moving faster still.

"Jason, for Christ's sake, the restaurant's the other way. We'll be late as well as frozen."

"Gotta shake this guy," he muttered.

"Now there's just one?"

He propelled them three blocks out of their way to the west, then turned downtown again. Despite the icy air Kate began to sweat as they flew along, now zigzagging east, now heading south once more. When they arrived at the restaurant her hair was crackling where it had frozen from the sweat on her cheeks. Jason's eyebrows were rimed and his face almost fuchsia.

Returning home after dinner, they shared a cab with Jason's agent, who dropped them at their front door. Kate made a mental note to tell the patrol it needn't accompany her when she was with her husband. When Jason raised the possibility of calling in the police, Kate said absolutely not. Probably what he had felt tonight, she said, was his own guilt, trailing along behind him like a persistent, inescapable presence.

The next SWEAT center to be demolished was in Reading, Pennsylvania, as the Bomber, being charted now like a burgeoning hurricane, continued on a steady eastward path.

There had been no loss of life in any of the explosions, nor any conclusive evidence found to point to the Bomber's identity. The newspapers and television networks churned out daily speculation on this question: the perpetrator might be a disgruntled trainee, a jealous fellow author, a member of a right-wing sect that had attacked SWEAT as part of the creeping and corrosive humanism destroying the soul of America, a spurned suitor. (Who would have led the authorities to believe there might be such a person? Kate wondered.) The police and the FBI spun their wheels. And the Bomber moved on inexorably.

Kate could imagine Beryl's current state of mind, and she thought she detected signs in her press conferences of slight fraying around the edges. Although still, for the most part, presenting a confident front, turbulence was occasionally visible. Her voice tended to rise and threaten to go out of control when she spoke of the Bomber. Her gaunt fingers played incessantly with one of her stalks of hair, twisting it round and letting it go, curling and releasing, over and over again. She once slipped into ranting about presidential assassins and "other vermin who try to give themselves stature by striking at the mighty and powerful." Gone was the insouciance that had led her a short time ago to reply "Que sera, sera" in response to questions about her personal safety. She was definitely on edge. Each press conference was like a little morality play, and Kate felt the kind of pity for Beryl that she would feel for any character brought low by her own unchecked appetites.

A few nights later, when Kate and Jason ventured out for a cappucino after watching the late news (the Bomber, in an unprecedented concentration of activity, had struck the Philadelphia and Trenton centers on the same day), Kate was pleased to note that they were without shadows as they walked two blocks to the cozy little café that always seemed at its most inviting on cold winter nights.

"The Swarr must finally have gone around the bend," said Jason, as they settled into a booth by the front windows.

"Why do you think so?" Kate asked.

"What else could keep her from making an appearance?"

For the first time since the bombings had begun, Beryl had not, after today's disasters, held a press conference.

"Pure fear," said Kate. "Maybe she's gone into hiding."

"She could never do that. It would ruin her image."

"Well, I don't think going around the bend would stop her from going in front of the cameras."

"You're right," said Jason. "She wouldn't know, would she?"

"She's been borderline for some time, but I don't think she recognizes that."

"I'll go get the papers." Jason shrugged back into his jacket. "See what they're saying. Be right back."

Kate turned and through the frosted pane behind her watched Jason jog to the corner and disappear around it. She loved their winter ritual of coming out a couple of times a week for a hot drink and a look through the morning papers. It was something they had done throughout their marriage and it gave her a feeling of warmth and security.

As she turned back to her table, Kate heard a faint squeaking behind her and turned to see the chalky clown face of the bag lady, surrounded by its aureole of flaming curls, staring through the glass. My God, what it must be like to be out there staring in, out there in the bone-freezing cold, watching the people inside peeling off layers of clothing, raising steaming drinks to their lips? It was inhuman that anyone should have to endure such agony. Atrocious. Barbaric.

Kate rose and walked toward the door, noting a small empty table in the opposite corner. There was no reason she couldn't bring the woman inside, sit her down there, and buy her a drink of steamed milk with a dash of cinnamon on top. It was not as though she were a filthy, smelly derelict who would empty the place by her very presence. The several times she'd seen the woman Kate had noted, in fact, that she managed somehow to present a picture of impeccable cleanliness, despite her oddity. And really, was she all that odd in this neighborhood? There were lots of people who looked freakish enough to be recent victims of deinstitutionalization, even though one knew very well that they had gotten up that morning and deliberately assumed their facades. Mental hospital chic, they should call it.

When she opened the door the woman beckoned her outside.

"No, you come inside." Kate enunciated carefully and employed exaggerated gestures though there was no reason to assume that the woman's hearing wasn't perfectly good.

She became quite agitated, fluttering her hands, tossing her orange curls as she shook her head back and forth. Kate could see she would take some convincing. She closed the door behind her and walked down two short steps to the pavement, hugging her arms to her body to hold in the warmth.

"I'd like to invite you—"

She got no further. One of the woman's arms shot out and grabbed hold of her, yanking Kate in close to her bulky body. Once there she felt a hard object forced against her ribs. And then the woman was moving Kate along the street.

"Wait a minute," Kate protested. "Are you out of your mind?"

For an answer the woman raised the object from Kate's ribs and flashed it in front of her eyes. It was a gun.

"Wun permp undu gummat," the woman gurgled, exhibiting either an extremely crude attempt at vocal disguise, or a very severe speech impediment.

Whichever it was, Kate understood that she was to be silent and, with the gun waving in front of her face, her inclination was to comply. She did not cry out as she was pulled along. They passed no one to whom she might have signaled her plight. The same bitter cold that Kate barely felt now because of the adrenaline pumping through her system had emptied the streets.

Who was this woman? Had she been following her? What did she want? Was she connected with the SWEAT Bomber? Or was she just a local mad person, as Kate had originally judged her to be? Was Kate a random target or a carefully chosen one? The questions ricocheted round her mind as the woman tugged her through the streets. Kate tried to keep track of where they were, but by the time the woman stopped short and pushed Kate down the steps to a basement entrance to a brownstone, she had lost her bearings, though she knew she couldn't be more than a dozen blocks from home.

The woman pushed Kate flat against the door and held the gun to her back while she fumbled about in the unlit entrance, trying to use her key. When she finally succeeded, and the door flew open, Kate spilled into the darkness inside, losing her footing and landing face-down on the floor. The woman barked a command that sounded close enough to "Stay!" for Kate to remain still. Besides, she wasn't all that eager to know where she was.

She felt the woman step over her, and then a light went on. Looking along the floor, which was covered with straw matting, Kate could see two baked enamel stackable chairs in a bright yellow color, the legs of a card table, and a wastebasket set alongside it. Turning her head in the opposite direction, she saw two enormous pillows that were obviously meant to serve as seats and the shoes, ankles, and drooping coat hem of her captor.

Kate followed the woman's feet, shod in flat black oxfords that were in good condition, as they moved to another pair of stackable chairs, and then back to near where Kate lay. The legs of the yellow chair descended to the floor, just missing Kate's hand. She was yanked upward and thrust into the chair. Again she heard the command that meant she wasn't to move.

The woman rustled around behind Kate and then suddenly a rope slipped over her body, pinning her to the chair. She heard a ripping noise and wide strips of tape bound her wrists to the cold metal arms.

"I wish you'd tell me what this is all about," Kate said, trying to sound reasonable and calm. "Whatever you want, I really don't think it's necessary—"

The icy barrel of the gun bit into the back of her neck, causing the words to die in her throat.

As soon as the gun was removed, a cloth was drawn across Kate's eyes and secured with a tight knot behind her head. Then she could feel the woman standing in front of her and her fingers reached out and began to probe Kate's mouth.

"Oh, God," she pleaded, "please don't gag me. There's no need. I won't make a sound. I promise."

The woman hesitated and then Kate felt the gun's chilly metal being laid across her lips, pressed against them in silent threat.

Kate nodded to indicate that she understood and, to make certain there was no confusion, she repeated her promise when the woman removed the gun. "I won't make a sound."

And it was almost literally true, as she held her breath, listening intently to each move the woman made. Kate heard her removing her coat, hanging it up, then taking off her shoes, laces flicking against the leather. Why would she take off her shoes? Perhaps she didn't want Kate to be able to follow her footsteps. When Kate heard the distant sound of running water and judged the woman to be in another room, she tested her bonds by pulling against them, but found they were tight. After the water was shut off, there was no sound for some minutes.

Where was Jason now? What must he be going through? He had stepped out for a paper and returned to find his wife gone, leaving no trace. Had anyone in the café seen Kate snatched? Would anyone begin to know where to look for her?

Next Kate heard the approach of what could only be high-heeled shoes, tapping against the wood flooring of a hallway perhaps, muffling when they hit the sisal. Was the woman dressing for their night together? Why? Or maybe the shoes were mules and she'd put them on along with a dressing gown, though she hardly seemed the type.

Now the heels sounded again as they moved off the rug and onto . . . linoleum? Tile? She must be in the kitchen, a notion confirmed when a kettle whistled a high-pitched scream. Was she making them tea? Kate heard a popping noise. Toast?

As the woman returned, Kate heard rattling dishes and smelled orange pekoe tea, lemon, cinnamon. Had the woman made cinnamon toast? Had Kate been brought at gunpoint to some unknown place to have tea and toast at what must now be nearly one o'clock in the morning? It made no sense.

Now she felt the woman standing before her, unmoving, deliberative. Was she weighing Kate's fate? Deciding whether to share her tea and toast? Pointing the gun at Kate's head, execution style? Kate felt the mass of her body move forward, her clothing brushing against Kate's legs, felt her hands on the blindfold, untying its knot, felt the blindfold drop away from her eyes.

Standing before her, dressed in a lime green jumpsuit and matching open-backed spike heels, was Beryl, looking immensely pleased with herself.

"You had no idea, did you?" she said, as though she had just surprised Kate with a party on her birthday. "You never dreamed."

There was no need now to keep Kate quiet by resting the gun against her lips. She was speechless.

"I thought the jig was up that very first day when you turned around and looked right at me. Do you remember? After you ran into that little man? I was sure you'd recognize me. You looked right into my eyes. But I just kept on walking and when I got past you I realized you didn't know."

Beryl had placed the tea tray on a yellow metal table and now she sat down in the chair beside it and began to pour tea into two yellow plastic mugs.

"I think what really made the difference was stuffing my cheeks. I got that from Brando in *The Godfather*. Do you remember how that changed his whole face? I think if I hadn't done that you would have known me. Even with the makeup and the wig and the clothes, I think you would have known it was me if I hadn't stuffed my cheeks. But the point is, you didn't. The point is, I fooled you completely, didn't I?"

Beryl didn't seem to expect an answer to her question. She put a spoonful of sugar and a slice of lemon into each mug of tea. Then she cut the cinnamon toast into quarters. Not until she went to hand a mug to Kate did it seem to occur to her that Kate would have difficulty drinking it in her immobilized state. Obviously annoyed, as though Kate were a perverse guest who was being uncooperative, she slammed the mug down on the table and reached out to rip the tape from Kate's wrists, causing Kate to make her first sound in some time, a sharp cry of pain that Beryl ignored.

When Kate's hands were free, Beryl shoved the mug into them although Kate would still have been hard pressed to raise the mug to her lips, as her shoulders and upper arms were pinioned by rope. She certainly didn't feel much like trying.

"Believe me, I thought of a lot of different disguises," said Beryl, taking a sip of tea and nibbling on a piece of toast without offering any to Kate. "I even went to a place that rents theatrical costumes and looked at what they had. But then I realized that I could be traced through that so I decided to make my own. I sewed padding into the coat, which I got at a thrift shop. I even made the wig myself from some pieces of shag carpet. And you had no idea it was me, so I guess I did a pretty good job."

She ate another wedge of toast and drank some more tea, savoring a job well done.

Just how unhinged was Beryl? Kate wondered. What sort of tone should she take with her? She didn't want to do anything that would cause her to hurtle over the edge of the abyss on which she appeared to be teetering. She had to assume that she was dangerous despite the tea party atmosphere. Where was the gun? She looked around and saw it lying beside the tea tray.

"I didn't have much time to get things ready," Beryl said, "but I hope it will be comfortable and cheerful. That's why I picked as much yellow as possible. It makes me think of sunshine and we won't get much of that down here."

She sounded, Kate thought, as though the two of them were a couple of career gals who had decided to share an apartment.

"These pillows are a lot more comfortable than they look." Beryl got up from her chair, lowered herself onto one of the orange oversized cushions and bounced up and down. "And they make nice accents too, I think."

Kate pictured herself lashed to one of the pillows, her body arched to its puffy contour, and wondered how comfortable that would be.

"I haven't done much with the bedroom," Beryl said, "but we won't be spending much time in there."

She got up from the pillow and took the mug from Kate's hands, seeming not to notice that it was untouched. She replaced it on the tray, shoved another triangle of toast into her mouth, and carried the tray toward the kitchen.

"I think everything you'll need is on the table."

Kate looked over her shoulder and saw on the card table, whose legs she'd spied earlier, a typewriter, a tape recorder, and two reams of paper. Quickly she glanced back toward the table where the tray had been. The gun was still there. Beryl had not retaped her wrists. She shifted her weight from side to side and kicked out with her feet, trying to propel her chair forward. It moved slightly. She stopped for a moment and heard water running in the kitchen. Again, she wriggled her body and set the chair in motion, inching it closer to the table. With a final surge, she brought her hands within reach of the gun, grasped it and trained it on the kitchen doorway, waiting for Beryl to emerge.

At first she didn't see the gun. Then Kate raised it as high as she could, so that it aimed straight at Beryl's chest.

"Stay right there," Kate said.

Beryl made a little noise of irritation and kept coming.

"Stay there," Kate repeated.

Beryl grabbed the gun away from her. "You didn't think it was loaded, did you?"

Kate felt utterly foolish. She should have known Beryl wasn't *that* crazy, she supposed, not crazy enough to abduct someone with a loaded gun. And the idea that the two of them were going to live and work together in this hideous little apartment was probably just Beryl's final attempt to pressure Kate into doing her bidding, desperate certainly, and insufferable, but perhaps only mildly deranged. When Kate held her ground, when she refused once again to "collaborate," Beryl would let her go. What else could she do?

A clicking noise caused Kate to look toward the card table. Beryl stood beside it, opening the chambers of the gun, each one spilling a bullet into her hand, a smile twisting at the edges of her mouth. Six times Kate heard the click and saw a bullet eject. And when the gun was empty Beryl replaced each bullet, deliberately, carefully, beneath Kate's horrified gaze.

Then she set down the gun and came over to Kate's chair, tore two new lengths of tape from the large roll, and swiftl and securely bound her wrists to the chair arms, and her ankles to the legs. Kate noted that Beryl was good at this. Had she done it before? To her children maybe? Or to trainees during Lock-up?

"Now I think we understand each other," she said, standing before Kate with her hands on her narrow hips. "I'm very serious about this."

"I can see that," said Kate.

"It will be so much easier for us both if you just cooperate. We'll get the work done and that'll be that."

"I'd like to cooperate, Beryl—"

"Good. That's the spirit."

"But I'm not sure I can work under these conditions."

"Oh, I'll see that you're comfortable," said Beryl. "I don't expect you to work tied up.

"That's a relief."

"Let's be clear that there's no point going for the gun again. You saw you couldn't pull the trigger."

"Just give me another chance," Kate muttered.

"That sort of attitude won't be helpful or productive, Katherine. We'll get a lot more done, and we'll both be a lot happier, if you just decide to focus on the Work and put other considerations aside."

How could Beryl speak of work, and happiness? Did she really think she could imprison Kate and force her to write the sequel to *Captive Courageous*? And did she imagine that she could do this with impunity? Yes, Kate realized, that is exactly what Beryl thought and imagined.

"How long were you planning on our being here?" Kate asked, fighting to keep the panic from her voice.

"Only as long as it takes to get the job done. Not a moment more."

Kate supposed that was meant to be reassuring. "Don't you think people will be looking for us?"

"Of course they will. But they won't find us. I've made sure of that."

Kate wondered what measures Beryl had taken to prevent their being discovered, but decided she would rather not know. Instead, she would preserve the hope that even now the forces of law and order were closing in on them. Surely Beryl had slipped up somewhere. She wasn't clever enough to lay a flawless plan. Was she?

"Do you have any idea how long it might take us to do—" Kate refused to dignify Beryl's proposed enterprise by calling it a book, or even work. She'd seen enough war movies to know how important it was for POWs to buttress their self-respect in any way they could, no matter how minor. "—to complete your project?"

"That will depend on you, Katherine. We can be out of here in no time if you do your part."

Had it not occurred to Beryl that once they were out Kate might report to someone what had happened while they were in here? Did Beryl believe she would be free to enjoy the preordained success of *Captive Courageous*'s sequel? Again Kate answered yes to her own unspoken questions.

"I thought we'd get started first thing in the morning when we're fresh," said Beryl, pulling Kate and her chair backward a few feet until they rested against the wall, tucking a small pillow between the wall and Kate's head. "Is that comfy?"

How could she ask such a question? How could Kate possibly answer? What a pity that her sleeping sickness hadn't lasted a little bit longer. It would have been useful in this situation. As it was, there was no way, trussed up like this, the cold hard metal of the chair pressing on her flesh, her head inclined stiffly backward in order to hold the pillow in place, that she would sleep. And her mind would grow more, rather than less, muddy, and she would be unable to devise any way out of this nightmare.

Now Beryl was holding in her hands two pieces of cloth, one the size of a handkerchief that she was forming into a ball, the other a rectangular strip.

"I would rather not gag you," she said.

"You don't need to," Kate said quickly. "Really you don't."

"But I don't see how I can take the chance given your earlier behavior."

"What behavior? When I said I wouldn't make a sound, I didn't."

"But you went for the gun. That raised real control issues for me, Katherine."

"How do you think I feel?" Kate said plaintively, immediately regretting her tone and rushing on, desperate to avoid the gag. "I promise that I'll be quiet. If I don't have that thing in my mouth I'll sleep much better and be able to get much more done tomorrow."

Beryl was wavering, ball of cloth in one hand, strip in the other.

"Besides," said Kate, "if I started to scream you'd wake up and come out with the gun and—" She didn't want to plant any specific reprisals in Beryl's mind. "And what good would that do me?"

"But then the damage would be done."

Why hadn't she kept her mouth shut? Quit while she was ahead? "But it won't happen because I won't scream. I promise. I won't make any noise. None."

"You'd wake me up and I really need my sleep."

The stony look in Beryl's eyes told Kate the battle was lost, but she fought on.

"But I won't scream. I'm giving you my word. And I'll keep it."

"I've worked too hard to have this whole thing fall apart because of a little gag," said Beryl, advancing on Kate.

"It seems little to you because it's not going in your mouth. I also need my sleep and I think I'll sleep better if—"

Beryl's fingers entered Kate's mouth, cutting off her words, and Kate bit down, hard, feeling a satisfying crunch of flesh and gristle. Beryl yelped, but Kate held on, a dog with a prized bone. Beryl screamed, and yanked her hand about in an effort to break the grip. But Kate's clench did not weaken. Beryl screamed again, but only when she dropped the cloth she was holding and slapped Kate across the face, did her hand spring free.

In a cold, wordless fury, Beryl leaned down to retrieve the gag and roughly stuffed it, and the dust ball now adhering to it, into Kate's mouth. Then she whipped the rectangular strip into place and knotted it tightly behind Kate's head, pushing it back against the pillow when she was done.

She stalked off and when Kate heard water running in the kitchen, she pictured with pleasure Beryl holding her wounded finger under the cool stream.

A pounding at the door startled her and brought Beryl flying into the room, darting first toward the door, then away from it, arms fluttering with fear and uncertainty. The knocking continued and she looked to Kate, as though she could supply an answer. The strip across her mouth prevented Kate from smiling, but she endeavored to force as much glee as possible into her eyes. Beryl twirled about in the middle of the room. Kate felt a surge of hope. She could imagine Beryl going utterly mad, churning without cease before her in a parody of her dancing days. Eventually, the neighbor, or whoever was knocking, would get the police and break in. Kate would be saved. Beryl would be, finally and forever, finished.

"You all right in there?" a man called through the door.

His voice pulled Beryl out of her spin.

"Fine," she answered. "Sorry for the scream. I cut my finger chopping onions for a stew."

Kate willed the man to find it bizarre that this woman was making stew in the middle of the night. She willed him to be suspicious, to question further, to go home and call the police, despite Beryl's reassurance.

"Okay," he said.

"Thanks for checking," said Beryl.

She flashed Kate a blazing smile of triumph, then moved toward the hall that led to the bedroom, pausing when she reached it to turn toward Kate.

"Tomorrow we begin," she said. "I have the concept and the material. You'll help me whip it into shape. I even have the title this time—and I think it's a good one. *Free at Last*."

Then, giving one last look at Kate's roped, taped, gagged body pushed up against the wall, she turned and went down the hall to bed.

Chapter Twelve

*D*URING the night, which only lasted a few hours but felt, to Kate, like a decade or two, she took stock of her situation as dispassionately as she could, finding very little in her favor. The police were bound to tie her disappearance and Beryl's together, but they were also likely to attribute them to the SWEAT Bomber and to focus their investigative efforts in that direction. It was heartening to know that there was a vigilant neighbor upstairs (mustn't it mean something that one of this almost extinct species was overhead?), but the prospect of Kate making any significant noise was almost nonexistent. Beryl's present intentions, apparently, were to have Kate "whip together" the sequel, then release her. And if Beryl's twilight state continued, rendering her oblivious to the consequences of her acts, Kate supposed that could occur. But could she really bear to write *Free at Last?* A part of her felt a strong preference for being gunned down in cold blood.

Could she reason with Beryl, conjure up People's Bank &

Trust and play Beryl to Beryl's Rodney Flint, advocate surrender as the least of many possible evils? Her powers of persuasion seemed puny weapons to pit against Beryl's obsession. Might Jason recognize that her disappearance was not what it seemed, imagine what Theobold would do if he were assigned to "The Case of the Vanishing Wife"? It was possible, but certainly no guarantee of rescue. Jason's mystery-solving skills, as even he would admit, were stronger on paper than in real life. He had never, in fact, as long as Kate had known him, been able to solve so much as the disappearance of a wallet or a set of car keys. By morning Kate was fighting to keep despair at bay.

The sound of an alarm clock interrupted the snores that had issued from the bedroom all night long and Kate was startled, soon afterward, to see a stranger coming down the hall toward her. Was she an accomplice, hidden in the bedroom and now roused to take the early-morning tour of duty? An intruder? An hallucination? Only when the woman spoke did Kate realize it was Beryl, utterly unrecognizable without her eyebrows, lashes, color-slashed cheeks, vermillion lips, electrified hair. Indeed, the pasty sphere of her face appeared featureless, as though she had been erased in the night.

She was carrying a small television set, which she placed on the yellow table, attached to a length of cable emerging from the wall, plugged in, and turned on (Kate was pleased to see that one heavily bandaged finger gave Beryl some difficulty with those tasks), pulling up a chair alongside Kate's bound and gagged body in companionable fashion. It was just after seven o'clock and the "Today Show" was broadcasting the news.

"I watch this because I love Willard Scott," Beryl said,

flashing at her what Kate thought was a smile although she wasn't certain because she couldn't really see Beryl's mouth. "He and I were on 'Good Morning, Houston' together, promoting our books."

Beryl chatted through news items about Beirut, arms control, a new GAO study of government waste, but fell silent when her own picture flashed onto the screen and listened intently to the accompanying words.

"Author Beryl Swarr, founder of the SWEAT organization, which has recently suffered a rash of bombings at its centers throughout the Midwest and East, disappeared yesterday and authorities say they are uncertain whether Mrs. Swarr is in hiding or whether she herself has become the victim of the SWEAT Bomber."

"That's exactly what I wanted them to think," said Beryl, clapping her hands with delight and giving Kate's arm a congratulatory squeeze, as though they were in this together.

Kate felt the squeeze only faintly and wondered if she were losing sensation in her limbs. When Beryl removed the gag, she must remember to raise the specter of gangrene and point out how disagreeable a condition this would be in one's collaborator.

"Mrs. Swarr was named as the target of the attacks in a note received last week by a Pittsburgh television station, following an explosion at the SWEAT center there. Meanwhile, last night the Bomber struck again, destroying the Newark SWEAT center in what police said was the largest blast yet."

"That is just across the river," said Beryl, jumping to her feet and snapping off the television.

Didn't she even want to see if Kate's abduction was featured on the news? Had she forgotten that Kate existed?

Perhaps now in Beryl's mind she was just a lump of flesh strapped to the chair, about on a par with the lump of stuffing that comprised the pillows on the floor, the sole difference being that the pillows couldn't write.

"They're practically here," said Beryl, an unmistakable note of hysteria in her voice. "Probably in the city right now."

Was she talking to her? Kate wondered. Beryl's unadorned eyes melded with her sallow skin and it was impossible to tell where she was looking.

"But they won't find us here. Not a chance. No way. Still, we've got to *move*. M-O-V-E *move*."

She tore down the hall and vanished into what Kate surmised was the bathroom. Kate stared at the blank television screen, her only link to the outside world, and felt tears of hopelessness rise into her eyes.

Beryl was back in short order, with a face where there had been none, and what she must have considered a no-nonsense work outfit: a pants suit made of heavy striped ticking that made her look exactly like a mattress. Beneath it, like a garment thrown across a bed, she wore a pink turtleneck emblazoned with TAKE CHARGE! The black metal handle of the gun protruded from the waistband of the pants.

As she sped by Kate on her way to the kitchen, with no evident intention of stopping, Kate tried to push some strangled sounds through the gag and succeeded in getting Beryl to break stride, but only for a moment. She looked around, annoyed, wondering where the sound was coming from, then continued on her way.

Kate's frustration and rage had reached a fever pitch by the time Beryl returned with a tray of tea and toast (was that all the woman ate? She should publish *The Swarr Diet* and watch it go to the top of the lists), and when the horrid gag was removed, she spewed them out.

"Okay, Beryl, you want something from me? Here's what you're going to have to do to get it. You're going to have to untie me and untape me and let me move around freely for a while so that my circulation can start again. You're going to have to let me go to the bathroom and take a shower. You're going to have to get me something to eat besides tea and toast. And if I decide I want to take a nap you're going to have to let me lie down on the goddamn bed, although I don't think I'll do that because I want this nightmare to end just as soon as possible."

"I'm sorry you see this as a nightmare," Beryl sniffed, as though she'd been accused of being a poor hostess. "I've done everything I could to make it as comfortable as possible."

"You'll have to try a little harder," Kate said, pressing her advantage.

Blinking rapidly and making little snuffling noises, Beryl untied Kate's shoulders and removed the tape from her wrists and ankles.

"I'll get you something to eat," she said peevishly, and moved off to the kitchen.

Kate could not believe her good fortune. She was unshackled. Beryl was in the kitchen. The front door was perhaps fifteen feet away. Slowly she rose, supporting herself on the arms of the chair. She could feel how weak her legs were; she also felt she could make it to the door. Summoning all her energy, she took two steps forward and pitched face-first onto the floor.

Beryl, who had heard her fall, came to the kitchen doorway. "Don't try to do too much," she said. "I'll have your cereal in a minute."

And indeed she was back that quickly, ruling out another attempt.

Kate wolfed down the glutinous mass that was supposed to be oatmeal, ate two pieces of toast, drank a mug of hot tea, and felt much better afterward. She was even able to walk upright to the bathroom though she steadied herself by reaching out to the walls with her fingertips.

"Your towels are to the right of the sink," Beryl called out, eager to repair her reputation as a hostess.

Fearing that the force of the shower might knock her over, Kate chose instead to splash a great deal of cold water onto her face and upper body, rubbing vigorously afterward with a towel in hopes of aiding her circulation. She found, also on the righthand side of the sink, a toothbrush, which she assumed was hers, and which she used gratefully. She looked in the medicine cabinet but found nothing there to aid an escape effort. She checked the small window over the toilet, but it was barred.

Bossing Beryl around was not a tactic on which she could rely for long, Kate knew. But it had gained her a temporary advantage and she debated how best to use it. The first thing she would do, while Beryl was still feeling defensive about her hospitality having been called into question, was to suggest that they leave the television on, tuned to the Cable News Network.

Next, Kate supposed she ought to explore with Beryl her recent actions' ramifications, of which she seemed quite unaware. This probably would not gain her much leverage, but Kate felt she ought at least to try. In general, her most effective course was probably to play the agreeable collaborator, lulling Beryl with a sense of goodwill, awaiting an opening.

Kate hobbled back into the living room where Beryl sat by the tape recorder, earphone plugged in, eyes glazed with pride as she listened to the sound of her own voice, the gun resting in her lap.

"I think we should keep the television tuned to a news station," Kate said. "We ought to know what's going on."

Beryl hesitated a moment, nose rising as though to sniff out chicanery in Kate's seemingly sensible suggestion. Then she popped the plug from her ear.

"You're absolutely right, Katherine. We may as well know what we're up against." She rose, the weary warrior, and snapped on the TV. "I'll tell you, it's one thing to get to the top and another thing to stay there."

While Beryl was lost in a meditation on the burdens and cruelties of fame, Kate spun the dial over to CNN. A reporter was reading the scores of hockey games played the night before.

"If I had it to do over again . . ."

Beryl's ellipsis quivered with meaning and Kate saw an opportunity to reason with her.

"Are you feeling regretful?" she asked.

Beryl sank back into her chair, rubbing her furrowed forehead with the barrel of the gun. "They all want a piece of you."

Kate sat as well, taking the weight off her trembling limbs. But she leaned forward when she spoke, hoping to penetrate Beryl's defenses with her urgency.

"It's not too late to pull out," she said.

Beryl threw back her head and gave an exaggerated and spurious laugh worthy of the heroine of an amateur operetta. Kate thought for an instant of going for the gun, but Beryl's head suddenly snapped forward as though she had read Kate's thoughts.

"If you call this off now," said Kate, "I'll forget the whole thing." She wasn't sure that was true, but it certainly seemed worth saying.

Beryl's body quickened, her eyes flashed, her grip on the gun grew tighter. "This? You and me and *Free at Last*? That's what you want me to call off?"

"I want you to call off this kidnapping," Kate said.

"Kidnapping?" Beryl was outraged by the characterization.

"You're holding me hostage."

"Hostage?" A flush matching the red on her cheekbones spread over Beryl's face.

"I'm your prisoner. You're doing to me what Rodney Flint did to you."

"I am not!" The accusation obviously offended Beryl deeply. "I haven't killed anyone."

"Not yet."

"I'm not using you as a bargaining chip to gain my freedom. I have my freedom."

"Not for long. Don't you know what they'll do to you if you get caught? And you will get caught."

"I'm not keeping you here to protect myself."

"You're keeping me here to write your book. It's the same thing."

"The Work makes its own demands, Katherine," Beryl said, assuming the uncustomary position of handmaiden. "Surely you can understand that."

Kate gathered herself for a final effort. "Beryl," she said, "you abducted me at gunpoint, you brought me here and tied me up and kept a gag in my mouth all night long."

"It was not all night," Beryl objected. "It was just for a few hours."

"You're holding me here against my will, threatening me

with a gun every move I make. You're committing a serious crime. This is not some pajama party."

"It certainly isn't," Beryl said, cutting in briskly, "and I'm glad you realize it. We've got work to do."

Kate slumped in her chair, feeling the full weight of the hopelessness of her situation, as Beryl moved to the card table and began sorting through the material laid out there.

While Beryl's voice hummed in the background, Kate tried desperately to focus on her diminishing options. She had, somehow, to get Beryl out of here. Perhaps then she could make something, as yet unthought of, happen. With Beryl here there was no chance at all.

What could dislodge her? Kate tried to think as Beryl explained each stack of papers, each pile of tapes. She tried to think as she sat before the typewriter, a sheaf of Beryl's notes to her right, the first one on the top page reading: "Waiting in green room of 'Dave Duncan Show.' Energy high, but feel centered. Now the real work begins and I'm READY!!"

Kate felt her skin crawl with embarrassment and her scalp break out in a sweat of desperation. She could not turn this into readable prose. She could not turn it into prose of any sort. Her fingers would freeze. The words would jam in her brain.

She turned behind her to Beryl who sat, gun in lap, listening to her tapes, smiling with contentment.

"Would you make me some more oatmeal and toast?" Kate asked. "I know it's strange, but whenever I begin working on something new I get ravenous and eat a second breakfast. It's an old habit. Stoking the fires of selfhood, I guess."

Although food sensitivity had honed Beryl to a wraith,

she could still understand the urge to eat and didn't appear to consider Kate's request odd in the least. It also didn't hurt that Kate was able to quote from SWEAT's catechism.

"If you're thinking of going for the door," Beryl said, on her way to the kitchen, "don't. It's locked from the inside with a key."

"I wasn't thinking of that," said Kate. "Never even occurred to me."

When Beryl went out of sight Kate moved quickly to the tray that held the breakfast dishes, grabbed her oatmeal spoon and shot back to the typewriter, hitting a few keys to reassure Beryl with the sound. Then she forced the spoon between two of the letter shafts and twisted it with all the power her attenuated arms could muster. The spoon bent nearly double in her hands and two of the letters splayed outward, tangling with their neighbors. She jammed the deformed spoon into the pocket of her skirt, sat down, and hit the keys again. Two struck cleanly, the third brought the snare she'd fashioned up against the paper where it stayed while the machine wheezed angrily in an effort to unknot itself. Just for good measure, Kate hit the keys several more times. Then she got up and walked to the kitchen.

Beryl stood at the stove, stirring the oatmeal with one hand, holding the gun with the other.

"There's something wrong with the typewriter," Kate said.

"That is a rented machine that they assured me was in A-1 shape," Beryl stated, as if that would make it so.

"Well, they were wrong. We'll have to get another. I can't possibly work on this one."

"Well, I can't possibly take it back to the place where I

rented it, which is in my neighborhood and where they know me."

"Beryl, come and look at it," said Kate. "There's no way it can be used."

Beryl pulled the spoon free of the cereal and slammed it onto the counter with annoyance. Then she stalked into the living room, leaving the fire lit beneath the pan. Perfect, Kate thought, turning it down low. If Beryl didn't remember and turn it off, the mess in the pan should begin burning in ten or fifteen minutes, sending a nasty odor rising to the floor above. It wasn't much, but it cheered Kate slightly.

Beryl was bent over the typewriter, trying to twist the deformed shafts into their original shape. Kate, when she looked into the snarl and added her voice to Beryl's complaints about the dependability level of merchants today, was horrified to see telltale flecks of oatmeal clinging to the metal, obviously sprayed there by the wrenching motion of the spoon. But Beryl didn't seem to notice.

"There's a rental place on Mercer and Canal," said Kate. "Are we near there?"

Beryl froze in a posture of suspicion, sensing a pitfall.

"All right, all right," said Kate. "I'm just trying to help. Don't tell me where we are. Not that it would do me any good if I knew."

"It would be extremely dangerous for me to go out," said Beryl, resuming her futile fussing over the typewriter's innards. "We'd lose time. I'd be paying for a second machine."

"The Work makes its own demands," Kate murmured.

Beryl wavered for another moment, then motioned Kate toward her chair. Kate submitted. Beryl would never leave unless Kate were tied up and gagged. And what could Kate do in such a state? While Beryl pinioned her with rope and tape, Kate's mind raced to answer the question. Then her eye fell on the small TV and a plan, farfetched but possible, took shape.

"Could you leave my ankles undone?" she pleaded. "I still haven't gotten much feeling back in my feet after last night."

"I don't think that would be wise," Beryl said.

"I can't do anything or go anywhere." Kate demonstrated by shoving her feet out in front of her and bouncing in her chair. Unfortunately, she moved an inch or so forward.

Beryl gave her a disparaging look and peeled a long strip of tape from the roll.

Kate realized there would be no better time to raise the specter of rot and decay.

"I'm concerned about gangrene," she said.

"I'll do it a little looser," Beryl snapped.

When Kate was secured and gagged, Beryl disappeared into the bedroom, emerging soon after in her red wig, white makeup slapped on her face, shrugging into her padded coat and poking stuffing into her cheeks. In some ways it was an improvement, Kate thought. But what on earth would the typewriter rental people make of her? Maybe they wouldn't even do business with her. And they would need a deposit. What would Beryl do about that? She couldn't put it on her credit card. Whatever happened, it was sure to be odd enough to be memorable. And perhaps if police were combing the neighborhood, questioning everyone, the rental people would remember the weird lady with the white face and the red curls and . . . and so what? There was nothing to tie them together. Unless someone in the café had actually seen her snatch Kate. A long shot. Very long.

Kate felt herself winding down into despair again. Even the sound of the door closing behind Beryl didn't stir her. She gave a couple of halfhearted tugs against the tape around her ankles. It was not substantially looser than the previous night. She tested the sounds she was able to produce with the gag in her mouth, feeble grunts that barely carried across the room. She dropped, disconsolate, against her restraints.

It was the smell of the charred oatmeal that finally roused her from her apathy. The man upstairs. He'd been moving about not long ago. She had to reach him somehow, excite his concern and curiosity. The oatmeal alone wouldn't do it, not in the next half hour. Her plan had been to reach out with her feet and turn up the volume on the television as loud as it would go. Now her feet were unavailable. Well, she'd do it anyway. She'd tip over her chair, rub the tie across her mouth against the rough matting on the floor until it slid down over her chin; she'd spit out her gag, and turn the damn thing with her teeth.

Kate did not stop to examine the feasibility of any of this, but began rocking her chair from side to side, tipping this way, then that, picking up momentum, finally thrusting all her weight to her right and pitching onto the floor, her body and the carapace of the chair landing heavily, her head cracking against the edge of the table on the way down. Her cry, muffled by the gag, was so puny that she felt able to ignore both it and the pain that caused it. Besides, she felt if she stopped moving she might never start again.

With her cheek resting on the sisal rug, she lowered her chin, then pulled it upward, lowered and raised it again, scraping her skin on the prickly rope in an effort to dislodge the cloth tied round her mouth. It didn't budge. She repeated the maneuver, dragging her face back and forth over the coarse surface, feeling her skin burn. Had the cloth slid downward slightly? Again, she rubbed against the harsh rug, the scratches on her face stinging from salty tears of frustration. The tie stayed in place.

Kate lay still, feeling defeat seep through her exhausted body. A wisp of smoke floated before her eyes. The odor of incinerated cereal assaulted her nostrils. Maybe she would burn to death. That seemed all right. She only hoped it would happen before Beryl returned so that she would never have to see her again. She felt she could die happy if that one wish were granted. And what of Jason? Was it only last night, twelve hours ago, that she had been with him? Beryl's universe, in all its malign absurdity, had the power, as always, to make all normal life seem impossibly distant.

Kate heard Jason's voice. "We don't believe, as the police do, that she was abducted by the Bomber along with Mrs. Swarr."

That's right, darling, she answered him woozily in her head, feeling her words join his in a united stream.

"We feel, in fact, that there is a good chance that she was kidnapped by Mrs. Swarr."

Kate didn't care that she was hallucinating, the first stage of smoke inhalation, she imagined. Each figment conjured seemed like a message sent to Jason. And it was satisfying to know that he would understand what had happened, to be assured that he would see Beryl paid for it.

"My wife wrote Mrs. Swarr's book."

Ah, the greatest punishment of all, the true author of *Captive Courageous* revealed. Kate was just as glad she wouldn't be alive to take responsibility for her part in it.

"She was pressuring her to write the sequel and my wife

consistently refused, which infuriated Mrs. Swarr. The kidnapping may have been a last desperate attempt to get what she wanted."

"Have you gone to the police with your story, Mr. Wylie?" said another voice.

Who was that, horning in on her final moments? Kate twisted her head about to clear it, toward the smoky entrance to the kitchen over one shoulder, toward the little television set just beyond the other. There she looked directly into Jason's eyes.

"We have," he said, "but they don't seem interested. My son and I are pursuing this on our own and asking for all the help we can get."

The camera angle widened to include Igor. "Especially people in the neighborhood," Igor added, eliciting a nod of agreement from his father. "We're interested in anyone who's seen a woman in the vicinity wearing a dark coat, with red hair—"

The front door of the apartment flew open with a crash, obliterating Igor's description of the woman but admitting the creature herself. Beryl slammed the door shut and fell against it, gasping for air. Kate groaned beneath her gag, attempting to cover the sound of the television and to bring Beryl's attention to the smoldering kitchen lest her consternation keep her from noticing it.

She moved quickly and Kate heard the vicious hiss when a stream of cold water hit the pan. An old exhaust fan wheezed into action. Kate heard Beryl struggling to get open a window that had probably been sealed for years. The racket drowned out the sound of the television and the next time Kate twisted toward it, Jason and Igor were gone.

Then Beryl stood over her, massive and distraught in her disguise.

"Just what the hell do you think you were up to, sending me out there?" she demanded.

Kate, strapped into her chair, lay mute.

"I got extremely poor vibrations on the street, I'll tell you. P-O-O-R, with a capital P. I saw at least three cop cars. Flyers with your name on them. It didn't take them long to get those into circulation, did it?"

It certainly didn't, Kate thought, hope rising again.

"And how was I supposed to rent this typewriter?" Beryl raved on. "With a credit card in *my* name? I suppose you thought I'd fall for that, didn't you?"

She prodded Kate with the toe of her black oxford. Kate fought to produce some sound that would remind Beryl of how impotent she was, even though pushing against the gag made her feel like choking.

"Well, it didn't work. I didn't fall for it. And what about this little trick?" She waved a scornful hand over Kate's prostrate form. "What's this supposed to be?"

Beryl circled Kate, surveying her from different angles.

"I wonder what kind of story you'll come up with to explain this. The smoke blew you over? You sneezed? You don't remember because you hit your head? What's the story going to be?"

Again, she nudged Kate with her foot, poking it into her midriff, pushing it against her thigh.

"Well, whatever it is, save it, because I'm not buying. Besides, it didn't do you much good, did it?"

Beryl did not wait for an answer this time but headed down the hall.

When she returned, her disguise was gone and so was her fury. The fire in the kitchen was, apparently, not the only blaze that had been extinguished. She righted Kate and her chair absentmindedly, as though, together, they were a piece of furniture, upended by mistake. When Kate screamed behind the gag, Beryl removed it. When Kate said she was sick of hearing the same news over and over and suggested they turn off the television (it would not do to have Beryl know that the net was tightening around her), Beryl pulled the plug from the wall. She even, when she noticed Kate's abraded cheek, dampened some towels with cool water and dabbed them against the scratches.

"I smelled something burning and saw the smoke and I was going to try to get to the kitchen somehow," Kate said, explaining the position in which Beryl had found her.

Beryl didn't seem to care.

"I suppose I could work in longhand," Kate offered. "At least we could make a start."

Beryl did not respond.

Did she know somehow that the end was at hand? Was it?

The next few hours with Beryl in the basement apartment were rather what Kate imagined it must have been like in the bunker with Hitler at the end. Beryl moved about aimlessly, wrapped in the air of a dying dream, glancing through a sheaf of papers, extracting one and reading it, a smile of fond recollection playing round her mouth, popping a cassette into the recorder and listening for a few minutes, head nodding with evident satisfaction, then switching it off, vanishing for long periods into the bathroom where Kate imagined her looking into the mirror, staring into her own opaque eyes and attempting to rally, to "Take charge!" (Futile efforts, apparently, as she returned to the living room listless and brooding.) When she stood framed in the kitchen doorway, trails of smoke from the oatmeal fire curling around her body, eyes lit briefly with the glow of remembered triumph, the sense of götterdämmerung was complete.

But when bullhorns sounded outside the apartment shortly after dark, and the spotlights that had been set up glinted through the windows, Beryl did not hold the gun to her temple and pull the trigger. Instead, high color sprang into her cheeks, her body grew taut and purposeful. Moments before, she had seemed on the verge of extinction; now a life-giving transfusion had animated her spirit and given her flesh new vigor. Police, reporters, cameras, and microphones were outside her door. Did it matter that they were here to effect and record her arrest? Apparently not.

"I'll have to change," she said, looking down with distaste at the gray cowl-necked sweater and muted plaid pedal pushers she was wearing.

Had she brought an outfit for this eventuality? Kate wondered.

"And I'll want to make a statement," Beryl added, moving down the hall. "Maybe you could get started on that. You know the sort of thing—everything I did I did for SWEAT, for hostages everywhere, for the Movement ..."

"I can't do much while I'm tied to this chair," Kate called, but Beryl had vanished into the bathroom and didn't hear her.

When she returned ten minutes later, in full stage makeup, she was wearing the lime jumpsuit, the open-heeled matching pumps, a bright flowered scarf knotted at her neck and flowing over her shoulder, large lemon-yellow enameled hoops suspended from her ears, and a bright red sash knotted at her waist.

"We would like you to come out voluntarily, Mrs.

Swarr," a voice boomed from outside. *"We'll give you five more minutes."*

"Take it easy, take it easy," Beryl muttered, once again the public figure pressed by insistent demands. "Do you have some notes for me?" she asked Kate.

"How was I supposed to write them?"

"Oh, it doesn't matter," Beryl said, still refusing to acknowledge Kate's condition. "I can speak off the cuff. I've certainly done it often enough."

She opened her purse, which lay on the card table, took out a mirror and looked into it, fiddling with the scarf at her neck, pushing upward with her fingertips on the stalks of her hair, flicking a bead of mascara off the end of one very long eyelash. Then, apparently satisfied, she turned back to Kate.

"Would you like to come out with me?" she asked.

Kate knew it was no small thing for Beryl to offer to share the limelight. Besides, if she was not fully aware of what awaited her outside, Kate was, and she felt strangely protective.

"You'll have to untie me," she pointed out.

Beryl, for the first time in hours, seemed actually to see Kate, tied and taped, and she moved swiftly to release her.

"One more minute, Mrs. Swarr," a voice bellowed.

"Coming," Beryl sang out, as though she had just been summoned to dinner.

Kate stood and tested her legs, jiggling them to stimulate circulation, putting weight on one, then the other.

Beryl stood by the door, waiting.

"You'll be cold, Beryl," she said.

"Well, I'm not going out there in that horrid old coat."

"No, I suppose not," said Kate, beginning to inch awkwardly across the room.

When Beryl stepped outside, Kate hung back slightly, the ghostly presence behind in the shadows. The night was illuminated by the lights trained on the front of the building. Reporters and cameramen, uncontained by the ragged police lines, clustered in a buzzing knot on the pavement.

When Beryl felt the warmth of the lights and heard the shouted questions, lobbed like projectiles over the heads of the police waiting for her, she responded reflexively, hands shooting up over her head, fingers spreading into the victory sign. Kate watched the familiar silhouette, arms swaying in time with the pulse of the crowd, then saw it freeze as a loud report cracked through the din. Still reaching upward, as though she could grasp the frigid air and keep herself erect, Beryl hung suspended for a moment before falling backward against Kate, whose arms went round her and felt the warm blood seeping against them as the two of them sank to the ground entwined in a kind of parodistic pieta.

She looked down into Beryl's face and watched death catch at the heavy lashes against her cheek, overtake the gasping mouth, drain the color from beneath the painted mask. Then Kate raised her eyes and saw Norma Van den Haag, standing at the edge of the stunned crowd, holding the smoking gun.

Chapter Thirteen

*W*HEN Kate needed sol-
ace in the days ahead—and she did need consoling for the
part she had played in the macabre and bloody spectacle
that had unfolded only four blocks from her home—she reminded herself how humiliated Beryl would have been by
the revelation of Kate's place in the creation of *Captive
Courageous.*

"Look at it this way, Katie," Jason said, holding her the
day after, as she lay between clean, cool sheets, trying to ex-
orcise the frightful images playing over and over again in her
mind. "She'd probably rather be dead."

"Than what?" said Kate, shocked by the suggestion.

"Than have people know she didn't write her own book."

"But they do know."

"But she doesn't know they know."

As harsh as this sounded, Kate realized that Jason had a
point. The fact that Beryl had not written a word of her
book certainly did call into question key parts of the

SWEAT program, all that business about self-confrontation and journal writing, those insights that can only come as one struggles to put words on paper. Maybe Beryl *would* rather have been dead than face the dissolution of her credibility and, as a consequence, her SWEAT empire.

Kate, at any rate, chose to cling to that idea rather than entertain for long more disturbing notions: mightn't Beryl have bluffed her way through the authorship crisis and landed, unashamed, on her feet, alive and well and spreading the SWEAT gospel more fervently than ever? Would Kate rather Beryl had died than have had *that* happen?

Jason also tried to get Kate, when she threatened to sink into a slough of despondency, to focus on the horrific thing Beryl had done to her before her sad and spectacular demise.

"That which ye sow," he said.

"Live by the gun, die by the gun? C'mon, Jason, this isn't Theobold. The formulas aren't so neat."

"Kate, do you forget that this woman kidnapped you, held you prisoner, gagged you, tied you till your blood stopped running, tried to coerce you into writing her unspeakable book, and would have done God knows what to you if she hadn't been found? Don't you see how monstrous that is?"

Kate assured Jason that she had not forgotten. What she could not make him understand was that her feelings were tempered in some inexplicable way by her own part in Beryl's conception.

"But if she hadn't been your monster, she would have been someone else's," Jason argued.

"I suppose so," said Kate, "but the fact remains that she was mine."

While Kate mourned privately and ambivalently, she followed the public mourning for Beryl, which was prolonged and extravagant and in no way diminished by the fact that she had become a felon in the last few days of her life. Candlelight vigils were held round the clock at all the SWEAT centers that had not been in Norma Van den Haag's demonic path. Even at some of the sites where explosions had occurred, small knots of SWEATees huddled amidst the rubble, tapers guttering, for as long as the winter winds would allow. Giant crepe-draped pictures of Beryl stood in the centers' windows. Black-bordered memorial boxes with Beryl's name and the dates of her birth and death appeared on the book pages of newspapers around the country.

At SWEAT's New York headquarters, in Petrucci's old bakery, Beryl's body lay in repose, the bier surrounded by Swarrguards, extending to their fallen leader in death the protection they had been unable to afford her in life. Busloads of followers from all over the country arrived to pay their last respects, the stream of vehicles creating a constant rumbling hum that was audible in Kate's apartment several blocks away.

The day of the funeral Beryl's coffin was borne through the streets by SWEATees and members of Hostages Anonymous, platoons of Swarrguards fore and aft, to a small neighborhood church that could not begin to accommodate the mourners who spilled down the front steps into the square across the street, and listened to the service over loudspeakers set up for that purpose. When Beryl was cremated, her ashes, in accordance with her will, were flown to Harbor View, where she had asked that they be placed in a vault at People's Bank & Trust, "the spot where it all began."

Watching television coverage of the interment, Kate recognized many of the town's citizens to whom she had talked when Harbor View's numero uno was just beginning her ascendance. Stanley, loyal to the end, was there, looking stricken, Lance beside him, Melody skulking in their wake. (Kate thought she detected an intimation of pleasure in the normally lusterless eyes of Beryl's daughter as the vault clanged shut.) Absent, of course, were the Van den Haags and, Kate noted, Beryl's mother, who declared in a later interview, that she'd "gone off" Beryl from the time she decided to write a book about her experiences.

"Just because something happens to a person is no reason it has to be a book," Acacia said. "Besides, she didn't even really write it, as everybody knows by now. Why, I've had plenty of things happen to me in my life—Mr. Wease locking me in the fruit cellar for days at a time, three babies born dead, my father killing himself at the Sunday dinner table with the whole family there—but did I write a book about any of that? No. And if I ever did, I can tell you this: I'd write the damn thing myself."

This one discordant note aside, Kate felt Beryl would have been pleased with the pomp and circumstance and with her glorification as a martyr, and might indeed have deemed these rewards worth dying for. She would have been less pleased, Kate was sure, with the amount of attention given to the woman who had made it all possible.

For every grief-stricken member of SWEAT or H.A. who went before the cameras to tell what Beryl's life had meant to his or her own, someone who'd known Norma Van den Haag was interviewed. The concensus was that Norma, deranged by her daughter's death, had come increasingly to hold Beryl responsible for that tragedy, and to resent what she saw as Beryl's exploitation of it. Even so, most professed

273

themselves surprised that Norma had blasted to smithereens nearly a dozen buildings and murdered a former fellow citizen of Harbor View in cold blood.

"Oh, I knew she had a grudge," as one neighbor put it, "but I didn't know it was quite so big."

When reporters caught her outside court on the day of her indictment, Norma herself, a wicked glint in her eye, explained it this way: "I just looked inside myself and I found that self-energy and I said, 'Norma, take charge!'"

Norma had been led to Beryl, Kate learned, by following Igor and Jason, who in their first, but surely not last, collective effort decided that Beryl was behind Kate's disappearance and set out to find her. Igor's "boys," recipients now, along with Igor, of Jason's affectionate respect, connected Kate's abduction to the bag lady's absence from the street, went door to door in the neighborhood questioning people who might have seen something, talked to the super of the building where Kate had been incarcerated, and got a match on the description of Beryl in disguise.

Jason and Igor, together, brought Kate home after the shooting and tended her in the days that followed, the new union between them a balm that broke over her in healing waves. Jason regaled Kate with tales of the cleverness and common sense Igor had displayed during the search. Igor credited Jason by saying he must, after all, have inherited some of his father's character traits. Kate told them, repeatedly, that they made a wonderful team. She said it so often, in fact, that they finally told her to stop, assuring her that their affinity would survive and endure without her prompting.

A week to the day after Beryl's death, Kate received a letter from her grandmother that read:

Ghost of a Chance

Dear Katherine:
Although my whole life contradicts it, and I proba-
bly wouldn't admit it to anyone but you, I do agree
with what you say. Why don't you and your family
come to visit me so that I can thank you in person for
giving me a second chance?

> *Affectionately,*
> *Your grandmother*

The next day Kate began to work on her long-delayed novel, the requiem for her parents with which she hoped to bestow on them the peace they had never enjoyed in life and to grant eternal rest to some old conflicts of her own. She had written a page, not a perfect one, but a bona fide beginning nevertheless, when the phone rang.

"Ron Nadler calling Kate Wylie," she heard when she picked it up.

"Yes?" The name wasn't familiar.

"I'm representing Norma Van den Haag," he said.

"Oh, yes." Kate recalled her last glimpse of the woman as she was being led away by police, looking back over her shoulder to make sure her prey was dead. "How is Norma?"

"A lot better than she was a few weeks ago."

"Really?" Kate would have thought that imprisonment and a murder charge might have lowered, rather than raised, Norma's spirits.

"Well, she's gotten a lot off her chest, let off some steam. It all helps."

"I'm not sure I'd characterize what Norma did as letting off steam," said Kate.

"The point I'm making," he said, "is that this is a lady who's been through hell and now she's experiencing some relief."

Linda Crawford

"What can I do for you, Mr. Nadler?"

"Norma asked me to get in touch with you. She'd like you to come to see her."

"Oh, I don't think so. I don't see what purpose—"

"Hang on. Wait a minute. It's not a social call. She has a proposition to discuss with you."

"What's that?"

"Norma feels that what she's been through could be helpful to other people in the same boat and for that reason she's thinking about doing a book. She'd like to have you sign on as the writer."

"Mr. Nadler," said Kate, "please thank Norma for thinking of me, but tell her I'm no longer in that line of work."